INTERPOL CONFIDENTIAL

A LAW ENFORCEMENT FARCE

MICHAEL E. ROSE

SilverWood

Published in 2016 by SilverWood Books

SilverWood Books Ltd
14 Small Street, Bristol, BS1 1DF, United Kingdom
www.silverwoodbooks.co.uk

British English spellings have been used throughout.

ISBN 978-1-78132-493-6 (paperback)
ISBN 978-1-78132-494-3 (ebook)

British Library Cataloguing in Publication Data
A CIP catalogue record for this book is available from
the British Library

Set in Adobe Garamond Pro by SilverWood Books
Printed on responsibly sourced paper

MICHAEL E. ROSE is a Canadian author, journalist and broadcaster. He has worked for major media organisations around the world, including the Canadian Broadcasting Corporation, Maclean's Magazine, Radio France International, *The Sydney Morning Herald* and the Reuters news agency in London. He is also the former Chief of Communications for Interpol at the agency's global headquarters in Lyon, France.

His usual genre is spy thrillers, with the Frank Delaney series winning new readers year after year. The first thriller in that series, *The Mazovia Legacy*, won critical acclaim and was shortlisted in the prestigious Arthur Ellis Awards for Best First Novel. The second volume, *The Burma Effect*, drew similar attention. The third, *The Tsunami File*, was shortlisted in the Arthur Ellis Awards for Best Crime Novel of 2009.

Rose has travelled extensively to many of the world's trouble spots including Nicaragua, Haiti, Sierra Leone, Ivory Coast, Burma and East Timor. He has drawn from those experiences for the gripping stories and characters in his thrillers, and now for *Interpol Confidential*.

After spending a number of years in the UK and France, Rose now lives with his Australian wife and Burmese cat in Sydney. For more about him and his books, visit www.michaelrosemedia.com.

PRAISE FOR *INTERPOL CONFIDENTIAL*

"Rose writes with a deft hand, a twisted wit, and an insider's knowledge of Interpol. A hilarious page-turner."

Terry Fallis, award-winning satirist and author of *The Best Laid Plans*

"Michael E. Rose's hilarious satire takes us into a massive bureaucracy faithfully dedicated to combating crime and corruption, breaches of security, evil plotting and disloyalty – all in its own ranks. Departmental warfare and buried animals in the Interpol HQ garden are just the beginning. Add a paranoid, philandering Secretary-General who likes dressing up in silk kimonos, his wife who packs a mean Heckler & Koch, an executive of careerist back-stabbing multinationals, and bent cops who won't share what they know with anyone, least of all other cops, and comedic stress leave is definitely in order!"

Tony Maniaty, journalist and author of *Shooting Balibo* and *Smyrna*

"A contemporary, character-driven farce that works wonderfully. The author of several previously-published crime thrillers, Rose skilfully draws on his own experience working within Interpol to fashion an entertaining mix of incompetence, scheming, and paranoia that will have readers gripping their sides with laughter. When delegates from around the world convene in Munich, ostensibly to re-elect the vain and ambitious Secretary General to another term, it all comes deliciously unglued in an entertaining farce that once suspects is closely rooted in fact. There are naïve junior technocrats struggling to comprehend what their boss requires (and who are unable to provide it), paranoid senior officials and their equally suspicious wives, and a CNN news crew eager to penetrate the walls of Interpol in search of scandal and incompetence, both of which abound. Once this tale hits the streets Rose should expect to find himself dropped from Interpol's Christmas-card list."

Jim Napier, reviewer at Deadly Diversions

Everyone sees what you appear to be.
Few know what you really are.

Niccolò Machiavelli

ONE

It was, everyone agreed afterward, not a good thing for the giant Interpol sign to suddenly fall off the side of the headquarters building and smash itself, two storeys below, into a catastrophic pile of broken glass, billowing dust, twisted aluminium and hissing, sparking electrical wires.

It was not a good thing because the Interpol sign was a mere three weeks old when it plunged to the tiled entry forecourt, narrowly missing an arriving delegation of clearly intoxicated police officers from Belarus and a fetching young French data compiler from the stolen motor vehicles database department. And because it was a pet project of Interpol Secretary General Didier Herriot-Dupont.

Few inside the glass and steel fortress that housed the world's largest international police organisation dared voice the opinion that the incident was perhaps a bad omen of some sort. Or that it was divine retribution for Secretary General Herriot-Dupont, who was known almost universally as DHD. He was also known secretly, to certain of his many detractors, as ADHD, with no apologies to sufferers of attention deficit hyperactivity disorder. No one would dare venture such opinions just months away from the Interpol General Assembly at which DHD's re-election by the world's police was at stake, and, it was said, in serious question.

Few inside the glass and steel fortress on the banks of Lyon's Rhone river dared venture an opinion in public on any topic anymore. Herriot-Dupont ran a very, very tight ship. He did not suffer fools, or dissenters, or pretty much anyone, gladly. To run afoul of

Herriot-Dupont as he went about the business of putting his stamp on Interpol was to put oneself in great peril.

He was a short man, very short, but his physical presence could strike fear into the hearts of even the most seasoned Interpol officers. He was stocky, solidly built. He was the product of Normandy peasant stock; broad-shouldered, ham-handed and small-bottomed. He had the gleaming, close-set eyes of a predatory bird, a similarly bird-like beak, and a mane of salt-and-pepper hair, always immaculately coiffed, it was said, to better impress his female admirers, real or imagined.

Indeed, in his heart of hearts, Interpol Secretary General Didier Herriot-Dupont wanted very much to be a boxer, or a bricklayer or an ill-tempered riot cop. Instead of a career officer, a bureaucrat, from the highest echelons of France's Police Nationale.

DHD wanted to be a man's man, a policeman's policeman. But he was, alas, not. He was, inescapably, the former head of the least interesting, the least respected of the French police divisions.

Only the bravest of Herriot-Dupont's detractors would suggest, in public, that the Directorate of Resources and Competencies was anything but a crucial element of the French law enforcement system, doing essential work to keep frontline police officers well trained and well supplied.

The fact that some unkind members of the law enforcement community found the DRCPN to be a bit of a minor-league outfit was something no one would dare point out to him. That sort of unfounded criticism was not something Herriot-Dupont wished to hear. Though he would, in dark moments, acknowledge, only to himself, that running around making sure the French police had enough boots and handcuffs and whistles and procedural handbooks was not glamorous work.

For reasons perhaps best known to France's byzantine foreign policy establishment, it had been decided that a Frenchman must at all costs succeed the brash American woman who had attempted to drag Interpol kicking and screaming into the twenty-first century. That the American Secretary General had instituted a scorched earth policy in her reform drive, that there had been much collateral damage of various sorts during her tenure, was only half the story. The French had simply decided it was time to wrest control of Interpol away from the upstart Americans and steer international police cooperation once again into a European orbit.

That campaign, after intense diplomatic manoeuvring in world police circles, had succeeded. DHD won the vote at the Interpol General Assembly in Belixico City almost five years earlier and France had its diplomatic victory.

The Secretary General was very, very upset about the smashed sign. He had summoned his Chief of Staff for an emergency meeting as soon as security sent up the news. Freiderikos Milonakis was an outstanding Chief of Staff who, Herriot-Dupont clearly assumed, would have already ascertained the cause of the incident and taken steps to punish, severely, the guilty parties.

"What the hell has happened with my sign, Freiderikos?" Herriot-Dupont hissed, even before Milonakis was fully inside the office.

The Secretary General liked to pepper his conversation with the sort of swearing used by case-hardened American cops. A frightened appointments assistant in the anteroom hunched closer over her keyboard as Milonakis closed the door.

"It almost killed those inebriates from Minsk," DHD said. "How will it look at the General Assembly if important visitors to headquarters are being crushed by debris falling from my building?"

Milonakis was usually, almost always, unflappable. He had learned from his days in the Hellenic Police how to deal calmly with victims of testosterone poisoning, and superior officers suffering from small-man syndrome, or, in this case, stocky Normandy peasant womaniser small man syndrome. He was determined not to let the sign incident ruin his day.

The new Interpol sign had, in fact, already ruined a good number of Milonakis' days. When the Secretary General decided that something needed to be done, something public, something that would enhance Interpol's somewhat chequered image, that something would have to be done at top speed, with no handwringing about cost or operational fallout, or how many nervous breakdowns were induced among his police or civilian staff.

Indeed, the sign project had just about killed Interpol's long-suffering Chief of Communications, Alf Mortman, a lugubrious, overweight, extremely unhealthy police officer seconded from Estonia. Mortman had the sorry task of managing, or failing to successfully manage, the organisation's communications with the outside world, with the world's police, and with the world's frequently unappreciative media. Milonakis had passed to Mortman the poisoned chalice of the Interpol sign project and Mortman had immediately become a target for obsessional DHD wrath.

Mortman had at one point very unwisely argued in a meeting with the Secretary General that the debate over security regarding the sign was beside the point, as the Interpol headquarters was clearly indicated on the bus stop outside. The Interpol headquarters was also marked on all maps distributed by Lyon's tourism authority. But the debate, led by the Secretary General himself, had raged for weeks as to whether putting a giant illuminated Interpol sign on the outside of the building, the first time any Interpol headquarters building would be thus identified, might make it a target for terrorist attack.

Secretary General Herriot-Dupont had begun professing concern that the building would indeed become a target, despite the sign having been his idea in the first place. The Secretary General liked any discussion, among his senior advisors or among certain high-ranking police visitors from key member countries, that added an element of drama to the life of Interpol. He liked anything that made it seem that he, Herriot-Dupont, was at the helm of a crime-fighting organisation with major challenges and threats on all fronts.

"Have you even *thought*, Monsieur Mortman, about the security risks involved in having a sign installed on the outside of this building?" DHD had thundered in a recent meeting whose main agenda item seemed to be humiliation of the defenceless Estonian.

"Secretary General, you yourself asked to have the sign put up," Mortman had said, sweat beading most unattractively on his doleful face.

Mortman's one saving grace in DHD's eyes, Milonakis knew, was that he was short as well as being overweight. This pleased the Secretary General when official photos were to be taken of him alongside his Communications Chief. Mortman – and Milonakis, for that matter, himself not an overly tall man – did not draw undue attention to the Secretary General's vertical challenges. Milonakis hoped there were other reasons for his continued tenure as Chief of Staff than the fact that he helped make the Secretary General look less short in official photos.

"So no risk assessment is required, in your view, Mortman," Herriot-Dupont asked. "Is that correct? Putting the world's largest international police organisation in danger just so we can have an *advertising* sign out front?"

"Everyone in Lyon knows that this is the Interpol headquarters, *monsieur*. It's on the bus stop. It's on all the maps."

"I see," Herriot-Dupont hissed. "And what have you been doing to rectify this communications problem?"

Milonakis had watched the ritual humiliation with a slight sense of guilt, but also with the relief of those whom a schoolyard bully had chosen, on this day anyway, not to target. Other senior Interpol staff in the meeting room cast their eyes downward; very quiet, very careful not to draw undue attention to themselves.

"Can you tell me, Monsieur Mortman, why I pay you more than 100,000 euros a year virtually tax free, and plead every year with the Estonian National Police to extend your secondment here in the south of France, if you have not even thought of why bus stops outside this building have the name Interpol inscribed on them for every terrorist operative to see? Have you ever spoken to the Lyon bus company about this problem? As my highly-paid *Chef de Communication?*"

"The bus stops have always had that on them, *monsieur*," Mortman ventured. "Long before any of us came along."

Survival Rule Number One at Interpol was to never engage the Secretary General in debate. DHD slammed his fist down onto the boardroom table.

"*C'est de la merde!*" he shouted. Sometimes shouting in French was the only way DHD seemed sure he was making himself properly understood. "I don't want to hear about problems! I want only to hear about solutions!"

Mortman went silent. He was onto his third heart attack. The Interpol doctor had told him that his ulcer was about to perforate and that he should avoid stressful situations at all costs. He ate lunch alone in his office each day, listening to Vivaldi and hoping the telephone would not ring.

"Freiderikos," Herriot-Dupont said. "Can you now take responsibility for this project as I wanted you to in the first place, and get a proper risk assessment done before we go further? Ask that new FBI man on the third floor to help out, and then send a note to his superiors back in Washington praising his work here. I haven't heard from the FBI Director for a long time. What's the young man's name again?"

"O'Brien," Milonakis said.

"*S'il vous plait*, get O'Brien working with you and send a note to the FBI saying what a wonderful officer he is. Give the Director my regards and ask if he will attend the General Assembly."

"I will," Milonakis said. He was a man of few words when the Secretary General was in a rage.

"How would it look in the United States if we put up a sign without looking properly at the risk?" Herriot-Dupont said to the meeting at large. "Do we want Homeland Security to think we are fools? It is a dangerous environment we're in. It's a powder keg waiting to explode. We are living, as our American friends say, in a post-9/11 world. So let us all please get serious on risk. And I want that infernal sign installed by the end of next week. We have an Executive Committee meeting coming up and we will need to get every member's picture taken out front to send home with them. Are you able to assist me on this, Freiderikos? The highest priority, *vous comprenez?* Mortman, I want you to stick with whatever inconsequential communication dossiers you've got going at the moment and stay clear of this sign project. And where is that CNN profile you've been promising me since last year?"

Milonakis, despite being a very proud Greek, was a student of Machiavelli, a devotee. He kept a small portrait of the Italian political genius in a metal frame on his desk, as one would with pictures of a wife or children or a favourite pet. The image faced inward, so as not to generate unwanted queries or discussion among those who visited him in his office. But if Machiavelli had been a rock star, Milonakis would have camped out all night to get concert tickets in the front row and bought the T-shirt after the show.

When Secretary General Herriot-Dupont was in a Level One or Level Two rage and heading toward gale-force incoherence at Level Four or above, Milonakis always drew on Machiavelli for inspiration before taking action. There was nothing in *The Prince* that dealt directly with such things as fallen Interpol signage, but there was always guidance. Milonakis kept in his upper right-hand drawer a well-thumbed copy of this indispensable manual for those serving as advisors to the powerful and the capricious.

This time the advice for Milonakis' latest problem was obvious. Milonakis didn't even have to look up the relevant quotation: *Whosoever desires constant success must change his conduct with the times.*

This had been one of Milonakis' guiding principles since arriving at Interpol from the Greek police eleven years ago with his third wife's lawyers snapping at his heels. Before Herriot-Dupont had wrested the top job away from the incumbent American, Alexandra McGraw, and during the reign of the redoubtable Welsh Secretary General, Jonathan W. Holmesworth.

Milonakis had been Holmesworth's devoted and unflappable

Chief of Staff. He had served, devoted and unflappable, under McGraw, and he was now Herriot-Dupont's devoted and unflappable Chief of Staff. He intended to be the Chief of Staff for the next Interpol Secretary General, and quite possibly the one after that. The better to avoid a return to Greece and the complications of ex-wives and ex-children. The better to amass large piles of tax-free euros and work on his retirement fund, his collection of exquisitely tailored suits and his racks of handcrafted shoes.

Milonakis made it his business to know where all the bodies were buried, no matter whom he worked for. In the case of Secretary General Jonathan W. Holmesworth – a flamboyantly eccentric former Deputy Chief Constable or Assistant Chief Constable of the North Wales Police; Milonakis could barely remember now – the metaphoric bodies in the last tumultuous year of his reign were everywhere. There was even an actual (i.e. non-metaphoric) body: that of his small dog, Toodles, beloved by both Holmesworth and his neurasthenic wife, Gladys. Toodles had been buried in the Interpol headquarters garden in a bizarre, secret late-night ceremony attended by a select group of trusted staff, among whose number had been one Freiderikos Milonakis.

When it became clear during Alexandra McGraw's subsequent tenure that Herriot-Dupont, then France's representative on the Interpol Executive Committee, was going to make a move for the American's job, Milonakis offered the Frenchman, and powerful players in the French Interior Ministry, his services. Discreetly, very discreetly.

Herriot-Dupont's campaign for election as head of the world's largest police organisation was not pretty. Milonakis had been invaluable in orchestrating the damaging whispering campaign about McGraw's (alleged) blunders and misjudgements, about her (alleged) losing battle with Cotes du Rhone wine, about (alleged) ineptitude in the latter stages of her previous career at the US Postal Inspection Service. Allegations do not have to be true to be damaging.

Just as effectively, Milonakis had also orchestrated the whisperings, when he was assisting previously with Secretary General Holmesworth's departure, about, among many other things, a deceased Yorkshire terrier having been buried, at the insistence of Holmesworth's wife and against all imaginable organisational regulations, security procedures and/or French national health standards, late at night on the Interpol grounds.

Herriot-Dupont had swept to power in a landslide vote at Interpol's General Assembly in Belixico City, at which every trick in Machiavelli's book had been employed. That victory involved, among other things, extravagant funding for delegates' travel and hospitality, provided ever so discreetly by various supportive law enforcement agencies in Europe wishing to depose the American and install one of their own at the Interpol helm.

Quite why it was deemed appropriate for the latest French Secretary General of Interpol to be the former head of the least interesting and least respected of the French police divisions was not clear. And why it was appropriate for that new Secretary General to be a broad-shouldered, ham-handed and small-bottomed product of Normandy peasant stock, with a legendary predilection for extramarital affairs and dalliances with hotel chambermaids, bargirls and university students, was also a question so far unanswered.

Perhaps, some suggested, DHD knew where certain political bodies were buried in Paris or Brussels. Perhaps somebody in Paris owed him a very large favour. Or perhaps, the most uncharitable of observers suggested, incoming Secretary General Didier Herriot-Dupont, from an obscure department of the French national police, a man with lofty ambitions, would be easy to control.

Control would be easier still if a French intelligence agency mole were to be installed inside Interpol to keep track of things. Indeed, the existence of a French mole was an open secret at Lyon headquarters, just as was the existence of the CIA mole. It was common knowledge even among the lowliest of the building maintenance and cleaning staff who looked after the little offices on the second floor set aside for Interpol's various moles.

Absolutely clear as well was that Freiderikos Milonakis had survived the recent transitions in style. And would go on surviving. Though the challenge of winning unanimous re-election for Secretary General Herriot-Dupont, his latest assignment, was of an unprecedented order of difficulty.

"Freiderikos, it has to be unanimous, you know that, don't you?" Herriot-Dupont had told him one night as they sat in the Secretary General's private quarters.

One of the many perks of office was a spacious apartment for the Secretary General on the top floor of the headquarters building. It had sweeping views of the Rhone and the verdant hills beyond. It also housed the Secretary General's impressive collection of rifles and shotguns, mounted in all their phallic splendour on every available wall.

"Nothing else will do. No one will ever take me seriously again as Secretary General if even one member country votes against me in Munich. You know that, don't you, *mon ami?* Tell me you understand this absolutely."

"I will do my best, you can be sure of this, *monsieur*," Milonakis said.

"Call me Didier, Fred," the Secretary General said. "I invite you to do so."

Herriot-Dupont routinely invited Milonakis to dispense with formalities when he (a) was meeting with the Chief of Staff in his private quarters and (b) needed something from his Chief of Staff very, very badly. Milonakis had never been able to bring himself to address the Secretary General in this way because (a) he had come up through the ranks of the Greek police, where such informality was unheard of and (b) such familiarity would make betrayal, if betrayal ever became necessary, somewhat more difficult, though never impossible.

"I can only do my best. Your record, however, speaks for itself." Milonakis delivered this along with his best princely-advisor smile. His opened his palms to the ceiling in a gesture of submission and devotion. "I am here to serve."

Milonakis kept a notebook of the finest black leather, in which he recorded, among many other things, a list of the Secretary General's enemies (ever-expanding) and Interpol's foul-ups and failings (ever-expanding). A unanimous re-election at the Munich General Assembly, in light of what was in that notebook, was achievable. Possibly. But it would be far from easy.

Milonakis had successfully taken on for the Secretary General a large number of seemingly impossible tasks in the previous four-and-a-half years. His salary had risen accordingly over the same period.

He had helped clear out what Herriot-Dupont considered, in the first heady weeks of his mandate, to be dead wood. That this group included a disproportionately high number of those loyal, or seen to be loyal, to the previous American and British Secretaries General was a mere detail. That the clearing away of dead wood had generated a number of extremely expensive appeals to the full Administrative Tribunal of the International Labour Organization in Geneva, and a spate of scathing media coverage, was, in DHD's view, beside the point. He had pledged to draw Interpol back into the European orbit, tribunals or no tribunals, unions or no unions, collateral damage or no collateral damage.

Milonakis managed that project, as he had managed the incessant tinkering with Interpol's allegedly state-of-the-art electronic police communication system, X-24GT. This had replaced, by order of the previous Secretary General, the organisation's antiquated (some would say laughable) reliance on telephone, mail and fax to communicate with the world's police.

The new system installed by Alexandra McGraw had run millions of euros over budget and it was still, some eight years after conception, gripped by major teething problems. Much high-tech X-24GT equipment lay unused and gathering dust in faraway Interpol offices in places like Panama City and Brazzaville and Bishkek. Herriot-Dupont had seen this as his cue to recreate the system in his own image and make it the triumph the American contingent had so badly desired. He and France and Europe would be seen to be creating a truly new Interpol, with appropriately high-tech communications. In a post-9/11 world. Et cetera.

And of course all such innovation would certainly look very good on a CV someday, perhaps someday soon, when DHD made his move back to the French law enforcement arena where he longed to be taken seriously at last.

Milonakis had helped the Secretary General shift Interpol, at great expense and even greater upheaval, further and further away from its bread-and-butter police work of worldwide Red Notices for wanted persons and fingerprint files and stolen vehicle registration number databases and the tracing of stolen works of art, into uncharted waters of terrorist watch lists and intelligence-gathering and chemical weapons interdiction.

That a large number of member countries were clearly reluctant to have Interpol sail into those post-9/11 waters, that many of the world's police who had in fact even heard of Interpol actually preferred it to stick to the basic police business of apprehending fraudsters crossing borders or chasing drug dealers was, in DHD's view, irrelevant.

That many of the new Interpol projects and initiatives flew in the face of what experienced cops the world over knew to be true – police, in their heart of hearts, do not want to share information with other police forces unless they really have to, and police forces the world over want to be the ones taking credit for all possible arrests, all pos-sible successes, and not share the glory with Interpol officers or anyone else – was, in the Herriot-Dupont view, entirely beside the point.

The new Interpol was now clearly in the twenty-first century, like it or not, and one Didier Herriot-Dupont was indisputably at the helm.

The good ship *Interpol* was a much more modern ship, yes. And it was, thanks in large part to the policies of Alexandra McGraw, in many ways a more dynamic organisation and effective in some of its endeavours. But, as Milonakis was the first to admit, the headquarters building under DHD's stewardship was a pulsating glass cauldron of grievances, disagreements, unfinished projects, abandoned initiatives, recrimination and discontent. Casualties lay everywhere, victims were regularly carried away. The headquarters building was boiling over with palace intrigues and plots and machinations.

Member countries, meanwhile, many of them, were up in arms over increased annual dues, inexplicably rejected applications from their national officers, trampled jurisdictions and public criticism by the Secretary General of their operations. Enemies literally abounded.

"Unanimous re-election, Freiderikos. Every single member country must vote for me. This is our priority. Are you with me?" Herriot-Dupont had said that night.

"I am, Secretary General," Milonakis had said.

"Call me Didier. I invite you to do so."

The emergency meeting about the fallen sign, involving only the Secretary General and his Chief of Staff, was not, therefore, a moment for passing the buck.

"What the hell has happened with my sign, Freiderikos?" Herriot-Dupont asked again. "And who is looking after the Belarusians?"

"I believe the problem must have been with the installation," Milonakis said. "I'll call the company. I already have a crew out front cleaning up debris. I've sent the Belarus delegation over to Le Passage for a late lunch and I've told the manager to order in more vodka for the evening."

DHD's harried senior secretary – one of a retinue of four assistants who toiled in cramped conditions outside his office – knocked lightly and pushed open the door a crack.

"*Monsieur?*" Yolande said tentatively. "*Permettez?*"

"Yes, yes, Yolande, what is it?" Herriot-Dupont barked.

"The Chief of Security is here to see you. It is *très urgent*, he says, *monsieur*."

"*Merde*," Herriot-Dupont said. "*Merde*. Excuse my language, Yolande."

"*Je vous en prie, monsieur*."

Bernard LeBlanc strode into the office, looking flushed. He was a career functionary at Interpol, ineffectual as security chief but, with no real threats to speak of, also relatively harmless. Most of his job consisted of supervising guards who quickly passed mirrors under all arriving vehicles and looked in visitors' bags for explosive devices and unspecified contraband.

"Monsieur Herriot-Dupont, there is a problem," the Chief of Security said.

"*Merde alors*," DHD said.

"What is it, Bernard?" Milonakis asked, getting up.

"A body," LeBlanc said. "The crew has uncovered a body."

"A what? A what?" Herriot-Dupont shouted, leaping to his feet.

"Where?" Milonakis asked.

"In the garden bed out front. Where part of the sign fell."

"Impossible!" DHD shouted.

"However, I think it may just be a dog," LeBlanc said.

"A dog!" Herriot-Dupont shouted.

"They have dug it up. It is badly decomposed. Perhaps you should have a look."

"I am the Secretary General of Interpol!" Herriot-Dupont shouted. "I am a graduate of the École Nationale d'Administration. I'm not going down there to inspect the body of a decomposing dog!"

"Are you sure it's a dog, LeBlanc?" Milonakis asked quietly.

"Is it a Belarusian?" said Herriot-Dupont. "Are you certain it's a dog, Bernard? *Très certain?*"

"The head is very small," LeBlanc said.

"But this could be almost anybody around here," Herriot-Dupont said.

"And, *monsieur*, there is something else. The media are here," LeBlanc said. "Television."

"What?" Herriot-Dupont shouted.

"What?" Milonakis shouted.

"They have heard about the body somehow. But it is local TV only. French TV, not foreign."

"How on earth…" Herriot-Dupont looked over at Milonakis in disbelief. "Fred, can the media possibly be here so fast?"

"I will get Mortman out there," Milonakis said. "Or a press officer."

"No, no, no. Handle it yourself, Fred. It is a media leak. We must have a leak."

"And, *monsieur*…" LeBlanc said fearfully.

"What? What else?" Herriot-Dupont barked.

"Your wife has arrived."

"What? But she's not due back here until late next week. What is she doing back here?"

"She left Washington early, she said, *monsieur*. She is here now, downstairs with security. Still at the entrance."

"Well why in the name of God did she not just come up to the apartment?"

"My men didn't know just what to do," LeBlanc said, looking imploringly over to the Chief of Staff. "She was carrying a gun…"

TWO

Interpol Secretary General Didier Herriot-Dupont was alone in the living room of his top-floor apartment in the headquarters building, practising before a floor-to-ceiling mirror his idiosyncratic and, to the uninitiated, somewhat alarming style of the Japanese martial art of kendo.

He was dressed in a crimson silk kimono, not the traditional Japanese black kendo armour and face mask. This, in fact, was also unusual, for he would normally, even for an early morning session, be dressed in any one of a number of the police uniforms presented to him as gifts from law enforcement agencies in Interpol member countries he had visited in an official capacity.

Most unusual, from the point of view of kendo traditionalists, was that Interpol Secretary General Didier Herriot-Dupont wielded in his practice sessions not the bamboo *shinai* sword but any one of the many rifles and shotguns from his personal collection. He wielded these guns in the correct and precise kendo style – as one would expect from an expert sixth-dan practitioner – but the visual effect of a stocky, silver-maned Norman peasant dressed in a policeman's uniform and swinging a rifle or a shotgun in graceful, potentially lethal kendo arcs was, to say the least, memorable.

Very few, however, had had the privilege of seeing DHD practise kendo, whether kimono-clad or in police uniform. His Chief of Staff had done so, for Freiderikos Milonakis was his most trusted associate, and frequently in his private quarters. Certain cleaning ladies, usually timid, headscarved migrants from Morocco or Algeria who would never dare recount what they saw or heard in the Secretary General's apartment, had glimpsed the practice sessions. And his American wife – known to all at Interpol as Madame DHD, despite her actual name being Julia Smith – had also seen this sight.

Secretary General Herriot-Dupont was dressed in a silk kimono on this day because his wife was in the apartment, still sleeping off the effects of her flight from Washington, the unpleasantness with security personnel when she had arrived at headquarters with a ten-shot Heckler & Koch 45HK pistol wrapped up in her suitcase, and the aftermath of a lengthy, gale force, post-arrival shouting match with DHD.

Herriot-Dupont had donned the kimono after the shouting and general unpleasantness had subsided in the early hours, as no matter how long their very frequent arguments and disagreements lasted, a sexual coupling surely followed. Madame DHD had once, long ago, ventured that she found the Secretary General fetching in a kimono. So it was traditional in their post-conflict couplings for him to be kimono-clad as he thrust himself triumphantly at his wife's slim hips.

Madame DHD was a criminologist by trade, an appropriate profession for the consort of an Interpol chief. She was petite, slightly shorter than DHD, and this was also appropriate, indeed essential, for anyone taking on the consort's role. Herriot-Dupont had made very sure to find a partner not one centimetre taller than he. The correct choice of a life partner, he had long ago concluded, was a crucial element on the road to power and greatness, in law enforcement or any other realm.

There had been, of course, murmurings in certain European circles about that fact that Madame DHD was American. But others saw the strategic wisdom of such a transatlantic union; saw the diplomatic finesse involved, if not a certain irony. Didier Herriot-Dupont could never, despite his ferocious campaign against the previous American Secretary General, be accused of anti-American sentiment, could he? Not having taken an American wife.

As he swung his weapon and practised elegant kendo moves – on this day using a vintage Boxall & Edmiston double-barrel twelve-gauge shotgun with profuse plate engravings, one of the finest and costliest weapons in his collection – DHD considered his latest marital travails. For it must be said that while the marriage to Julia Smith had been brilliantly strategic – a union not just with an American but with a respected criminologist, and carefully timed to coincide with DHD's original bid for the Secretary General's post so as to head off any vulgar suggestions that he might be too fixated on a law enforcement career or without the usual requirements for love, affection and family life – the marriage had not, to be frank, been a happy one.

Madame DHD had for some reason resented the subsequent interruption to her academic career, the frequent travel required to France, the frequent public humiliations she endured when her husband was in a temper, or when he merely sublimated his own marital disappointment into scathing remarks about his wife's personality or professional achievements or physical appearance or sexual appetite.

To be very, very frank, and this was something that Herriot-Dupont himself only acknowledged in moments of deep introspection, Julia Smith had been a major disappointment. Perhaps any consort would have been, for in his heart of hearts, Herriot-Dupont was not the marrying kind. He was the absolute caricature of the womanising French male, prone to dalliances, born to be an unfaithful, feckless, inconsiderate husband. That French society very often ignored, condoned or even applauded such behaviour among powerful politicians and public figures was lost on the Americans, and in particular on Herriot-Dupont's American wife.

Julia Smith simply wasn't woman enough for him; that was just the sad truth of the matter. The marriage had for many months simply remained at the point, at least until now, of unarmed standoff. That Julia had now been stopped by Interpol security from bringing a gun into the headquarters building gave the Secretary General pause, to say the least.

Madame DHD had argued strenuously, first with security and then later in the privacy of the apartment with Herriot-Dupont himself, that the gun was a gift for the Secretary General. That the Secretary General's collection comprised nothing but rifles and shotguns did not seem to trouble Julia whatsoever.

"I bought it for *you*, Didier!" Julia had shouted repeatedly, once released by security and the gun duly confiscated. "It was a *gift*, for God's sake."

Her round, wire-rimmed eyeglasses slipped down the overlong bridge of her nose, something that always infuriated the Secretary General, particularly when this occurred at official functions. That, and her somewhat (by French standards) inexpertly coiffed female university professor's hair. Julia looked, Herriot-Dupont always thought, too academic. Too, well, American.

"I don't collect handguns, Julia," he had shouted.

"You need to branch *out!*" Julia shouted back. "You've got too many damn rifles now anyway. Start a *new* collection, for God's sake. It was a gift!"

After he had punished her severely in bed for this latest misdemeanour, DHD lay awake for a long time, considering, with regret, his marital fate.

Truth be told, Herriot-Dupont very much regretted the day he had swept Julia Smith off her feet at a criminologists' convention in Phoenix, Arizona, and taken her back to the hotel to have his way with her. The benefits of the partnership had in the end been too few, the downsides too many. Julia was not exactly a liability to him at present, but neither was she an asset. The marriage could still be endured, but only just. The extramarital consolations he had frequently allowed himself, the utterly secret assignations and the occasional bit of rough trade he had indulged in with a series of nubile young women, occasionally in pairs, were little enough.

The immediate question, Herriot-Dupont asked himself as he

swung the shotgun back into a new kendo move and observed himself closely in the floor-to-ceiling mirror, was whether security had in fact foiled a possible assassination plot. Involving his own wife.

True, a foiled assassination attempt on the life of a French Secretary General of Interpol would play out extremely well in the media, in a post-9/11 world and in the run-up to a General Assembly at which he was seeking re-election. It would, as it were, look pretty good on a CV. But less impressive would be the marriage angle: a foiled assassination attempt involving his own wife as the would-be assassin was not quite the news story he needed in the pre-election period. Or at any time, for that matter.

She doesn't have the guts to try to do me harm, Herriot-Dupont thought. No. She does not.

"Re-election, re-election, unanimous re-election," he chanted aloud as he swung the shotgun over his head. The mantra soothed him. "Then, then, then, Didier, *mon vieux*," he chanted, "we can begin to solve the other problems we have before us."

He swung the shotgun swiftly to his shoulder and pointed it expertly at the closed door leading to the bedroom wing of the vast apartment, then at the door leading to the offices outside, then at the windows overlooking Lyon. He pulled back the trigger of the left barrel and let off one imaginary, devastating blast.

Die, all you bastards, he intoned silently. Die.

Interpol Chief of Staff Freiderikos Milonakis was in his well-appointed private office down the corridor from the Secretary General's bevy of assistants. He was making a fresh list in his leather-bound notebook.

Secretary General issues, Milonakis wrote. *Current as of today's date. Vis-à-vis Munich General Assembly.*

He paused. Updating the list, though something he did regularly, even religiously, was never a pleasant task. The sheer size and complexity of the list would make any Chief of Staff break into a sweat. Indeed, on many a morning did Freiderikos Milonakis wake from his slumbers in a damp chill, having dreamed of his list, dreamed of disastrous scenarios, dreamed of plots and allegations.

He was paid handsomely to be the Secretary General's professional worrier and confidant and fixer, but it was an extremely daunting task. The enemies list in his notebook told that tale.

Already entered, among others:

- *Executive Committee members Valon Dragusha and Yoko Watanabe.*
- *Other EC members?*
- *Japan Criminal Investigation Bureau.*
- *Dutch Police Agency.*
- *Europol (all!).*
- *FBI Director Mike McCrindle.*
- *Alexandra McGraw.*
- *Belixico Federal Police Commander.*
- *The Government of Iran.*
- *German organising committee for Munich Gen. Ass. (especially Adolph Fenstermacher).*
- *Interpol stolen motor vehicle unit (all).*
- *Interpol stolen works of art unit (some members of).*
- *Interpol cafeteria manager.*
- *Former Sec. Gen. Holmesworth, and wife.*
- *Fired Interpol staff members (various), and their lawyers.*
- *Le Monde newspaper (editor, et al).*
- *Le Progrès newspaper, Lyon (editor, et al).*
- *SG wife??*

This was merely the A List. Lists B and C, also duly entered in Milonakis' notebook, contained the names of other of the Secretary General's foes, victims and targets, but those who posed less of an immediate threat or who were merely to be monitored carefully at this stage.

How did one get onto Milonakis' A List? Well, in the case of Valon Dragusha, an Interpol Executive Committee Member for

Europe, and a Chief of Commissariat of the Serbanian State Police, it had to do with a range of complex factors. Dragusha was unspeakably corrupt and hopelessly alcoholic. He was known to run, in addition to his law enforcement duties, a lucrative business selling on confiscated items – particularly ladies' cosmetics and booze – to wholesalers in the capital, Virana, and elsewhere. It was an open secret that he wanted to be Secretary General one day, a prospect that filled Milonakis, not to mention Herriot-Dupont, with dread.

Dragusha was also a rumoured pornographer and he was definitely an inveterate pincher of ladies' bottoms, in Serbania and elsewhere, anywhere, around the world. He expected, whenever he travelled to Lyon for Executive Committee meetings, to avail himself of the services of Lyon's choicest ladies of the night, at Interpol expense. He had not yet made his move to take Herriot-Dupont's job, and Milonakis doubted he would move this time. But Dragusha was rumoured to be orchestrating Herriot-Dupont's fall, and a less than overwhelming re-election in Munich would make his bid all the easier when the next ballot was held five years hence. Or earlier if Dragusha had his way.

Dragusha was also extremely unhappy that Milonakis, on Herriot-Dupont's orders, was now refusing to procure female companionship for him while he was in Lyon and, again on DHD's orders, regularly questioning the exorbitant expense claims racked up by the Serbanian on supposed Interpol business in Lyon, Virana and other cities. Dragusha could quite likely swing swathes of Eastern Europe's vote at the Munich General Assembly and possibly elsewhere. Dragusha was a major concern. DHD would need to work harder to keep Dragusha happy.

Yoko Watanabe was a major concern as well, though for quite different reasons. She was a successful and respected Japanese detective, and now a Chief Superintendent in Japan's National Police Agency. Watanabe was one of two members for Asia on the Interpol Executive Committee. Her issue with the Secretary General was, in her view and the Japanese finance ministry's view, the profligate spending on a range of new and ill-considered Interpol projects, resulting in regular proposals from Herriot-Dupont that member countries' annual dues be increased.

Watanabe was the very model of personal and professional rectitude. She did not like the fundamental and rapid changes Herriot-Dupont was introducing at Interpol, and she did not at all like Herriot-Dupont's frequent invoking of his European law enforcement background as a less-than-subtle way of denigrating the Japanese or other Asian police. Watanabe had routinely voted against Interpol budget and dues increases at Executive Committee meetings, and there was a rumour she was marshalling support in certain Asian nations for a protest vote against the Secretary General in Munich. Just to give him a scare, it was said.

Why did the entire senior Japanese national police hierarchy hate the Secretary General? That had something do with a Japanese TV interview given by Herriot-Dupont approximately one year earlier, during which he had accused the nation's police of general ineptitude, and particularly in their investigation of an alleged Japanese criminal connection to a stolen vehicle used in a political assassination in Lebanon. That the Secretary General had all but gutted the Interpol stolen motor vehicle department to pay for a range of other grandiose projects was an irony not lost on senior Japanese police.

The Dutch police? Well, the Chief of that particular law enforcement agency had not taken kindly to the public dressing-down he had received from Herriot-Dupont at a recent Interpol European Regional Conference. The Secretary General had ridiculed what he regarded as the failure of the Dutch police to get tough on drug traffickers in Amsterdam, and he had even ridiculed the Dutch police uniforms. The Dutch police were clearly offside, and might take some European member country votes with them in Munich. Not good.

Europol? Arch rivals of Interpol, though the two organisations exchanged liaison officers, and in public repeatedly professed eagerness to cooperate. The fact of the matter was that senior staff at Europol did not want to share police information with Interpol, did not want

Interpol sniffing around on European cases, despite a European being at the helm, did not like the Secretary General's style and did not like the fact that he was, in their view, never a true police officer. Relations with Europol were sour, very sour indeed.

FBI Director Mike McCrindle hated the Secretary General as a result of some slight or series of slights from the days when Herriot-Dupont was still with the French police. The FBI as a result consistently refused to send as many seconded agents to work at Interpol as DHD requested. The two FBI agents currently serving in Lyon were not – Milonakis saw this clearly – of the highest quality. They had simply been put out to pasture. The FBI Director needed to be carefully watched.

Alexandra McGraw was an enemy for obvious reasons.

The head of the Belixican federal police was, like Serbania's Dragusha, corrupt, powerful, and, like Herriot-Dupont, a ladies' man. Alonso Gomez did not appear to want to be Secretary General (yet) but he badly wanted a spot on the Executive Committee and seemed to have formed an alliance with Dragusha to get there. He sent expensive gifts of all kinds to Executive Committee members, at all times of the year. He would attend, and cast Belixico's vote at, the Munich assembly.

The government of Iran was upset because Interpol had issued Red Notices for the apprehension of alleged Iranian terrorists. Iran did not think Interpol should be hassling them about terrorism. Iran did not like the Secretary General as a result. Simple.

The German organising committee for the General Assembly, and in particular its chairman, Adolph Fenstermacher, did not like the Secretary General either. Fenstermacher was old-school, a senior *Bundeskriminalamt* man who did not like Herriot-Dupont's, or for that matter Milonakis', incessant and very costly demands as regards the staging of the conference in Munich. Herriot-Dupont had already personally travelled twice to Germany, with Milonakis and Interpol's communications chief, to inspect plans for the General Assembly and to make demands. Adolph Fenstermacher was reported to have spoken in very unflattering terms about Herriot-Dupont to senior German officials. Fenstermacher was too German and too reliable to ever deliver anything other than a perfectly staged General Assembly. But whether the staging would be to his taste, or to the Secretary General's, remained to be seen.

All members of the Interpol stolen motor vehicle unit were angry about a major reallocation of resources from their heretofore highly successful and hugely popular police work to some of the Secretary General's other, far more glamorous, projects. That member countries' police forces valued and frequently availed themselves of the stolen motor vehicles databases was, in Herriot-Dupont's view, beside the point. That was 'old Interpol'.

Some members of the stolen works of art unit hated the Secretary General for similar reasons.

The manager of the Interpol cafeteria, André Julien, hated the Secretary General because he never ate there but had nonetheless ordered that Julien stock various costly Lyonnais delicacies to impress foreign visitors who lunched in the building. Julien hated the Secretary General because he insisted on hiring outside caterers for all after-hours functions in the building. Julien was said to be stirring up resentments among Interpol staff.

Former Secretary General Jonathan W. Holmesworth, and all of those employees fired in the legendary post-Holmesworth era purge, hated the Secretary General for obvious reasons.

Le Monde's editors hated the Secretary General simply because they felt like it. A number of highly critical *Le Monde* articles and opinion pieces had eventuated as a result. The main Lyon newspaper hated the Secretary General because he consistently refused to be interviewed, to meet editorial staff or to pay the paper any attention whatsoever. Reporters from *Le Progrès* were, as a result, always searching for negative stories, and for disgruntled staffers with tales to tell.

And among the many threats to DHD was almost certainly his wife, terribly sad though that may be. Milonakis did not share the Secretary General's newly developed theory that Julia Smith was planning an assassination. The incident with the Heckler & Koch pistol was, in Milonakis' view, not to be overemphasised. But the undeniable fact remained that the marriage was not a happy one, that there was frequent and frequently noisy conflict, and that anyone would agree that a disgruntled and often humiliated spouse was an enemy well worth watching. And, yes, the Heckler & Koch HK45 was one wicked-looking gun.

Milonakis closed his leather notebook with a heavy sigh. He could not face the B and C Lists this morning. Perhaps he would update those later in the day. Suddenly he was plunged into despair. Why do I do this? he thought bitterly. Why? Then the glowering images of his three ex-wives and, more importantly, the images of their high-priced lawyers in Athens came before his mind's eye. Suddenly, things became clear again.

Interpol Senior Staff Meetings took place at least once a week, or more often if the Secretary General was in a rage about something, or if he had become obsessed with a new Interpol law enforcement initiative or project, or some operational failing by a police force somewhere in the world, or some real or imagined public slight dealt either to him personally or to Interpol as an organisation by a police officer somewhere, by a member of the media, or by anyone, absolutely anyone, else.

In the electronic appointments calendars of the senior Interpol officers invited to attend – usually all officers at the Director level plus some unfortunate Assistant Directors invited to explain a foul-up – these meetings were noted with the initials *SSM*. They were widely known, however, as 'S&M meetings', with the sadism to be dealt out by Herriot-Dupont and the masochism among those who attempted to explain themselves to, or worse, to debate law enforcement or any other matters with, the Secretary General.

First item on the agenda on the day after the fallen sign debacle was, naturally, the fallen sign. The Head of Building Services, Jacques Buisson, was taking his verbal beating like a man. He was a sturdy, swarthy man of Franco-Algerian stock, and known to be himself a dispenser of angry words to members of his own staff.

"And did you personally inspect those bolts before the sign was installed to make sure they would be able to do the job required?" Herriot-Dupont asked.

"*Non, monsieur*. I did not. I thought of course that the installing company would provide us with quality materials," Buisson said.

Other SSM participants kept their heads lowered. Milonakis was taking notes.

"You *thought?*" Herriot-Dupont hissed.

"*Oui, monsieur*," Buisson said. "*Malheureusement*, some of the bolts appear to have failed."

"Because you failed to inspect them properly, Jacques," Herriot-Dupont said. "Would you agree with that suggestion?"

Buisson blinked, only once. He knew what was required. "*Oui, monsieur*. I fully accept this. Yes."

"And you have ruled out sabotage?"

"*Oui, absolument, monsieur*," Buisson said forcefully.

"My sign will be reinstalled when, exactly?"

"As soon as possible, *monsieur*."

"Which is when, exactly?"

SSM members willed Buisson not to say the wrong thing. Pick a date, any date, they all urged him silently.

"I cannot say exactly at this stage, *monsieur*. I am in negotiations with the company."

Wrong answer. Wrong, wrong, wrong. SSM participants waited for the verbal blows to rain down.

"I, on the other hand, *can* say exactly when, Jacques," Herriot-Dupont said. "If my building manager cannot, I can. That sign will be repaired and reinstalled in forty-eight hours from now. And we will have launched a lawsuit against the installation company by then. Cynthia, get your department on that today."

Director of Interpol Legal Services Cynthia Payne, an urbane, world-weary lawyer from Scotland, nodded and slowly wrote something on her lined yellow pad. She was an SSM veteran.

"Noted," Payne said briskly.

"Freiderikos, get me the phone number of the sign company," Herriot-Dupont said. "I will call the owner personally."

"I can make that call for you, *monsieur*," Milonakis said. He knew what the consequences of an irate Secretary General phone call could often be.

"Freiderikos, what did I just say?"

"I will get you the number."

"And we have completely ruled out the possibility of sabotage?"

"I think so, yes," Milonakis said cautiously. "I will continue to make enquiries."

"That is your job, Freiderikos," Herriot-Dupont said.

"Yes," Milonakis said.

"And the dead dog?"

"A mystery," Milonakis said. "I will continue to make enquiries."

"TV? Stories about the sign or the dog?"

"Nothing aired last night. It was too close to their deadline. I have calls in to the station's editor-in-chief."

"I will call," Herriot-Dupont suggested.

"Not necessary at this stage, *monsieur*."

"Is someone trying to embarrass us, Freiderikos?"

"I will continue to make enquiries."

Next on the agenda: preparations for the African Regional Conference in Zambezi. It was the last big regional meeting of police from Interpol member countries before the General Assembly. Herriot-Dupont wanted it to be a major success, with no hitches, with major and positive media coverage, with new cross-border crime-fighting initiatives and training programmes agreed to. Milonakis had already been to Kulsaka City twice in recent months to check on preparations.

Interpol's Events Manager, Antonio de Caldevilla, had just returned from his own visit to Kulsaka. Caldevilla was a most unlikely man for the job, as he was the most undiplomatic and quite possibly the most unpleasant senior staff member in the entire organisation. Except, some argued, for the Secretary General himself. Caldevilla had risen high in the Maltese national police echelons, then he ran into some major hushed-up difficulty late in his career and had been farmed out to Interpol until he was of pensionable age. The Secretary General had agreed to take him on in return for favours as yet unspecified from the Maltese authorities. He had wanted to bolster support among Interpol's Southern European member countries, and it was good to be owed a favour or two from Malta, a malleable minor player in European policing. Herriot-Dupont had therefore been willing to ignore many, indeed most, of Caldevilla's failings.

Caldevilla lacked all people skills, all empathy, all charm. This despite keeping various reference books about protocol ostentatiously displayed on his office shelves. He was a huge fan of the British royal family, and indeed of royalty everywhere. He wore his Maltese Civil Protection Order of Merit lapel pin on any suit jacket he chose for the day. He ordered his staff around unconscionably. He liked to see secretaries cry. And his fractured, impossibly convoluted English made him an extremely poor communicator, no matter where his assignments took him. Listening to him struggle in English brought tears to eyes of all but the most charitable.

"We are under control. It is good," Caldevilla said. "All extremely alright, OK."

Caldevilla very much enjoyed reporting to high-ranking officials anywhere. He always sat bolt upright in his chair when he did so. He applied extra oil to his black helmet of hair on the day of any such encounter. He grinned an obsequious, nicotine-stained grin as he made his reports.

"The opening ceremony?" Herriot-Dupont said. "This is crucial. The Zambezin Interior Minister will attend?"

"It is good, very OK," Caldevilla said.

"The Zambezin police band? Photographs?"

"Yes. Good, good."

"Seating?

"Extremely arranged."

"Media?"

"Aha, *monsieur*, well, this is of course not of my area. Mr Franklin has, I think, this area."

Caldevilla flicked his head, distaste apparent, in the direction of Frank Franklin, Interpol's Assistant Director for Media Relations. A Canadian, a civilian and a former newspaper police reporter from Toronto, Franklin reported to Chief of Communications Alf Mortman. Together they generated enough anxious energy to power a small city. Franklin was drinking far too much and sleeping far too little since he had arrived in Lyon. Caldevilla and Franklin hated each other. They often travelled on Interpol business together – far too often.

"I have done up a written report on the Kulsaka media preparations," Franklin said. He wore a crumpled brown corduroy jacket that would have been the latest style in Toronto newsrooms in 1975. He wore lightly tinted aviator-style eyeglasses indoors. No one knew why. Some suggested it was to mask eyeball redness. He had a round bald spot on the top of his head that peeled when touched in the slightest way by sunlight.

"I've not seen it," Herriot-Dupont said. "I need these documents before you come into SSM."

"You have it there, I believe. In the purple folder. I did up copies for everyone," Franklin said.

"And CNN?" Herriot-Dupont asked, picking up a loose-leaf folder.

"Looking very positive at this stage, Secretary General," Franklin said.

"We need that profile before Munich," Herriot-Dupont said.

"Looking very positive," Franklin said.

Herriot-Dupont glanced at Franklin's report, apparently unsure whether to reject it totally before having had a chance to read it in full. Franklin was lucky. The Secretary General decided to wait and to attack all aspects of the plan later, probably in writing.

"Antonio, anything else to report from the Zambezi mission? No problems at all?" Herriot-Dupont asked.

"Well…" Caldevilla said. He picked a piece of lint from the sleeve of his impeccably cut navy blazer. He fingered his Maltese Civil Protection Order of Merit lapel pin.

The tension level in the room rose instantly, palpably. Interpol's long-suffering Director of Operational Police Support, Jean-Marc Moulin, tried unsuccessfully to catch Caldevilla's eye. The meeting had been going on for too long already, and Moulin clearly wanted to avoid extending it with some protocol problem raised by Caldevilla.

Moulin, seconded from Belgium's Federal Police, was, almost all agreed, the best and most effective officer in the entire organisation. Moulin just wanted to be able do his job. He wanted Interpol to be all that it could be. That aim, however, was constantly being thwarted.

"Real police work is a very simple matter," Moulin would say repeatedly, in private, to his trusted colleagues "It is to find and apprehend wrongdoers. That is all. At Interpol, these days, real police work is not easy."

"Well," Caldevilla said after a pause, "among the Zambezin police organisers and the support staff I had, I must say, some little, small problems. But not too big."

DHD looked sharply at Caldevilla and then at Milonakis. "Like what, Antonio?" he asked.

Now it was Milonakis who tried to catch Caldevilla's eye.

"I could not tell any of them apart," Interpol's Events Manager said.

"What?" Herriot-Dupont said.

"I could not tell any of them apart," the Events Manager said. "These dark African people, they all look exactly very much the same to me."

"Antonio," Herriot-Dupont said warningly.

Caldevilla smiled warmly. He opened his palms to the ceiling.

"It is so, yes. Always when I travel to Africa I have this problem, *monsieur*. In Ngheria even more so I find than in Zambezi. They are darker there, I think."

"Antonio—" Milonakis said.

"I can't believe I'm hearing this," Herriot-Dupont said.

"Yes, it is always like this. It is a common problem. To tell these dark people apart."

"Antonio—" Milonakis said again.

"You find this also, Freiderikos?" Caldevilla asked.

"Antonio, best to shut up now," Payne called out.

"Yes, Antonio. Thank you very much, *merci*," Moulin called out.

"I can't believe I'm hearing this," Herriot-Dupont said.

"It is a common problem in the African places," the Events Manager said.

The strategic value of keeping this esteemed representative of Malta's Public Security Police, and his senior officers back in Valetta, onside apparently outweighed for the moment the necessity of correcting certain racist assumptions held by Interpol's Events Manager. Herriot-Dupont merely shook his head sadly and turned to the next agenda item, somewhat to the amazement of SSM attendees. There was no way of predicting how an SSM session would go on any given day, no way at all. Herriot-Dupont moved quickly on to the next, and last, item.

"Moulin? Databases? How is the terrorist watch list project proceeding?"

Moulin and his team had been given the heavy task of expanding, virtually overnight and literally at any cost, Interpol's array of databases. Some of the databases most popular and useful among the world's rank-and-file police officers were thought by the Secretary General to be old-fashioned, not interesting.

More interesting, more modern and far more impressive on a Secretary General's CV would be to drag Interpol into the post-9/11 world of terrorist watch lists. The problem, as Moulin would tell any trusted colleague, was that none of the world's truly important law enforcement agencies had any genuine interest in sharing such data with Herriot-Dupont's Interpol. This reluctance infuriated Secretary General Herriot-Dupont. This made Moulin's life unbearable.

"We are making steady progress, *monsieur*," Moulin said.

In fact, the number of names in the database was still below five thousand, and most of those names came from B-grade databases of minor national players in the so-called war on terror. And the backgrounds and details of many of those listed could not be properly verified. Few member countries took any notice of the launch of Interpol's new terrorism-related databases, few ever used them, and fewer still contributed any significant data. This infuriated the Secretary General. This, too, made Moulin's life unbearable.

"I want ten thousand names, minimum, before the General Assembly," Herriot-Dupont said. "Minimum. And I want all 190 member countries wired in to the X-24GT communication system by then as well. *All.* I want to announce this in my speech on the first day. Everybody has to be connected."

"Understood," Moulin said sadly.

"I am counting on you, Jean-Marc," Herriot-Dupont said.

"*Oui, monsieur,*" Moulin said sadly.

"And my new bioterrorism project?" Herriot-Dupont asked. "This must be operational. Training courses, booklets for police officers everywhere in the world. Posters for all police stations. I want to see Interpol bioterrorism project posters on the wall of the police headquarters in Ouagadougou. You can have all the resources you need for that, Jean-Marc. Until after the General Assembly in any case."

"Understood," Moulin said.

THREE

Even the most paranoid Interpol Chief of Staff would have reason to worry about what Secretary General Herriot-Dupont said immediately after the SSM.

Milonakis was alone with him in the boardroom. They were looking at their diaries together.

"Cancel my eleven o'clock meeting, Fred, please. I've got something else on now," Herriot-Dupont said.

Alarm bells rang in Milonakis' head. "The Egyptian delegation won't like that very much," he said.

"You can go along to that. That will be fine," Herriot-Dupont said.

"What can I help you with, Secretary General?" Milonakis asked.

"Nothing, thank you. I'm just meeting Broussard from IT about the General Assembly preparations. I don't need you for that."

The alarm bells clanged louder. Ordinarily, the Secretary General would not deign to meet the Assistant Manager of Interpol's computer department at all, for any reason. Or an assistant manager from any department, for that matter. Gilles Broussard was too junior to merit Secretary General-level attention. That such a meeting had been scheduled, that Chief of Staff Freiderikos Milonakis was not required to attend, that this was being announced suddenly – this was all reason for concern.

"I'm happy to come to that," Milonakis said. "We can see the Egyptians after lunch. I'll cancel your meeting with the BMW man."

The Secretary General wanted an appropriately post-9/11

armour-plated car, and was to look at the most expensive available model that afternoon.

"No, leave that," Herriot-Dupont said.

"Troubles with Broussard?" Milonakis asked.

"No, no. Nothing wrong. Just a little chat," Herriot-Dupont said.

"I am happy to help out if there is a problem with Broussard," Milonakis said.

"No, that will be fine. Thank you, Fred," Herriot-Dupont said in the husky voice he used when he was not being entirely frank with his Chief of Staff. "You deal with the Egyptians for me. Tell them I think they're doing excellent police work down there."

Gilles Broussard was a career Interpol *fonctionnaire*; a classic. He was old Interpol and proud of it. He had seen various Secretaries General come and go. He was in for the long haul, on a coveted *contract durée indèterminée*, an open-ended contract, iron-clad in France, which meant that only an unspeakable crime of some sort would ever be enough to oust him from his not terribly well paid, not terribly senior, but oh-so-secure post at Interpol headquarters.

Broussard was fifty-seven years old, a native son of Lyon. In France, for a career *fonctionnaire*, being fifty-seven meant retirement was a matter of a few years, perhaps even a matter of months, away. He was reed-thin, of somewhat less than average height and weight, and suffered from the cold. He wore a brown cardigan sweater to work, even at the height of the Southern French summer.

He was no genius, to be sure, but he knew the Interpol computer systems inside out, if only because he had helped manage them for so many years, had helped implement changes of various sorts, had lovingly nurtured them along. He was rather like a gifted motor mechanic who knew a senior official's car so well that he could diagnose complex problems merely by listening to the way an engine sounded on any given day.

He could daily be seen lining up at the Interpol cafeteria at precisely 11.50 am, ten minutes before doors opened for lunch, heavily subsidised by Interpol member countries. He limited himself to one airline meal-sized bottle of red wine each lunch hour and a little *rondelle* of Saint-Marcellin cheese as a post-meal treat. He drove a sensible Renault Clio, grey in colour. He lived in a very small apartment in the unfashionable third *arrondissement* of Lyon. He went home each night, however, to his wife Claudette and his adoring children, a happy, somewhat heroic figure, with gripping tales to tell his family of the fight against international crime and his crucial role therein.

Broussard was startled and flattered in equal measure when the Secretary General's senior appointments assistant had called him to say he was to attend a meeting, *très importante et très confidentielle*, with Herriot-Dupont in his office on the fifth floor. In his twenty-six years at Interpol, Broussard had been to the fifth floor perhaps half a dozen times, and never, until now, to meet with Herriot-Dupont or any other Secretary General one-on-one about a very important and very confidential matter.

His immediate thought, however, was that this breach of Interpol procedure, this failure by the Secretary General, and therefore by Broussard, to respect the old Interpol norms of institutional hierarchy, would send his manager Pierre Cholet into a spasm of envy and despair. Cholet was even closer to retirement than Broussard, an even more entrenched *fonctionnaire*, and would therefore be extremely unhappy that his deputy, the lowly, cardigan-clad Broussard, had been summoned to see the Secretary General, any Secretary General, on an important and confidential matter.

"*Impossible à refuser, Monsieur Cholet*," Broussard said repeatedly when his manager had indeed protested. "*Impossible.*"

Inside, Broussard was aglow with pride and anticipation. What could this important and very confidential matter be, he wondered? Claudette will be so very proud. And the little ones as well.

Monsieur Herriot-Dupont had been *charmant, très charmant*, Broussard would tell his wife the evening after the meeting. Broussard had worn a necktie that day, something he usually only did for funerals and family weddings. He had considered not wearing his cardigan, but then recalled that the Secretary General's private office was said to be icy cold, and overly air-conditioned. He hoped he would not catch the flu.

He was much taken aback when Herriot-Dupont grasped his hand and shook it energetically, the other hand on Broussard's elbow, as if greeting a long-lost friend.

"Sit, sit," the Secretary General had said, pointing to a leather armchair near the balcony window of the office. "Coffee?"

"*Non, merci beaucoup, Monsieur le Secrétaire Général,*" Broussard said. "No coffee, not at this hour, thank you very much."

"And the family? All are well?"

Broussard was aglow with pride that the Secretary General of the world's largest Interpol police organisation would take time to enquire about his wife and children.

"In excellent form," Broussard said. "*Merci beaucoup, monsieur.*"

"That is a very nice sweater you are wearing today, Gilles," Herriot-Dupont said. "Very chic. *Très practique.* I must get one like it for myself."

Broussard resisted the temptation to remove his cardigan and hand it to the Secretary General as a spontaneous gift.

"Ah, well," Herriot-Dupont said, again flashing his best European diplomat's smile at the Assistant Manager of Interpol's computer department. "Yes. Yes."

Broussard was again aglow, from the warmth of the sweater and the warmth of the Secretary General's welcome. Claudette will be so very proud tonight, he thought.

There was at that moment a slight pause in the proceedings. Broussard was not sure what he could or should say next. The Secretary General sat smiling his incandescent diplomatic smile at him. Broussard smiled a slightly crooked smile back.

"*Eh, bien,*" Broussard said awkwardly. "Yes, well…"

He began to wish he had taken up the offer of a coffee, if only to have something to do with his hands.

"Gilles," the Secretary General said at last.

"*Oui, monsieur?*" Broussard said.

"Gilles, my friend, I am going to take you into my confidence."

Broussard's cheeks burned with pride. "You are?" he said.

"Yes. I have something very important and very confidential I would like to discuss with you today. And you must tell no one else about this conversation. You will see why in a moment."

"Not even my manager, *monsieur?*" Broussard asked, incredulous.

"Not even Cholet," Herriot-Dupont said. "No."

There was another pause. Herriot-Dupont's smile was extinguished.

"You are in charge of the computer installations for the General Assembly in Munich, I am told," he said.

"*Oui, monsieur,*" Broussard said. "Under the direction of my manager, of course."

Any good French bureaucrat will always make sure there is a superior who can be held to account for a problem or an error, should something unpleasant occur.

"But I am told that it is you who will oversee installation of our systems for the Assembly. The computer workrooms for Interpol staff, some laptops for delegates' emails, the voting system, all of that. Correct?"

"Yes. Under the direction of my manager, of course."

"Of course."

"You have been to Munich, I'm told. For planning and to inspect the situation."

"Yes, so far twice."

Claudette had been very proud of Broussard's travel to exotic locales.

"Your impressions?"

Broussard hesitated. Here he was being invited to make a judgment, something with which he had little experience or comfort. This was normally something for a manager, not an assistant manager, no?

"Well…" Broussard said.

"You may be frank with me, Gilles," Herriot-Dupont said.

The diplomat's smile flashed on again, though briefly.

"Well, I would say, I think, to be frank, that preparations are going quite well. I would say."

A droplet of sweat rolled down Broussard's spine. He shifted a little in his chair. The black leather squeaked alarmingly.

"Let me ask you something, Gilles. Very confidentially," Herriot-Dupont said.

"Of course," Broussard said.

"Is there a possibility of sabotage?"

"Sabotage?" Broussard said.

"Yes. Can our system be tampered with? Any part of it? Say, for example, the voting system?"

Interpol general assemblies and regional assemblies used a cumbersome and rather dated system of remote handheld voting devices. Delegates pressed one of two buttons on what looked like garage door openers. These sent a wireless signal to a computer in the room. An Interpol technician, usually Broussard himself, would examine the incoming data and arrange 'for' and 'against' numbers and bar charts with results of important votes to be displayed on a screen for all delegates to see.

"We have had no such trouble in the past," Broussard said. "Very infrequently there has been a small problem with batteries in the voting units used by the delegates. I always ensure, therefore, that all batteries are replaced, in all of the units, before an assembly anywhere. It is a little expensive, but we do it. It is only Interpol people who handle these units. And I myself always ensure that installation of the system is *parfaitement correcte*."

"These are troubled times, Gilles," Herriot-Dupont said sadly.

"I agree with that, *monsieur*."

"I need trusted people such as yourself to work with me to make sure that all is well, always, everywhere. You are my expert lieutenant, Gilles. My indispensable expert lieutenant."

Broussard thought his heart would burst with pride. Claudette would be so very proud. "*À votre service, monsieur*," he said. "Always. *Je vous en prie.*"

"I will need to take you into my confidence, Gilles," the Secretary General said. "From time to time. On important and confidential matters. You must be my eyes and ears. These are troubled times we live in, you would agree with me on that, wouldn't you, Gilles?"

"*Absolument, monsieur*," Broussard said.

"Are you sure you would not like a coffee, Gilles? Some cakes, maybe? A glass of wine?" Herriot-Dupont said.

The Secretary General's smile once again bathed the room in brilliant light: steady and very, very warm.

Freiderikos Milonakis was perhaps the only person inside Interpol who could get away with interrupting a closed-door meeting in the Secretary General's office. Even so, he did this rarely. And even so, the secretaries at small desks clustered around the office door looked terrified when Milonakis came through that morning and knocked twice, briskly, before opening the door slightly and putting his head in.

"Secretary General? If I may?" he said.

His unease about Herriot-Dupont's mysterious meeting with the computer man made this a risk worth taking. The secretaries took a collective fearful breath, anticipating a blast of flame and shrapnel from inside.

Milonakis went through, then stopped immediately, stunned at what he saw.

Secretary General Herriot-Dupont looked up, startled, as if caught in flagrante delicto with a lover. He was sitting beside Gilles Broussard on the leather couch – very close, very close. Milonakis could have sworn DHD's hand had been on Broussard's thigh and swiftly removed.

Broussard was extremely flushed, blood-red in the face. His tattered cardigan was askew. He gave Milonakis a dazed, yellow, toothy grin. Before him on the coffee table were cups, a plate of crumbling cakes and three airline-sized bottles of wine standing empty beside one smudged wine glass.

Surely not, thought Milonakis, a man familiar with the extramarital appetites of the Secretary General. Not with a man. Not with little old Broussard.

"I'm in a meeting at the moment, Freiderikos," Herriot-Dupont said, visibly annoyed.

"*Très confidentielle*," Broussard said, grinning wider.

Frank Franklin was in Mortman's office, grieving. He grieved for his lost innocence at the *Toronto Star*. He grieved for his lost calm, lost health, lost hope for the future. He rued the day he had been seduced by the notion of a cushy media relations job in the south of France, with extremely generous Interpol pay in virtually tax-free euros, a duty-free automobile and a rental subsidy.

He had planned to do a little light communications work, drink vast amounts of excellent French wine and write the Great Canadian Novel in his spare time. Instead, he had never worked harder in his life. His mobile phone rang incessantly with calls from journalists from around the globe, all of whom were, to very tight deadlines, about to file stories almost certain to enrage the Secretary General.

If the phone did not ring with media calls, it rang with calls from the Secretary General, demanding corrections in articles or broad-cast reports, demanding increased coverage of Interpol achievements, demanding success stories, profiles, feature articles about Interpol officers and especially about Herriot-Dupont himself. Or the phone rang with calls from Chief of Staff Fred Milonakis, reiterating the Secretary General's various concerns and desires. Or it rang with calls from the unfortunate Mortman, Franklin's boss, who was clearly at death's door from dyspepsia, disappointment and despair.

Franklin's life was also made difficult by the fact that most people, and most journalists, very badly misunderstood what Interpol did, what powers it had and what results it was realistically able to achieve.

Franklin's staff received call after call from bewildered reporters or citizens asking why notorious criminals were not immediately being arrested as a result of Interpol Red Notices (because national police in member countries were under no legal obligation to act on them), why Interpol officers didn't carry guns (because member countries would be most unhappy if Interpol people started running around national jurisdictions firing unlicensed weapons at wrongdoers) and why Interpol couldn't immediately locate anyone in the world who was wanted or missing (families of backpackers routinely called the press office asking in vain which hotel various wayward offspring were staying in).

Franklin and Mortman met each day at 11 am to review a press digest assembled by a team of two perpetually disgruntled female *fonctionnaires*. These ladies, Interpol lifers on open-ended contracts, saw no qualitative difference between a routine one-column-inch wire story about Interpol picked up by the *Des Moines Register* and a major attack piece in the *Asahi Shimbun* or the *Tempo of London*. They simply scanned media sites and subscription databases and bashed all the stories together into one jumble of news reports that he and Mortman would have to evaluate and be ready to defend each day before the first complaint call came from the Secretary General.

"Oh, Frank, oh dear oh dear oh dear," Mortman moaned on this day as he flipped thought the mass of photocopied material.

"Which one?" Franklin asked. "Which page?" Almost any page in the press digest could be a problem, depending on the Secretary General's mood or his latest project or his irrational crime-busting exuberance.

"The sign," Mortman said sadly. "Page 17."

Franklin had already read that one. *Le Progrès* had done a knife job. World's largest international police organisation can't even hang a sign properly over its front door. Falling sign kills local puppy.

"Local only," Franklin said.

"Look over at page 18," Mortman said. "*Agence France-Presse* has picked it up as a bright. Two hundred and fifty pickups from the wire. Print, radio and TV, in French, English and Spanish. The US also."

50

Franklin's heart sank. He very much wished it was after noon, any time after noon, so that he and Mortman could justifiably have their first glass of cafeteria-quality Cotes du Rhone.

"Page 31," Mortman said.

Franklin flipped forward in his coil-bound sheaf of papers. "Fuck," he said.

"Exactly," Mortman said.

The *Tempo of London* had done a major piece about the Zimwabse police chief serving as an honorary vice president of Interpol, alongside a litany of alleged police human rights abuses and corruption allegations. Headline: *Zimwabse's Hard Man Lauded by Interpol.*

"Christ," Franklin said.

"*Interpol could not be reached for comment,*" Mortman read.

"They didn't call me," Franklin said quickly, trying very hard to remember which media calls he had neglected to return the week previous.

"Nor me," Mortman said. "I don't think so, anyway."

Mortman's upper right-hand desk drawer was a nest of missed-call memos, bright pink in colour. He occasionally dipped into them, when he was feeling strong.

"It's just an honorary thing. Those Brit papers will always beat something like that up," Franklin said.

"It's on their website," Mortman said. "BBC and Reuters have called for comment. Amnesty International has issued a press release."

"Fuck," Franklin said.

"There's another bad local one," Mortman said.

"What page?"

"Thirty-eight."

Franklin read it in silence. *Le Figaro* in Paris had got from an unnamed source, apparently an Interpol source, the story of an unfortunate incident of four weeks previous. A small crowd of Australian and British Interpol officers had poured out of headquarters late one evening, bellies full of subsidised wine from the Interpol bar. They had encircled the French Police Nationale car always parked outside the entrance as part of an obscure security arrangement instituted in the days of Secretary General Holmesworth.

Teams of very bored French policemen sat for their entire shift inside the car, three shifts daily of eight hours each, smoking cigarettes and listening to the radio. No one ever saw any of them get out of the car. It was some kind of subtle statement by France that even an international police organisation was on French turf and therefore to be overseen, though with requisite French indifference, by their own cops.

The drunken crowd had ridiculed the tiny Renault patrol car, had intimated in colloquial and rather coarse Australian and British phraseology that the two French officers inside must, if they drove such a small and unmanly car, have correspondingly small guns and small penises. Et cetera. The car had been rocked violently from side to side, *Le Figaro* alleged. The French policemen who had undergone the ordeal were now on medical leave and would receive counselling. The incident indicated a profound lack of respect for French law enforcement and France generally, a senior French official was quoted anonymously as saying. An Interpol spokesman could not be reached for comment, the newspaper said.

"We're dead," Franklin said.

"I am already dead," Mortman said, ever the lugubrious Estonian. "This is a corpse you see before you. I am a victim of the arrows and, um, the slingshots of outrageous fortune."

The telephone on Mortman's desk rang. He froze. A terrified look crossed his ashen face. He reached for a cigarette. He turned up the volume slightly on his Vivaldi recording.

"You are my Chief Press Officer, Frank," Mortman said. "You should get that. It's line two. Get it in your office."

"You're Chief of Communications and Publications," Franklin said.

They sat watching the telephone, united in grief and apprehension. An Interpol spokesman could not, for the moment, be reached for comment.

*

Marianna Ozols had risen rapidly through the ranks of the Latvia State Police. She had done extremely well as a cadet, had had some early successes on important crimes and had therefore become a First Sergeant at an unusually early stage of her career.

Some who worked with her in the early years, the unkind, had suggested that she rose fast because of her prowess at fellatio in the offices of certain more senior law enforcement personnel in Riga. These rumours Marianna had always dismissed as nothing more than the product of jealous, sexist minds, the minds of men whose police careers had not worked out as planned. This sort of rumour about successful women in the police world was all too common.

Marianna Ozols had similarly ignored the gossip generated when she was seconded to Europol headquarters in The Hague. She ignored suggestions from jealous colleagues that a certain Latvian Lieutenant Colonel had hurriedly organised the secondment when his wife got wind of some alleged extramarital untidiness. Marianna had not expected the posting but had taken it happily, though the Dutch weather was, in her view, only a slight improvement on Latvia's.

Marianna Ozols had enjoyed her time at Europol, brief though it was. She had ignored the gossip among jealous, sexist colleagues that she had in turn been seconded to Interpol as Europol's liaison officer there when a certain wife had got wind of an alleged bit of extramarital untidiness. Marianna had not expected the posting, but had taken it happily. The Lyon weather was a distinct improvement on The Hague.

She was an effective, dedicated police officer and she had not allowed herself to be disheartened by the fact that she was assigned at Interpol, consigned, to a dreary, cramped and windowless office in the basement of the headquarters building. She was not disheartened by the fact that she had no real assignment at Interpol, no staff or cases or responsibilities. She was well aware of the bad blood between Europol and Interpol, the inter-organisational distrust, and the profound mutual dislike between the Interpol chief and the Europol chief.

Marianna Ozols spent her days at Interpol as productively as she could, writing reports back to Europol and also, even more confidentially, to the Latvia State Police, about Interpol's activities, initiatives and difficulties. Occasionally she would appear at a public event somewhere in Europe, proof positive of the fine working relationship between the two international police organisations. An Interpol liaison officer, a Romanian policeman of highly questionable skills, had duly been seconded to Europol in The Hague. On the surface, all was as expected, and as it should be.

However, she had not at all expected a very heavy piece of her office ceiling to suddenly come crashing down onto her head and her desk. Yes, the office was dingy and ill equipped. Yes, it was in the basement in a neglected part of the headquarters building. But for a heavy piece of ceiling to come crashing down on her head, in a cascade of noxious dust and framework and debris, was completely unexpected.

When the collapse occurred, shortly before lunchtime on that fateful day, Marianna had sprung to her feet and run in panic out into the corridor and up the stairs to the grand atrium entranceway on the main floor. Dozens of startled Interpol *fonctionnaires* filing toward the cafeteria spoke afterward of their distress at having seen a dust-covered female officer collapse to her knees in tears, calling out for assistance and explanations.

Interpol's Chief of Security Bernard LeBlanc had been masterful in his handling of the situation. He had led Marianna gently to sickbay, surrounded by security guards. He had ordered his minions to the scene of the incident to investigate and take photos. He had ordered the basement area in question to be cordoned off. Then he took the express elevator to the fifth floor. Lunch had been served somewhat later in the cafeteria than usual on that day, and the fight against international crime was ever so slightly interrupted.

Secretary General Herriot-Dupont, having completed his daily perusal of the press digest, picked up the telephone in a gale force rage.

He dialled the Press Office number, while calling out to his secretaries through the open office door, "Get Milonakis in here immediately!"

The gale intensified when there was no answer in Press Office. Milonakis rushed in, thankfully carrying his own copy of the digest.

"Where is my press team, please?" Herriot-Dupont shouted. "Why don't they answer their telephones down there? Have you seen today's press digest? Get me the editor of *Le Figaro* on the phone right now. Get me the editor of *Le Progrès*. Who is the editor of the *Tempo of London* anyway?"

"Let's go through the issues one by one, Secretary General," Milonakis said quietly.

"Who is leaking this *merde* to the media, Fred? Tell me, who is leaking all of this to the media?" Herriot-Dupont shouted.

"We'll find out," Milonakis said.

"You will absolutely find out!" Herriot-Dupont shouted. "I am two months away from the General Assembly, Freiderikos. You're my Chief of Staff. Do something. *Immèdiatement.*"

Francine Tremblay, the most timid of the Secretary General's assistants, had been elected by her colleagues to attempt the dangerous task of interrupting a DHD rant. She knocked ever so gently on the frame of the open office door.

"*Monsieur, permettez?*" she whispered.

"What? What? What is it?" Herriot-Dupont shouted.

"This is not a good time, Francine," Milonakis said gently.

"The Chief of Security is here," Francine said. "He says it is *très urgent.*"

"Good Christ!" Herriot-Dupont said, slamming a fist down on his desk.

Bernard LeBlanc rushed into the room, flushed, dishevelled, afraid. "*Excusez-moi, monsieur, mais c'est très urgent,*" he said.

"What? What? What?" Herriot-Dupont shouted.

"A piece of the building has fallen unfortunately onto the head of the Europol liaison officer, *monsieur,*" LeBlanc said, with an imploring sidelong glance at the Chief of Staff.

"A what? On who?" Herriot-Dupont shouted.

"Is she dead?" Milonakis asked.

"Alive, *monsieur*," LeBlanc said.

When Julia Smith was in Lyon, she had very little to do. When she was in Washington, she had classes to teach, student essays to mark, learned papers on criminological matters to prepare, prisons to visit, consulting work to do. In Washington, Julia Smith was somebody. At least, if she was in Washington and her husband was in Lyon or elsewhere.

When Julia Smith was in Lyon she wandered, most of the time, alone in the vast official apartment, unless she, as the DHD consort, needed to attend some sort of official function, at which she would routinely be ignored by her husband or humiliated in some subtle way.

On this day, Julia had done her routine wandering around the apartment, had gazed out of various windows at the Rhone, had inspected the DHD gun collection on the walls, had made herself a sandwich for lunch in the kitchen. She rarely went to the Interpol cafeteria to eat, dreading as she did the eyes of dozens of *fonction-naires* and police officers on her as she disconsolately pushed her tray of food along to the cash register and then carried it to the table where she always sat alone. Madame DHD longed for the comfort and familiarity of her little house in Georgetown, where she had her books and her academic work, and a succession of sexually naïve undergraduates – nice boys, all of them, truly – to help along on life's way.

On this day, Julia stopped at the door separating the official apartment from the Secretary General's office on the other side. She heard murmurings of conversation from the other side, and occasionally the sound of her husband laughing heartily at something a guest said. She stood in the dim corridor and peered through the peephole that had been installed in the door, at her husband's insistence, for security purposes in a post-9/11 world.

DHD was sitting on the black leather couch beside a small and rather mousy-looking man wearing a cardigan sweater. Julia thought she had perhaps seen the man, late middle-aged, somewhere in the headquarters' hallways. The Secretary General's guest did not look at all like a policeman. He did not look interesting enough to be a policeman.

Through the peephole Julia watched her husband pour his guest a glass of wine from a very small bottle. She saw him offer the guest cake from a tray of treats on the table before them. She saw the guest take a cake, nibble on it, sip hesitantly from his glass of wine, grin shyly.

Julia Smith was no fool. She was a criminologist by training. No detective, true, but criminally inclined, so to speak; a woman who was well aware, though from an academic vantage, of the seamy side of life. She had no doubt whatsoever that her husband liked to seduce young women whenever and wherever he had a chance. She knew; she was sure beyond any reasonable doubt of where her husband's voracious sexual appetites had led him over the years.

But a reedy little male *fonctionnaire* in a ratty little cardigan? In an office only a door's breadth away from his own long-suffering wife? And was DHD actually touching this grinning little man on the thigh? Right there and then?

No, Julia Smith said angrily to herself as she peered through the peephole at the unsavoury scene unfolding before her. No. This is not alright. This is a bit much. This is really and truly too much.

FOUR

Marianna Ozols, everyone agreed, had been very brave indeed. Shortly after being escorted to Interpol's sickbay she was actually sitting up unassisted, holding a crumpled Kleenex to her nose and blinking rapidly, holding back tears. Interpol's long-suffering doctor, more accustomed to signing off one staffer after another onto stress leave, actually had to call upon his medical training to examine someone for physical, as opposed to psychological, injury. He tapped and prodded and listened and then ordered the Europol liaison officer to the Clinique du Parc for observation and an overnight stay.

Ozols had protested, but then allowed herself to be transported in a wheelchair to the Secretary General's personal vehicle for the short run to the hospital. Herriot-Dupont had ordered that his driver and bodyguard both accompany her right into the hospital reception. As she was assisted into the large black Peugeot, a sprinkling of Interpol plaster dust still lay on her tousled hair, giving her something of the appearance of a decaying Renaissance statue.

The Secretary General watched from the broad terrace of his fifth floor office as the car sped off, hospital bound. His mood was dark, despite the brilliant autumn sunshine.

"Good riddance," he said bitterly.

"Sir, I think perhaps…" Milonakis, standing beside him, protested feebly.

"When is the last time she shared any Europol information with us, Freiderikos?" DHD spluttered.

"I can check," the Chief of Staff said.

"Don't waste your time. And now I will have to call her bosses in The Hague to say that a piece of my building has fallen on their liaison officer's head."

"I'm afraid so," Milonakis said.

"Let's hope the doctors send her home to Latvia for a very long time," DHD said.

"Sir, I think perhaps you are—"

"Get me LeBlanc and Buisson," the Secretary General said. "We will get to the bottom of this. Then get me that fool Franklin."

LeBlanc and Buisson sat like guilty schoolboys on the uncomfortable black leather couch, backs to the windows, where people were installed for reprimands and ritual humiliations by the Secretary General. The river and the verdant hills of Lyon lay spread out behind them, splendour visible, however, only to DHD and Milonakis as they sat facing the guilty parties.

"LeBlanc, you are my head of security. Buisson, you are in charge of the physical integrity and safety of this building," Herriot-Dupont said in his huskiest voice.

"*Oui, monsieur*," the guilty parties said in unison. It was impossible to deny such allegations.

"Is there any reason that either of you can think of that bits of this building are now beginning to fall down?"

LeBlanc and Buisson looked nervously at each other. What could be the safe answer to such a complex question?

"Well, gentlemen?" DHD snapped.

LeBlanc and Buisson looked imploringly at Milonakis. The Chief of Staff said nothing. The situation called for a stern demeanour. The Secretary General would accept nothing less from his Chief of Staff.

"Sabotage is unlikely, *monsieur*," LeBlanc ventured unconvincingly.

"Unlikely," the Secretary General said.

"So I believe, *monsieur*," LeBlanc said.

"But not out of the question," the Secretary General said.

"In life, *monsieur*, I have found that nothing is absolutely out of the question," LeBlanc said.

"A philosopher security chief," DHD said. "How reassuring it is to have someone of this calibre on my staff."

The Secretary General smiled broadly at his Chief of Staff.

"Would your philosophical researches extend perhaps to making enquiries for me, LeBlanc, and of course only if you are not busy with your other learned work, as to the theoretical possibility that someone is sabotaging my building so as to create maximum embarrassment and distraction for me in the run-up to what is the most important General Assembly this institution has ever faced, and only days before police delegates arrive here in Lyon from around the globe for the pre-General Assembly Executive Committee meeting? Could you perhaps find some time to do this for me, LeBlanc?"

"Why yes, of course," LeBlanc said. "*Immèdiatement.*"

"You are not a police officer, however, if I recall," the Secretary General said, looking triumphantly over at his Chief of Staff.

Milonakis thought this was something of a low blow. He said nothing.

"I am not," LeBlanc said.

"How is this the case, Freiderikos?" DHD said, wishing to raise in the mind of the head of security and the mind of his head of building maintenance intimations of the most horrible fate that could ever befall a French *fonctionnaire*: cessation of steady, formal, predictable employment in an establishment with a heavily subsidised dining room.

"It has never been the case here at Interpol, sir, that it was thought necessary to have a law enforcement officer as security chief," Milonakis said in a grave tone.

"For discussion at the Executive Committee level, possibly?" DHD said.

"Noted," Milonakis said.

"And you are not an engineer or an architect, I take it, Buisson?" DHD said.

"*Malheureusement, non,*" Buisson said, deeply shaken by the direction the conversation was taking.

"Unusual in an institution of this sort, Freiderikos?" the Secretary General asked.

"Somewhat," Milonakis said. "Somewhat unusual."

After LeBlanc and Buisson had been dispatched, the Secretary General's face had taken on the testosterone-reddened hue of a man who had subdued formidable opponents in bloody combat.

"Fools," he said after they had left.

"They are motivated now to get results," Milonakis offered.

"Precisely," DHD said.

"Franklin is next," Milonakis said.

Frank Franklin came in to the office smelling very strongly of breath mints. This was the result of a Canadian phobia about halitosis, and, often in Franklin's case, an attempt to mask the aroma of beer, wine or spirits, depending of the time of day and day of the week. Even this early in the morning, for an urgent meeting with and ritual humiliation by the Secretary General, Franklin had allowed himself a small bracer in the privacy of his office before coming to the fifth floor.

He quietly took his place alone on the cold leather couch, waiting for the verbal blows to rain down.

"Where is Mortman?" the Secretary General demanded to know.

"You only asked me to come up, sir," Franklin said, reaching for his mobile phone. "I can get him to come up."

"No, no, I don't want that man up here now. I mean where is he now?"

"Not sure, sir. Why?"

"He is my Chief of Communications, Franklin. It is a key position in this organisation. I need to know where he is and what he is doing at all times. As I do with you, though you would agree your position is not as crucial to the organisation?"

Milonakis tensed slightly. A trick question. He hoped Franklin would answer correctly.

"Well…" Franklin said, looking over to Milonakis for a clue.

"This is Interpol's Assistant Director for Media Relations, Freiderikos. See how agile he is intellectually."

Milonakis assumed a moderate frown, a slight grimace.

"I…" Franklin said. "It's…"

"Apply all of your intellectual powers to this question instead, Franklin. Who would want to leak damaging stories about my organisation to the press? In your professional opinion?"

Another trick question.

"I can't imagine there would be anyone inside here who would want to, um, you know, do you any harm in that way, Secretary General."

"Harm me?" DHD said sharply.

"Interpol," Franklin said quickly. "The organisation."

"So there are no leaks, then."

"Well, it is true that some of the recent stories haven't been terribly, you know, um, positive," Franklin said. Milonakis would not make eye contact with him during an interrogation.

"And the source of those stories, Franklin? The source?"

"Um. Well, it is a difficult thing to…"

"You of course would have excellent lines in to the press here and overseas, Franklin. Would you not? Considering what we pay you each year. You have contacts among editors, senior journalists everywhere."

"I know some people, yes," Franklin said. He sometimes drank with a very attractive young CBC chase producer when he was in Paris, but mainly to justify his claim for an expense account lunch at Café Marly or Fouquet's.

"What are they telling you?"

"About what?"

Milonakis winced noticeably. Wrong question, after a series of wrong answers. Franklin was doing very badly today.

"Freiderikos, please," the Secretary General said. "Can you help Monsieur Franklin here? Please?"

"The Secretary General wants you to assist us in tracing the origin of the negative stories that are appearing in various news outlets, Frank," Milonakis said, speaking slowly, as if to an ungifted child. "He wants you to use your contacts to find out where these stories are coming from, and he wants the leaks to stop."

"Bravo," DHD said. "Bravo."

"I can make some enquiries, yes, certainly, I'll do that right away," Franklin said.

"See that you do," DHD said.

The Secretary General let a moment of silence pass, for effect.

"When does your contract come up for renewal, Franklin?" he asked.

"In approximately eighteen months' time, sir," Franklin said. The thought of returning to Toronto filled him with dread. Toronto was a lot of things, but it was not the south of France.

"We will of course need these leaks stopped well before that, Franklin," DHD said dryly, looking over at his Chief of Staff. "You would agree?"

"Yes, of course," Franklin said. "Yes."

"In fact they must stop well before the next General Assembly, you would agree. A meeting the date for which is considerably closer than eighteen months away."

"I understand, sir," Franklin said.

"Aha!" DHD said. "Fred, our media man understands what is at stake."

Milonakis said nothing, instead simply training his stern gaze on the unfortunate Canadian.

"I have read your report on preparation for the African Regional Conference," the Secretary General said.

Franklin had been struggling to get an answer from anyone in the Zambezin police, or the Interior Ministry, or the Zambezin Federation of Journalists as to how preparations for media coverage of the event were proceeding. His arch enemy, Events Manager Antonio de Caldevilla, had, for his part, not got any answers whatsoever as to more general questions about venue preparations, hotel accommodation for police delegates, or any other matter. Preparations for the African Regional Conference, which would very soon bring together in one place senior police officers from across the continent, were, truth be told, in an extremely dire state.

"Um…" Franklin said.

"I need things to go well there, Franklin, you are aware of this," DHD said.

The Secretary General was concerned about a rumoured softening of support for him among African chiefs of police. He did not wish this weakness to manifest itself in the vote for his re-election at the General Assembly in Munich.

"We'll need some positive stories in the African media, Frank," Milonakis said. "In the main African newspaper, for example."

"Well, there isn't really one, sort of, pan-African newspaper," Franklin said. "It's not like that down there. There are a lot of, um…"

"A lot of opportunities for positive coverage?" the Secretary General offered.

Many of the most senior African police paid more attention to the *Financial Times* or the BBC's *World Business Report* than they did the local media. The better to track the value of their personal investment portfolios in Swiss and other nations' banks. Franklin did not offer this information.

"I have been working very hard on that, sir," Franklin said.

This was, in effect, true. His stomach knotted further. Despite his efforts, however, the daily press digest during the African Regional could prove to be a very slim volume indeed.

"This is crucially important, Franklin," DHD said.

"Understood," Franklin said. He hoped Mortman would ultimately be blamed for the paucity of positive stories out of Kulsaka. He wished he could renew his five-year contract before, not after, the African Regional. No chance of that, he knew. None.

"And CNN?" DHD asked. "My profile?"

"I spoke to them again this morning," Franklin said.

Not strictly true. It had been a conversation in his head only, in anticipation of an actual conversation with the features producer in London, if that apparently very busy journalist would ever return Franklin's calls. Such interior, head-only conversations were, for Franklin, a little like prayers.

"Not much time before Munich, Frank," the Chief of Staff said darkly.

"They can turn something like that around very quickly these days," Franklin said.

"First they have to come here to meet me, no?" the Secretary General said.

"Or they could do a two-way by satellite," Franklin offered without hope.

"No, no, no, no," DHD shouted. "We want them here. We want them to see the building. We want them to see the X-24GT system. We want them to see the Command Centre."

"They will have to come down here, Frank," Milonakis said. "Soon."

"They'll be wanting a news peg," Franklin said. "This is what's delaying things, I think."

"A what?" DHD demanded.

"A news peg, sir. Something in the news recently that will get people thinking about Interpol, about world policing. International police cooperation."

"People are thinking about these matters every day, Franklin. The terrorist attacks on New York and Washington were surely enough to generate this interest, no?"

Franklin did not ever want to be the one to tell the Secretary General that ordinary people the world over went about their daily lives thinking very little about Interpol. Or that the ones who did think about Interpol almost invariably thought of the utterly inaccurate Hollywood version, in which members of a super-effective world police force rushed around in exotic locales brandishing weapons and making dramatic arrests.

"Of course, yes," Franklin said. "But the 9/11 attacks were a while ago now."

"They are still extremely fresh in my memory, Franklin," the Secretary General said gravely.

"Offer CNN unrestricted access," Milonakis interjected. "The Command Centre, everything."

"Anything they want," DHD said.

"Jean-Marc Moulin will be uncomfortable with that, I think," Franklin said.

The Director of Operational Police Support abhorred the idea of journalists inside the Interpol headquarters building. He would be beside himself if they were allowed to film anything of a sensitive nature. And if the telephones and the temperamental X-24GT communications system were not running hot during the filming, what would CNN think of the world's largest international police organisation then? And if they wanted actual statistics about police use of Interpol's databases? If they wanted facts?

"I will deal with Moulin if he puts up any objections," the Secretary General said. "Tell him to call me on my personal mobile if he has any qualms about this CNN feature report."

Franklin blanched. "Interview," he said.

"Feature report," the Secretary General said. "I would imagine something around twenty to thirty minutes in length would be sufficient to tell the Interpol story."

"Twenty minutes," Franklin said.

"More or less," Milonakis said helpfully. "Approximately."

Freiderikos Milonakis was trying to calculate in his head how many hours of his day-week-month-life he spent in Herriot-Dupont's office. The numbers, he decided eventually, were simply too depressing for sustained contemplation and he terminated this line of thought for his own good. The Secretary General was seated before him, as always, at attention in his usual leather armchair. Franklin had departed, adequately panicked at the challenges before him.

"And now, Freiderikos, we must discuss in detail our plans for the Executive Committee meeting," the Secretary General said. "It is coming up very soon."

"Yes it is," Milonakis said, taking out his notebook.

The Interpol Executive Committee comprised thirteen senior law enforcement officials from around the globe, all with a taste for international crime-fighting and some with an even stronger taste for the lavishly-catered meetings three times a year in Lyon.

"Catering," DHD said.

"Very important as always," Milonakis said.

There was a pause.

"Our Serbanian colleague being a man of – how shall I put this delicately? – voracious and varied appetites," the Secretary General said eventually with a wry smile.

"Indeed," Milonakis said. He did not, of course, raise the issue of DHD's own voracious appetites, mainly sexual in nature. He very much hoped that one of DHD's mistresses in France and elsewhere would not, as they sometimes did, have some sort of personal or financial crisis in the run-up to the Executive Committee meeting or the General Assembly.

"Everything must go smoothly," DHD said. "This being the last EC meeting before Munich."

"As you have made clear," Milonakis said.

"We need everyone to go home from the EC meeting happy. Profoundly satisfied. Sated. If you get my meaning."

"Yes, I think I do. Indeed," Milonakis said.

There was another pause.

"We will also need success stories," the Secretary General said.

"I'm assembling some," Milonakis said. This was easier said than done at this stage of Interpol's development.

"Arrests, Freiderikos. Arrests," DHD said. "We need some arrests."

That arrests were still the prerogative of national police forces;

that Interpol officers simply assisted with information or crime data for policing operations in national jurisdictions, had once again been lost on Herriot-Dupont.

"Child pornography," the Secretary General said. "The EC likes that sort of thing."

"The Swedish police are working on something," Milonakis said. "We have assisted them. Photographic analysis."

Whether the Swedes would give Interpol any credit for such technical assistance was still an open question.

"Arrests are possible before the EC?"

"I hope so."

"Before the General Assembly, then, yes? You must push them, Fred. I'll need success stories in Munich also. For my speech."

"I am assembling some, sir," Milonakis said.

"And database use, Fred. We must populate our databases. Foster their frequent use globally."

Use of Interpol's criminal databases under Herriot-Dupont's stewardship was becoming spotty. Stagnant, in some cases. Falling in others. Member countries were now even more reluctant to share certain sensitive crime data or the names of suspects in major crimes. Or, too often, they were simply remiss in their filing obligations to Interpol. Milonakis did not want to have to go into the sad detail today.

"The cutting edge, Fred. That is where this organisation must be."

"Agreed."

"And the EC members must of course enjoy their stay in Lyon, always. Our Serbanian friend, for example," Herriot-Dupont said, returning to what seemed to be his major concern.

"He was not happy at the last EC," Milonakis acknowledged. Dancing girls had been denied the member, as it were.

"Perhaps we were, how shall I say, somewhat inflexible in his case the last time?" Herriot-Dupont said. "Too rigid. That is, with a man of such appetites."

Milonakis raised one eyebrow ever so slightly. The Secretary

General raised one of his own. Almost imperceptible communication eventuated.

"I will see what can be done this time," Milonakis said.

"Discreetly, discreetly," DHD said.

"Of course."

"And the main dinner? At Restaurant Paul Bocuse once again? All is in order?"

"Absolutely."

The main dinner during the quarterly Interpol Executive Committee meetings had become legendary in world policing circles, Lyon being the gastronomic capital of France. Positions on the Interpol Executive Committee were much sought after.

"And our friend the Japanese delegate?"

"Ah," Milonakis said.

"Ah yes," the Secretary General said gravely.

"A woman of modest appetites," Milonakis said.

"Everyone has their needs, Fred."

"Madame Watanabe would say that she only needs a reduced Interpol budget. Or a frozen budget."

The Secretary General chuckled softly. "Frozen budget is not on the menu at Bocuse at this time of year, I'm afraid, Freiderikos," he said. "Not with my re-election coming up."

They chuckled softly together. Eyebrows were ever so slightly raised.

After a moment's silence, Herriot-Dupont said, "There is something else."

Milonakis did not like the sound of this.

"I've been doing some thinking, Fred, about our staff," the Secretary General said, lowering his voice slightly, taking his trusted Chief of Staff even further into his confidence.

A very bad thing, the Secretary General spending too much time thinking. Milonakis knew this from bitter experience.

"I believe that we do not adequately recognise excellence among certain members of staff who occupy crucial positions, and who do outstanding work," the Secretary General intoned.

Could special recognition be headed the Chief of Staff's way? Milonakis asked himself this question with no genuine hope.

"I believe we should institute a new system of rewards for exemplary, extraordinary service to the organisation, Fred," the Secretary General said.

"Rewards," Milonakis said.

"Yes."

"For staff."

"For outstanding staff, Fred. Only for outstanding staff. Those who deserve special recognition, and therefore a special reward."

"What kind of reward?" Milonakis asked with a sense of impending doom.

"Cash, I would say. Yes, cash. And a car perhaps."

"A car," Milonakis repeated.

"People love to get a new car from time to time, do they not?"

"This sounds expensive, Secretary General. The budget… The Executive Committee… The Japanese will not…"

"Details, Fred, details. Is the concept a good one? That is what I am asking you."

"Well, in principle, I think one could argue that…" Milonakis said.

"Excellent," DHD said, beaming. "Let's begin this programme immediately. A pilot programme. No need to involve the Executive Committee in any decisions at this stage. Budget for the pilot could come out of, say, the stolen motor vehicles section. A little irony, no?"

DHD chuckled happily. Milonakis did not.

"You see?" DHD said. "A car. From the stolen motor vehicle section?"

"Not literally," Milonakis said sharply.

"No, no, no, my friend. You are far too literal. I refer to the money for the car, in this pilot programme. And the cash component to come from the stolen motor vehicles section budget."

"They won't like that, sir," Milonakis said. "It is still a very popular service to police. That database is among our most used. Staff and a lot of police forces will not—"

"To hell with them!" DHD shouted. He chuckled again, delighted with his new idea. When the Secretary General was hatching an expensive new programme or project he very often chuckled maniacally in this way.

"You will organise this for me, Fred. If you please. Choose the initial recipient," the Secretary General said. "The inaugural prize. I leave this up to you."

"Me," Milonakis said.

"I can help, of course, with some suggestions. A suggestion, perhaps. A nomination."

Milonakis saw now where this was going. "Do you have someone in mind?" he asked.

"Well, it is just a thought, really," DHD said. "I wouldn't want to, at this stage…"

"Who are you thinking of?"

"Well, for this pilot project stage…" the Secretary General said. "Yes?"

"Well, we know how crucial the information technology section is for effective international policing these days, Freiderikos. We know how hard that section has worked on the X-24GT communications system for us in recent years."

Virtually wrecking the system that had first been installed, adding costly and unnecessary features and sending several members of the team off on stress leave, Milonakis thought.

"Reward the entire team?" Milonakis asked.

"No, no. Not everyone," the Secretary General said.

There was a pause.

Broussard, Milonakis said to himself.

"Broussard," the Secretary General said. "He's a very good man. Instrumental in the X-24GT project. A very good man on that job. Outstanding. This is just a thought, however, Fred. I will leave details of this new programme and the inaugural recipient up to you, of course.

I would not wish to interfere. That's not my way of doing things, as you know."

"Broussard," Milonakis said again.

"Some cash, perhaps. For whoever is actually chosen. In recognition of exemplary service to international policing. Perhaps cash and a certificate of appreciation. And a car."

Freiderikos Milonakis had further cause for alarm later that day. One of his various informants from among the administrative and support staff, who had been trained to bring him bits of information the way puppies are trained to fetch sticks, or the way magpies will bring shiny items back to their nests, had stopped him in the paved forecourt of the headquarters building. Workmen there were readying the fallen sign to be re-hoisted into position. Other workers were repairing tiles damaged in the incident.

The informant in question was Chantalle Duquesne, a data compiler of approximately thirty years of age. She was known to suffer from any number of physical and psychological ailments and was often absent on medical leave of various sorts. The Interpol doctor, like many French doctors not terribly troubled by matters of patient confidentiality, kept Milonakis up to date on her ailments. Duquesne, for her part, kept Milonakis up to date about goings-on in the building.

She had stopped, years prior, offering sexual favours to the Chief of Staff. She was, he had wisely decided years prior, far too unstable for him to take into his bed. She was also, he had decided, far too skinny. He liked women with slightly more flesh on their bones. And he liked them to be less of a pharmacological experiment ready to explode than young Chantalle.

Her report this day was troubling in the extreme. The Secretary General's wife had been spotted having lunch in the staff dining room. A highly unusual event. Her customary lunching arrangement when she was residing in the headquarters building was to eat in the Secretary General's apartment, or to ask one of the Interpol drivers to bring her to any number of excellent restaurants in Lyon's historic Presqu'île quarter. She had no friends in Lyon or in France, it seemed. So she avoided dining alone in the cafeteria for all staff members to see.

This day, according to Chantalle, Julia Smith had entered the cafeteria shortly after noon. She had actually pushed her tray along the stainless steel rack, filing in behind other Interpol staff to the place where a young chef in a white jacket and cap expertly and swiftly made omelettes to order. She had ordered an *omelette mixte*, with extra sautéed mushrooms on the side. She had taken a small bowl of salad, some bread from a basket, a pat of butter, a small bottle of Badoit mineral water and a tiny bottle of wine, airline-sized.

Wine, Milonakis had thought as he listened to Chantalle's report. At lunchtime. In the staff cafeteria. Highly unusual for Madame DHD. And for an American.

The Secretary General's wife had been observed carrying her tray alone into the hubbub of the staff dining area. It was filled with many rectangular tables seating eight people, and a very few tables for two. Some of these tables for two were vacant, the perspicacious Chantalle had reported. But Madame DHD had not chosen one of these. *Mais non*. She had instead spied a vacant chair at the table used each day by computer section personnel, and she had seated herself beside the Assistant Manager of Interpol's computer department, Gilles Broussard. To his astonishment, Chantalle had reported, and to the astonishment of his departmental colleagues and the dining room generally speaking.

Broussard! Milonakis had actually called out the man's name when he received this news. His face had darkened. Chantalle became visibly alarmed. Had she inadvertently upset the powerful and handsome Chief of Staff in some way?

Madame DHD had chatted amiably with the Assistant Manager of Interpol's computer department Gilles Broussard, but, it seemed, with Broussard only. She paid scant attention, Chantalle reported, to his computer section colleagues also at the table. Madame DHD and Monsieur Broussard had engaged in animated conversation for some twenty to thirty minutes.

Long enough for a CNN feature segment, Milonakis had thought ruefully. A substantial amount of time.

Chantalle had been unable to discover the topic of this animated conversation between the wife of the Secretary General and the Assistant Manager of Interpol's computer department. Eventually, she reported, Madame DHD had stood up to go, touching Monsieur Broussard fondly on the shoulder. Touching Monsieur Broussard; touching him *fondly* on the shoulder. The dining room had gone silent. Madame did not give Broussard a goodbye peck on the cheek, as some observers at this point fully expected her to do. For a moment the watching Interpol staff, the lunching Interpol staff, had thought such a cheek-peck might indeed be offered. By the wife of the Secretary General to the Assistant Manager of Interpol's computer department.

Chantalle Duquesne thrust forward her pert breasts in pride at having brought such a shiny bit of information to the Chief of Staff.

"*Merci infiniment*," Milonakis had told her. High praise indeed for a minor Interpol functionary to receive from someone of his elevated stature. Chantalle all but swooned before him. Milonakis momentarily, once again, felt a frisson of sexual energy between them.

Steady, he thought.

After Chantalle had gone, Milonakis walked alone in the Interpol garden, deep in thought, increasingly alarmed. The garden was his favoured place for contemplation and a smoke.

What would his trusted guide Machiavelli say? Milonakis wondered as he smoked his Marlboro alone. Perhaps this? *The vulgar crowd always is taken in by appearances, and the world consists chiefly of the vulgar.*

No, Milonakis thought, congratulating himself on remembering an appropriate Machiavelli quotation. They are a vulgar lot in that dining room, but there is more to this than mere appearances.

Perhaps this, then, which Machiavelli offered from beyond the grave: *No enterprise is more likely to succeed than one concealed from the enemy until it is ripe for execution.*

Yes, Milonakis thought. Thank you very much, my learned friend. Thank you, yes. But what is the secret enterprise in this case? What is that American bitch up to?

FIVE

Interpol Secretary General Didier Herriot-Dupont was very fond of going on overseas missions, and not just because of the motorcycle escorts that very often, and quite gratifyingly, accompanied him from airports to his meetings with the world's police. Less developed countries, with less developed police forces (indeed, some with police forces that were breathtakingly far from developed, except perhaps in terms of corruption and a penchant for extrajudicial violence) were the best bets for a large motorcycle escort and a cacophony of screaming sirens to welcome him.

Neither was it just because of the lavish hospitality and lavish praise heaped upon him by police and politicians in many of the countries he visited, particularly in the less developed countries, though a man of his rank and stature in the French police could never hope to be treated on foreign soil as some sort of law enforcement potentate. No, it was not this. Though he would miss some of the perquisites of high office, he sometimes mused, when he returned eventually to France's Police Nationale. But at that point, he dared to hope, he would be Commissaire, no? And this would have other consolations.

No, he thought wistfully as he gazed out of the window of the white Zambezin Police Service VIP van that was whisking him, duly escorted by careering police motorcycles, from Kulsaka airport to the city's very best hotel, such perks and consolations of high Interpol office were not what he loved so much about overseas missions. It was the sense, as he so often reminded himself, and all members of his entourage, and all local police and any members of the media who might be present, that the missions were, despite what ill-informed critics might say, *making the world a safer place.*

That phrase was in the speech he was going to make to the assembled cops at the African Regional Conference, or, more accurately, those who would be able to stay awake in the heat and humidity after their very large conference lunches, just as the phrase was in virtually every speech he ever made as Secretary General anywhere in the world. And to hell with those who dared dispute Interpol's role in, yes, making the world a safer place. To hell with those who demanded facts, statistics, proof that Interpol was having any such tangible law enforcement effect.

"To hell with them all!" he called out suddenly to his entourage, seated uneasily in the police van as the driver flung the vehicle through the rutted streets of Kulsaka's grimy outskirts. Children and street vendors ran for cover along the entire route. "We are making the world a safer place!" DHD called out again.

His entourage, or the senior members thereof who were privileged enough to ride with him in the lead van, on this occasion consisted of Chief of Staff Freiderikos Milonakis, Director of Operational Police Support Jean-Marc Moulin, Assistant Director for Media Relations Frank Franklin (not at all a good traveller and now a nasty shade of blue-green with motion sickness), Madame DHD (not normally invited or welcome on official missions of this sort, but who had for some reason insisted on coming on this one to Kulsaka), the Assistant Director for African Police Services Goodluck Okiro (a legendarily ineffectual Deputy Superintendent seconded to Interpol from Ngheria's legendarily ill-disciplined national police force, for reasons known only to that country's Interior Minister) and a highly unusual addition to the entourage, the Assistant Manager of Interpol's computer department Gilles Broussard, there at the personal invitation of the Secretary General himself.

Other, lesser Interpol staffers and technicians and translators and hangers-on followed behind in other Zambezin police vehicles, well behind the motorcycles leading the way.

The motorcade skidded to a halt in a ragged line at the entrance to the Hilton Hotel on Selassie Avenue. Doors of all vehicles flew open simultaneously; uniformed and plainclothes Zambezin police leapt out, and flunkies and porters rushed from the lobby to greet the arriving Interpol delegation. DHD disembarked as might a visiting head of state. He moved elegantly lobby-ward, dispensing weary smiles to all who looked his way.

As always in dusty, less developed countries, the Interpol Secretary General was assigned the presidential suite, or similar. And, as often was the case, the suite assigned would be redolent with the smell of fresh plaster, paint and carpet, the result of hurried and last-minute touches to bring the accommodation up to world diplomatic, not to mention DHD and Freiderikos Milonakis, standards of luxury.

DHD did not linger in his spacious suite on arrival. He simply inspected the accommodation swiftly, sniffed the paint and carpet fumes approvingly, released his wife into the custody of the wife of the Zambezin Commissioner of Police, and hurried back down to the lobby and the waiting van to immediately begin the crucially important work of making the world, and on this occasion Africa, a safer place.

The headquarters of the Zambezi Police Service was, like many police headquarters buildings in Africa and Asia, a rather faded and dusty structure, filled with feeble fluorescent lighting, labyrinthine corridors and tiny wooden desks at which faded and dusty civilian scribes scratched away with ballpoint pens on densely laid-out legal documents and forms. Didier Herriot-Dupont was greeted warmly on the steps by the Senior Assistant Deputy Commissioner of Police Malindu Ngoma, a strapping man whose military bearing, pencil-thin moustache, immaculate khaki uniform and swagger stick would make him at home in any British colonial law enforcement outfit, circa 1912.

"Secretary General, welcome, welcome, welcome, it is indeed an honour," Ngoma shouted as he embraced DHD firmly and at length. "Come, come inside, we shall have tea together and speak of many things. The Inspector General sends his regrets, as do the Commissioner and the Deputy Commissioner. They will see you this evening at the gala dinner, and of course tomorrow at the conference."

Herriot-Dupont was somewhat displeased at this breach of protocol, despite the presence of a sweating police photographer who recorded the encounter for posterity, and presumably for Zambezi's government-controlled daily newspaper. Herriot-Dupont was, therefore, in no mood for lengthy African gabfests over tea. He gave his Chief of Staff a dark look. Milonakis made a mental note to blame the Interpol Events Manager for the lapse.

"Mr Ngoma," DHD began.

"Malindu, please, sir," Ngoma said with a slight bow of the head. "I am at your service, and at the service of international police cooperation."

"Malindu," DHD said. "I do not believe it is the time for tea."

"Guinness, then, sir, yes?" Ngoma said with a broad smile and a wink. "You are a policeman's policeman, sir, this much is clear."

Ngoma tuned and made an urgent gesture to a terrified young constable, who hurried off, presumably to replace waiting cups of tea with quart bottles of well-chilled Guinness, the preferred drink of African police around the continent.

"No, Malindu, thank you very much, no," the Secretary General said. "I think, given the tight schedule we are on, it would be best to proceed directly to the communications area."

As always on such missions, Herriot-Dupont insisted on demonstrations of his pride and joy, Interpol's state-of-the-art X-24GT police communications system, in theory installed and working in police headquarters buildings in all 190 Interpol member countries. The brainchild of the previous Secretary General, to be sure, but DHD's pride and joy nonetheless. In theory, this was the case.

Ngoma was clearly alarmed.

"Now?" the portly African said. "Today? I was told that the demonstration would take place on Wednesday, sir, or perhaps on Thursday. Not today, no, not today, not at all."

"Not my understanding, Malindu," DHD said, with another dark look at Milonakis. "Shall we go?"

Ngoma looked this way and that. He made urgent gestures and gave whispered instructions to terrified constables who rushed off ahead of the Interpol visitors. Frank Franklin gave whispered instructions of his own to the police photographer, who began snapping away, seemingly at random. Gilles Broussard, who had been invited to attend the demonstration in his capacity as Assistant Director of Interpol computer department, looked distinctly hot and uncomfortable. It was his first trip to Africa, and no one had informed him that sweaters were not required in Zambezi at this time of year.

The group stopped behind Ngoma outside a closed wooden door in a dim basement corridor. A laminated sign on the door said simply, *Interpol.*

"The National Central Bureau of Interpol," Ngoma said nervously.

"Excellent," DHD said.

"We were expecting the demonstration to take place on Wednesday, sir. Or on Thursday," Ngoma said.

"I'm ready," DHD said.

Ngoma knocked, and waited. There was the sound of scurrying feet inside. He opened the door. Rats? No. Zambezin police. In the dim fluorescent light of a windowless room were arranged three small desks, at which sat three extremely young uniformed policemen. The sweating constable who had been dispatched ahead of the group stood nervously to one side. A cleaning lady in a pink smock was still flicking a feather duster over desktops and the keyboard of a single computer that sat on a battered table. It was a vintage Hewlett Packard model, with what looked like prehistoric carbon smudges on its sides.

"Ready, constables?" Ngoma said nervously.

"Sir," the three young policemen shouted in unison, leaping to their feet, locking their spines to attention and saluting smartly.

"Constable Niwabwino, if you please," Ngoma said.

Constable Niwabwino pulled his chair to the computer table, seated himself before the screen and groped around for the power switch. The police photographer snapped away in a storm of electronic flashes. Niwabwino eventually found the power switch and flicked it to the on position. The screen regarded all of them blankly, darkened still.

The cleaning lady reached helpfully behind the desk and plugged in a filthy power cord. The screen flickered to life. The message eventually displayed said, *Welcome to the Interpol X-24GT secure police communication system. Please log on.*

"Password, Niwabwino," Senior Assistant Deputy Commissioner Malindu Ngoma said sharply.

"I do not know it offhand, sir," Niwabwino said quietly. "It is a closely guarded secret. It is distributed on a need-to-know basis."

"We need to know, Constable," Milonakis said sharply.

"Precisely," DHD said. "Global police cooperation cannot wait for passwords to be found, Constable. The X-24GT system is designed for immediate use, twenty-four hours a day around the globe. Am I correct in this, Malindu?"

"Just so, Secretary General, sir, just so," Ngoma said.

"Sir," Constable Niwabwino said weakly, "I was told that this demonstration would be—"

"Abracadabra," the cleaning lady said shyly.

"What, what? What do you say, woman?" Ngoma shouted.

The cleaning lady lowered her head even further. She adjusted her headscarf. "Abracadabra," she said again. "It is the password, Governor."

"The closely guarded secret password," DHD said.

Ngoma glared at the cleaning lady, glared at his constables, smiled warmly at the visiting Interpol delegation, and gestured urgently to Constable Niwabwino. The constable flailed away at the keyboard. A horizontal bar outline appeared on the screen, and this began filling very slowly with colour. The words *Uploading Interpol X-24GT, please stand by* appeared above it.

Ngoma and all three constables stood by. They peered hopefully at the screen. The cleaning lady gave it another flick with her feather duster.

"Damn that Zamtel," Ngoma said. "Damn them. I shall have a word with the Telecommunications Minister. It is not usually this slow to upload, Secretary General, I assure you."

The demonstration of the operation by the Zambezin Police Service of Interpol's state-of-the-art X-24GT communications system did not, in the end, take place that day. The visiting delegation had stood patiently for some minutes, a significant interval. Gilles Broussard had pitched in to inspect the installation and the hardware, and had frowned at the modem blinking wildly beside the computer terminal. But none of Broussard's expert interventions had proved successful. After perhaps ten minutes, the blue upload bar on the screen had been filled just one third of the way. It was decided the demonstration would be best carried out on another day.

"Damn that Zamtel," Ngoma said again as he led the delegation out of the Interpol communications centre. "It is not usually this slow to upload, Secretary General, I assure you."

Julia Smith did not like travelling. She did not like hotels. She did not like Africa. She liked Washington. She liked her own little Georgetown townhouse. So she was in an extremely foul humour when the Zambezin Police Service driver let her off at the Hilton after the shopping expedition and an interminable lunch with the wife of the Zambezin Commissioner of Police, Ladybug Wakumelo.

Julia Smith, a criminologist and the wife of the Secretary General of the world's largest international police organisation, had requested a change of plan. She had asked to visit the women's prison on the outskirts of Kulsaka. This request had been refused.

"It is under renovation, madam," her Zambezin police minder, bodyguard and driver had informed her gravely. "A visit is not possible."

Ladybug Wakumelo had not been supportive of the idea in any case. "Why would one want to go to such a dingy and distressing place at all at all?" she said to Julia repeatedly as the driver weaved his way through dense traffic to Kulsaka's glittering and heavily air-conditioned suburban shopping mall, a very approximate facsimile of any number of upmarket malls in Miami or Los Angeles or even Cape Town. Madam Wakumelo's objective on the shopping expedition that day had been sunglasses, lots of sunglasses, and she would not be deterred.

Julia Smith, Madame DHD, had suggested in vain that they visit instead the Kulsaka central market; stocked, it was said, with local food and interesting local handicrafts and pickpockets and sexually transmitted disease.

"Not safe, madam," the driver had said, "for a Western lady. Not safe."

And so they had travelled to Kulsaka's facsimile shopping mall and Julia had trudged sullenly behind Ladybug Wakumelo as she tried on dozens of pairs of oversized and overpriced designer sunglasses before eventually choosing half a dozen pairs to take home. No money appeared to change hands in shops. The wife of the Zambezin Commissioner of Police merely handed the chosen sunglasses to the driver and sauntered on to the next shop. The sales assistants did not protest.

Lunch, in a glittering cafe for Zambezi's bourgeoisie overlooking the mall's indoor fountain, consisted of Perrier water, crustless white bread sandwiches filled with an unidentifiable paste, and much chocolate afterwards. Ladybug Wakumelo, extremely large and round, had until this point protested that she was on a diet.

"But life is so short, Julia, is it not?" she intoned gravely as she spooned up chocolate mousse. Her towering, intricately folded tie-dyed headscarf, worthy of a modern-day African queen, quivered delicately as she indulged.

Julia had purchased nothing, eaten very little, spoken very little. Ladybug seemed to take no notice. They had not bonded during their shopping and lunch expedition, that is true, but there had been no logistical or diplomatic gaffes, so the Commissioner's wife and the police driver sped away from the Hilton secure in the notion that their duty had been more than adequately done. Madam Wakumelo was wearing as she headed home the favourite of her new purchases: a very large pair of white-framed sunglasses with gold-coloured accents, not unlike those favoured by Elvis Presley in his final Las Vegas supper club days.

Back in her hotel suite, Julia Smith was exhausted, no longer sure that coming along to the African Regional Conference was a good idea. She collapsed on the king-sized bed, which that night she would unhappily and unwillingly share with the Secretary General. Then the image returned of her husband and Gilles Broussard sitting together, very close, thick as thieves, on the sofa back in Lyon. Then she remembered clearly why she had come to Africa.

She consulted the protocol booklet that all members of Interpol mission delegations were issued before departure from France. Among many other things, it included the mobile phone numbers and hotel room numbers of all travellers. She dialled Broussard's number. She summoned him to her suite; the Secretary General's suite.

Broussard had been resting in his room when Madame DHD called, not long back from the unhappy events at police headquarters. Like Madame DHD, he was exhausted by the rigours of a police mission, of international diplomacy and of Africa. But there had been so many surprises in his life of late, so much that was new and incomprehensible, that he had merely put the phone down after the summons, put his brown cardigan sweater back on, and proceeded immediately to the presidential suite.

Madame DHD had greeted him warmly, very warmly, with the perfunctory French-style kiss on each check, then a third peck, Paris-style, for good measure.

"How may I be of assistance, *madame?*" he said.

"Please," Madame DHD said. "Sit."

Broussard sat on the living room's giant black leather sofa. All rooms he entered recently seemed to have large black leather sofas. The room was freezing with air conditioning. He was glad after all that he had brought the sweater to Africa, as his wife had insisted.

"It's my computer, Gilles," Julia said, pointing to a laptop sitting on the desk. "It's just refuses to work for me here in Africa. It doesn't seem to like the Dark Continent very much, I guess. I don't either, really."

She flicked her hair slightly and laughed quietly. She pushed her wire-rimmed glasses up onto the top of her head.

"Can you help me?" she asked, looking as helpless as she could.

"But of course, *madame*," Broussard said, leaping to his feet. In a matter of seconds, he had opened the laptop, fired it up, logged on to the hotel's wireless Internet connection and patched into Julia's Smith's preferred email system.

"*Voila, madame*," he said happily. "*Je vous en prie.*"

"Oh, thanks so much, Gilles," Julia said. "You're a hero. Please, have something to drink before you go. I've just ordered up some coffee. Or there is a lot of other stuff in the mini-bar."

Broussard beamed happily, picking at lint on his cardigan. He returned to his place on the sofa. "Well," he said. "*Je suppose…*"

"I can surely see why my husband asks you to accompany him on these overseas missions," Julia said. "Coffee? Some wine, maybe? It's probably horrible wine down here compared to Lyon."

"Oh, perhaps a small coffee, *madame*. It is too early for wine perhaps," Broussard said. "And you are quite wrong, *madame*, about my coming on these police missions. This is my first one ever in my career."

"I see," Julia said. "So it's unusual."

"Yes, very much so, yes," he said. "In fact, to be *très honête* with you, *madame*, I am not absolutely clear as to my duties in Kulsaka. Although, yes, this morning I was called upon to assist a little in a police communications demonstration."

Julia sat down beside Broussard on the sofa. "But I'm told you are a key member of the computer department, Gilles. You won an employee award just last week, I understand."

Broussard beamed happily. "*Oui, madame*, it is true. There was a portion that was cash. And a car. It has been leased for my use. For how long I do not actually know. A Renault Clio, very nice. My wife was very proud. She can now use our other one. It was a very large surprise."

"Unusual," Julia said. "A new award…"

"*Oui, madame*," Broussard said. "Very new. Perhaps the next one could go to my manager, Monsieur Cholet. He would like this very much. He has told me that."

"And now you have been invited on this official mission," Julia said.

"*Exactement*," Broussard said.

"Exciting for you."

"*Oui, madame*."

"Unusual."

"*Oui.*"

There was a moment of silence as both parties pondered life's little twists and turns.

"My husband values your services a great deal, it seems," Julia said eventually.

"Apparently so, *madame*."

"You were up in his office last week, I noticed."

"*Oui*, it is true."

"Fixing his computer? Or something more mysterious, maybe? Hush-hush police stuff, I bet."

Broussard looked a little uneasy. Was Madame DHD asking about operational matters now? What could he be expected to say to the wife of the Secretary General when asked such a question? What would the Interpol regulation be for such a matter as this? Should he share with Madame DHD certain matters that he and *le Secrétaire Général* had discussed in private?

"For a little discussion," he said. "That is all."

"A little discussion?"

"*Exactement.*"

"Planning?"

"*Oui.*"

"Plotting and scheming, eh?"

Julia Smith flashed a giant American smile at Broussard, to show what a good-humoured woman she really was. A woman who liked a joke, who put people at ease, who could speak easily to any member of her husband's staff.

"*Pardon?*" Broussard said, perplexed. "Plotting? But I'm afraid I don't—"

"A little joke, Gilles," Julia said. "Don't mind me. I'm an American."

She slid closer to Gilles on the sofa. "I just take a very keen interest in my husband's work. In the work of Interpol. Like a good little wife. You see? I like to know a little about what goes on. When I am in Lyon. To share in my husband's work. And to get to know his trusted members of staff. His award-winners. I'm silly like that."

"*Je vous en prie, madame,*" Broussard said.

Madame DHD flicked her hair again. "I don't bite, Gilles," she said. "You can trust me. You can take me into your confidence. My husband trusts you, clearly. Takes you into his confidence, clearly. Gives you awards. And a nice little Renault car."

Broussard looked increasingly uncomfortable.

"There's no reason why you and I shouldn't have the same level of trust, Gilles. If I am to help my husband in his important work and give him all the support he needs," she said. "I'm a criminologist. Making the world a safer place and all that."

Broussard picked lint from his sweater. "Yes, well, I of course…" he said.

"Would you like a glass of wine maybe? From the mini-bar. I'll get it for you," Julia said, moving closer to him on the sofa. She patted his thigh affectionately. "Then we can talk for a while."

"Well, *madame*, I…"

As Broussard spoke, the door to the suite opened suddenly. It was Herriot-Dupont. He stopped dead in the threshold.

"Broussard!" he said. "Julia."

"*Monsieur le Secrétaire Général!*" Broussard said, leaping to his feet, flushed.

"Gilles has been helping me out, Didier," Julia Smith said brightly. "With a little problem I was having. He's a really helpful guy."

Before and during any regional police conference, or any important international meeting. Didier Herriot-Dupont liked to get briefings from his most trusted lieutenants. Jean-Marc Moulin was one of those. He was a policeman, a policeman's policeman. Moulin could be trusted to give the Secretary General a real sense of what the world's police, cops on the beat, were saying; what they needed. Take the pulse of world law enforcement.

Moulin did not look happy as he sat across from DHD in the office that had been provided to the Secretary General for the duration of the conference.

"Well, Jean-Marc, what are the police saying out there?" DHD asked again.

The plenary session was about to start. Workshops, dear to the heart of African police and bureaucrats continent-wide, had been duly held. Discussions duly conducted. Soundings taken.

"Drug trafficking, human trafficking, fingerprints," Moulin said. "Stolen cars."

"Nonsense!" DHD thundered. "That is the old Interpol."

"It is what they want, sir," Moulin said. "Assistance with basic police work. More emphasis on this."

"Nonsense!" DHD said again. "Bioterrorism. Terrorism watch lists. The new Interpol."

"I regret to say that is not what our African confrères are calling for, *monsieur*."

"We will pull them into the twenty-first century."

"This is Africa, *monsieur*. Perhaps not yet ready…"

"Nonsense."

"We shall see," Moulin said.

"Significant additions to the agenda?"

"Bestiality, *monsieur*."

"Bestiality?"

"*Oui*. There has been workshop discussion of this."

"Is this a crime, Jean-Marc?"

"That is what the discussion has been about, sir."

"Bestiality."

"*Oui, monsieur*. There has been discussion of how this should be approached: the legislation, the most effective police response. In certain African countries the police are unsure, the legislation is ambiguous…"

"There is legislation concerning bestiality?"

"In certain African nations, *monsieur*. Not all."

"For discussion at an Interpol conference."

"*Oui*."

"With media present?"

"Only for the plenary, *monsieur*. I understand that no press were admitted to the bestiality workshop."

"Get me Franklin," DHD said.

Franklin was at that moment engaging in some light communications work in the hotel lobby with the *Tempo of London*'s southern Africa correspondent, Christopher Winslow-Hague. A most unpleasant specimen of the British journalistic class, in a 1970s-era safari suit and a Panama hat. Winslow-Hague was not interested in bestiality, or at least he did not ask about this as a possible story. Word had not yet gone out that bestiality might be on the agenda of Interpol's African Regional Conference in Kulsaka.

What Winslow-Hague was interested in was Zimwabse's much-feared Chief of Police being an honorary vice president of Interpol.

"It's an honorary position, Christopher!" Franklin shouted to him again through his hangover. "It's no big deal. How many times do I have to tell you that?"

"No big deal. I can quote you on that?"

"We're off the record, Christopher. We agreed on that," Franklin said wearily.

"How could he have been appointed in the first place? The man is a thug. How do men like that get to be honorary anything in an international organisation?"

"He was chosen by police delegates to a General Assembly, I forget which one, to serve on the EC. Out of our hands. He has now retired from that post. When they retire, they are honorary vice presidents."

"For life."

"It's an honorary thing."

"How can you let a thug like that sit on the Executive Committee in the first place? Who would elect a man like that?"

"Out of our hands. The member countries decide. Police decide. It's Interpol."

"Unbelievable."

"Out of our hands."

"I'll need an interview. On the record."

"No way. Not with me."

"With someone else, then."

"No chance."

"*Senior Interpol officials refused to comment.*"

"Fuck you, Chris," Franklin said, drawing fully upon his legendary media relations skills.

"Fuck you too, Frank."

"Fuck off."

"Can I quote you on that?"

Interpol's Events Manager, Antonio de Caldevilla, was meanwhile making female members of the Zambezin organising committee cry. It was his usual procedure at gatherings such as this. He invariably found last-minute fault with many aspects of conference preparation

– venues, equipment, seating arrangements, menus for gala dinners, transport, accommodation, security, photography, cost. He vented his frustrations primarily at female members of organising committee staff, except if the event was being staged in Malta.

On this occasion, Caldevilla had just completed a ferocious verbal assault on a young woman from the Zambezin Interior Ministry. She was sobbing uncontrollably, her long black hair quivering, her shoulders heaving as she wept. She was holding a pair of reading glasses in one hand and a battered clipboard in the other.

"Crying is of no use," Caldevilla said, though he liked to see women cry.

"We have done the very best we can do," the young woman managed to say sadly, between sobs.

"This is, of course, not good enough," Caldevilla barked. He looked triumphantly around at the circle of uniformed and civilian Zambezins who were watching the scene unfold. It was a small sea of grave black faces.

"You are being beastly to me," the young woman said eventually.

"Accusations are of no use, none. They are not," Caldevilla said.

"I shall tell my uncle," the young woman said, looking up, tears streaming down her cheeks.

"This is, of course, no use," the Events Manager said.

"I shall tell my uncle, the Interior Minister," the young woman said.

SIX

Interpol Secretary General Didier Herriot-Dupont and his trusted Chief of Staff Freiderikos Milonakis were performing a postmortem on the proceedings of the African Regional Conference. They were doing so in the relative comfort and safety of the Secretary General's office. However, the remains of the African Regional Conference were no cause for comfort.

As always, Milonakis was expected to be the lead pathologist.

"And so, Fred," Herriot-Dupont was saying. "How was that particular situation allowed to develop?"

"I'm meeting with Caldevilla this afternoon. I'll get his report."

The niece of the Zambezin Interior Minister had collapsed in the hotel's grand ballroom, reportedly in tears after an encounter with Interpol's Events Manager. She had been rushed home with a motorcycle escort to rest and had been unable to attend the plenary session. She had somehow lost her clipboard and eyeglasses in the confusion. However, she had, very bravely, managed to drag herself in to the gala dinner. The Interior Minister of Zambezi was said to be much displeased.

"That Maltese idiot," DHD hissed.

"Sometimes Antonio does not understand the need for tact."

"He's an idiot!"

"We need Malta very much at this time, sir," Milonakis said. "This would not be the time to offend them."

"After the General Assembly we will offend Malta," DHD said.

"Depending on how the European vote goes, I would say," Milonakis said.

"And the plenary session," DHD growled. "A disaster."

"Not ideal," Milonakis said.

The African police delegates, those who attended the afternoon plenary session in Kulsaka, those who were sober and those who stayed awake, had not responded at all well to the Secretary General's speech. Milonakis had seen that very clearly. It was too long, for one thing. Even the translators appeared to have trouble staying awake for the duration. And the Secretary General's rousing call for African law enforcement to help lead the way to a safer world had fallen, it seemed, on deaf ears.

The Secretary General's proposal for more effective use continent-wide of the state-of-the-art X-24GT police communication system, for a state-of-the-art bioterrorism training programme to be attended by all senior African police at the expense of their own organisations, for more contributions from Africa's police to Interpol's state-of-the-art terrorist watch list and databases had, it seemed, fallen on deaf ears.

Then the highly unusual decision, taken at the last minute by DHD himself, to invite the Assistant Director of Interpol's computer department to demonstrate on a giant screen to some two hundred police delegates, in an overcrowded and overwarm conference room, the intricacies of the latest developments in the X-24GT system had not been a success either. Milonakis had already written a letter of complaint to the head of the Zamtel telecommunications company, and to Zambezi's telecommunications minister.

The stress of that ill-fated X-24GT demonstration had in fact proved too much for Gilles Broussard, unaccustomed to public speaking and to overseas police missions in tropical climes. Broussard had afterward been led away from the podium by two Zambezin paramedics, weak in the knees, extremely red in the face and sweating profusely. He was ordered by the Zambezin police physician to rest in his air-conditioned room at least until it was time for the gala dinner.

Jean-Marc Moulin, however, Interpol's Director of Operational Police Support, had, many agreed afterward, somewhat stolen the show with his presentation on the flow of stolen cars from Europe and Japan to Africa. His PowerPoint slides had been excellent; his use of graphics to show where hundreds of cars had been stolen and where in Africa they had been recovered through diligent routine police work, with expert Interpol assistance, was a highlight of the conference, many agreed. Moulin's presentation was greeted with sustained and very warm applause. The question period that followed was lively, relevant and interesting, many agreed.

The Secretary General did not agree.

"How was Moulin allowed to present such a thing?" Herriot-Dupont asked Milonakis testily. "This is the old Interpol, we have moved very far beyond this sort of thing, have we not, Fred?"

"The content of all presentations was approved by you some weeks ago, sir," Milonakis said quietly.

"No, that is not so. I did not see Moulin's presentation beforehand, no one showed that to me," DHD shouted.

"I'll ask Jean-Marc about this," Milonakis said.

"What's his little game, Fred?"

"I don't believe he's trying to do—"

"You are naïve, I think sometimes, Fred," the Secretary General said.

No one had ever accused Interpol's Chief of Staff of being naïve.

"Perhaps I am a little," Milonakis said. "Sometimes, perhaps. Yes, that may be true."

"Watch Moulin for me, Fred," Herriot-Dupont said. "And he is not to speak to the plenary at the General Assembly in Munich. You understand?"

"That would be very unusual," Milonakis said. "He is Director of Operational Police Support."

"He is not to speak."

"Understood."

"I am being undermined," DHD said. "On all sides."

"Jean-Marc has no reason to undermine you," Milonakis said. "He's loyal."

"Perhaps I'm even being undermined by my own wife?" the Secretary General said gravely.

"I think not," Milonakis said.

"The gun incident, Fred. And now I am told that she lunches with my staff. Why is she doing that? Why does she insist now on going to regional conferences in Africa? She doesn't like Africa. What was she doing with that fool Broussard in my own hotel room in Kulsaka, Fred? Tell me. You are my Chief of Staff. You are supposed to be my eyes and ears."

"I will investigate."

"We gave him a car, Fred. Why does he now betray me?"

"That's too harsh, sir. There is no evidence that he…"

The Secretary General went silent, as he did when lost in paranoid speculation. Milonakis indulged in some paranoid speculation of his own; not, as he knew, having been taken fully into the Secretary General's confidence on the Broussard matter.

"I am being undermined," DHD said again eventually.

"It was not all bad, the conference," Milonakis said brightly, looking for something positive.

"No?"

"The bestiality resolution did not get up."

A rueful smile appeared on the Secretary General's lips.

"And the gala dinner went extremely well," Milonakis said.

"A raucous affair," DHD said.

"It was," Milonakis said.

"They do know how to have a good time, those African police," DHD said.

Any other gala dinner, at any other conference that had got so out-of-hand in a five-star hotel would have definitely been a matter for the police. Milonakis knew this full well. But in this case, there would have been no use calling the police to restore order. The police – scores of them, from many countries – were already there.

*

Another serious problem was developing. Milonakis had been assigned to defuse it. Interpol staff – many of them; most – were up in arms over the Secretary General's precipitous decision to close the popular headquarters building bar. It was jammed every day, after work hours and into the evening, by seconded police and permanent Interpol officers and support staff and international visitors. Drinks were cheap, smoking was allowed; colourful insignia from the world's police agencies lined the walls. Everyone loved the Interpol bar.

The Secretary General had always hated the Interpol bar. He thought it was a breeding ground for gossip and innuendo and discontent. He thought it was a place where staff conspired again him. He had been waiting for months for an excuse to shut it down. When he returned from Kulsaka he believed he had that excuse. He believed the time was right, though Milonakis advised him strongly against it.

Australian and British police officers stumbling out of the building after a particularly rowdy night in the Interpol bar had once again humiliated French police sitting in their tiny patrol car outside the front gates. They had once again rocked the Renault and they had accused the French cops of having no penises whatsoever. Another complaint from senior French police officials had been sent to DHD. The bar was therefore to be closed indefinitely, with immediate effect.

The immediate effect was to infuriate Interpol staff. Clusters of disgruntled and very thirsty staff congregated for the first few days after the closure around the locked glass doors to the bar on the ground floor of the headquarters building, muttering darkly, seeking explanations, seeking resolution; seeking a target. The crowd thinned somewhat as the days progressed. The fury did not subside.

"It can't be permanent, Secretary General," Milonakis had said. "There will be a revolution."

"It is to be permanently closed," DHD said. "I will not tolerate drunkenness among my staff."

"This is France," Milonakis said.

"This is Interpol," DHD said. "It is the world's largest international police organisation. We are making the world a safer place. Why does that require a staff bar?"

"There will be a revolt."

"We can allow it to be opened on special occasions. Christmas."

"Christmas only?"

"Easter. Bastille Day. A few days per year. That is my compromise position. Inform the staff committee."

Milonakis' informants among staff were daily bringing him extremely alarming reports. The murmurings would only grow louder.

"Deal with it, Fred," DHD said. "You're my Chief of Staff."

Only the most paranoid would link discontent among staff to the subsequent catastrophic failure of the state-of-the-art X-24GT police communication system. Even Milonakis, a man only too familiar with the endless pageant of unscrupulous human behaviour, did not link staff discontent with the failure of that system, just days before the scheduled arrival in Lyon of the Executive Committee, and just weeks before the General Assembly in Munich. He did not immediately make such a connection.

The X-24GT screens had, one morning, simply gone dark. Puzzled technicians stood and stared. Manuals were consulted, clipboards brandished, phone calls made. There was no immediately apparent cause. Reports began to come in from around the world – or rather, from countries where X-24GT had actually been installed, and where it was being used correctly, or being used at all – that the system was not working in those places also. Interpol's battle against international crime was, possibly, being significantly impeded.

When the breakdown was not immediately rectified, Milonakis had summoned the Head of Interpol's computer department, the inscrutable Pierre Cholet, an Interpol lifer who had seen various systems come and go, had seen various Secretaries General come and go. He did appear sufficiently alarmed, in Freiderikos Milonakis' view.

"This must be fixed absolutely as soon as possible, Cholet," Milonakis said.

"I have assigned this to Gilles Broussard, *monsieur*," Cholet said, his hooded bureaucrat's eyes betraying no sense of urgency. "My deputy."

"You're the head of department, you should look after this yourself. It should be your first priority," Milonakis said.

"Monsieur Broussard is an award-winning member of my staff," Cholet said. "As you know. He has been judged more than capable by yourself and others. By the Secretary General himself. In Monsieur Broussard I have every confidence."

Could a man like Cholet be capable of sabotage? Milonakis asked himself, glaring across the desk at the head of the Interpol computer department. Does he have the balls?

"This must be fixed at once, immediately, today," Milonakis shouted.

"Perhaps Monsieur Broussard will need to call the Americans. They who first designed this system."

Key people in the X-24GT project team had been purged by the Secretary General soon after he took over the post. They had been victims of the purge of Americans loyal to the previous Secretary General. They had been critical of Herriot-Dupont's plans for major and costly modifications to the system.

"Impossible," Milonakis said.

"I shall ask Monsieur Broussard for a progress report," Cholet said.

"Get that imbecile Cholet up here immediately," the Secretary General had shouted when Milonakis made his report.

"He has assigned rectification to Gilles Broussard, sir," Milonakis said.

"Broussard?" DHD shouted.

"As Cholet points out, an award-winning member of the computer department staff."

*

Broussard was sweating profusely as he gave DHD and Milonakis his interim report. He was seated uneasily on the interrogation sofa.

"We have performed all of the usual software tests, *messieurs*," he said sadly. "At the present moment there is no obvious cause."

"There must be a cause," DHD shouted.

"It is not obvious."

"Make it obvious, Gilles," Milonakis said.

"Today," DHD said.

"I will get the technicians to investigate possible hardware defects," Broussard said.

"No one anywhere in the world is able to use X-24GT, Gilles," DHD said. "Do you realise the law enforcement implications of this? The implications for me personally?"

"*Oui, absolument, monsieur*," Broussard said sadly.

"X-24GT screens are blank around the world," DHD said.

"A little like Kulsaka, *non?*" Broussard offered helpfully.

"Take back that damn car!" the Secretary General had shouted after Broussard left the office. "Cancel the lease! He can take the bus. That man does not deserve to be driving an Interpol car."

"That would be counterproductive at this stage, *monsieur*," Milonakis said. "In my view."

Minutes, literally, before senior police from all regions began arriving at headquarters for the Executive Committee meeting, X-24GT screens began flickering back to life. No one among the computer department's troubleshooting staff, and neither Broussard nor Cholet, was able to explain, it seemed, what had gone wrong or why things were suddenly again going right.

Was this a warning of some sinister kind? Milonakis and the Secretary General were too preoccupied with the logistics and diplomatic niceties of a crucially important EC meeting to attempt to answer such a question; to do anything other than be grateful that X-24GT was once again at the service of the world's police, in countries where it had actually been installed, where it was being used correctly, or being used at all.

Restaurateurs around Lyon rubbed their hands in anticipation of the quarterly meetings in the Interpol Executive Committee. Not all were fortunate enough to be selected as venues for official dinners and lunches. Indeed, some of the lunching was actually done, less lucratively, inside the headquarters building, but catered, nonetheless, by some of the outside restaurants, much to the frustration of the manager of the Interpol cafeteria, André Julien.

To be elected a member of Interpol's Executive Committee in the era of Didier Herriot-Dupont was, in world policing circles, something like winning a handsome lottery prize. It was feather in any police officer's cap; it carried major prestige in home countries. It involved periodic business-class air travel to Lyon in the sunny south of France. It involved chauffeur-driven airport pickups, very fine hotel rooms in a charming *arrondissement* of Lyon, and a series of very fine meals, as previously described. It involved constant compliments and strokes from the Interpol Secretary General and his Chief of Staff and other minions and officials; much photographing of proceedings; much issuing of press releases by Frank Franklin and Alf Mortman and their colleagues in the Communication and Publications department.

In return, for a few days three times per year, the EC members gave densely laid-out agendas their occasional full attention. They deliberated gravely on challenges facing the world's police. They ticked a few administrative boxes here and there when required. They were, de jure, the trusted and trustworthy overseers of Interpol and the bosses of the Secretary General. But, de facto, with just three drop-in trips a year to Lyon and with the bellies of most members always full of fine French food and wine, few of the EC members did much to rock the global law enforcement boat. Except, perhaps, for the occasional Japanese member, or an

American from time to time, or a Canadian or Brit here and there along the way.

That is not to say that there were not challenges thrown up at EC meetings, or controversies or disagreements or even a little sulking from time to time. But with representatives from all global regions, and from some very questionable police forces in certain of those regions, and with little experience among such representatives in acting as members of a true board of directors, the EC did not, some would argue, truly manage the working of the world's largest police organisation. That was left, by and large, to the Secretary General of the day. That was, at the present moment, one Didier Herriot-Dupont.

At the EC meeting in question, his major challenges were to head off some anticipated hard questions from Japan about his proposed budget increase, to ensure that the various appetites of Serbania's delegate were more than adequately sated without violating too many French laws, and to make sure that Executive Committee President Jafar Kheir El-Mowab, from the esteemed police state of Sudan, was suitably flattered and awarded and photographed and rewarded, without, in his case, the use of any alcohol whatsoever.

Serbania's Valon Dragusha, known to consider himself next in line for the Secretary General's post, known to be angling behind the scenes before making an eventual move for the job, was as always the first to arrive. Several days ahead of all other EC members, as per usual. He had already made clear to the Chief of Staff that his room at the Hotel Grande Bretagne was inadequate, that his Interpol per diem would be insufficient as always, and that his chauffeur had not spoken to him even a word of greeting in the Serbanian language. Not, he pointed out repeatedly to Freiderikos Milonakis, an acceptable state of affairs for a weary senior police officer who had travelled all the way from Virana alone, without the support and succour of his wife; alone, alas, alone in a draughty suite of rooms in the increasing evening chill of autumn.

"I'll have something sent up, Valon," Milonakis had said on the telephone. "Something to chase away the chill."

"Something or someone? Ha! Ha! Ha ha!" Dragusha shouted. "I joke this time with you."

"A surprise for you. Wait just a little."

"Promising, promising, promising news, Freiderikos," Dragusha said. He sounded a little drunk already, on vodka likely pilfered from the plane. "I wait, therefore, wifeless in my room with a – what you French say? – a frisson of anticipation. A very big frisson! As you French like to say."

"I'm Greek, Valon," Milonakis said patiently.

It was a little game Dragusha liked to play.

"A Greek stallion, is it true? Not Italian? Ha!" Dragusha roared down the phone line from his hotel two blocks from headquarters building. "Rumours have reached even Virana, *mon frère*, my brother, my son!"

Dragusha went to ground for two days. Occasionally there was call from his room for an Interpol car to ferry him to a Lyon restaurant. When the member for Serbania showed up in the wood-panelled Interpol boardroom on the first official day of Executive Committee proceedings, he did not look good at all. His face was the ashen hue of a man who had seen too little daylight and had smoked too many cigars and cigarettes. Strands of his heavily oiled hair struggled to spring away from his mottled skull; clumps lay waiting to escape. His burgundy pinstripe suit was badly in need of pressing. He chewed mints distractedly throughout the morning's business. He glowered at his agenda documents. He belched discreetly from time to time.

Jafar Kheir El-Mowab of Sudan was to be chairman. He did not, unfortunately, understand or endorse the Western rules of order. Japan's Yoko Watanabe did. Watanabe would therefore be challenging a series of El-Mowab's rulings through the three days the EC members were to be together, making the world a safer place.

"I very stren…ruously object to this, my colleagues," Watanabe was already saying. The meeting was just fifteen minutes old and she had lodged an objection. Milonakis would have to remind himself as to the details of his salary and benefits package many times that day, and the following, in order to make it through.

As a good part of the budget increase being proposed was earmarked for improvements to Interpol's state-of-the-art global police communications system, the Assistant Director of Interpol's computer department Gilles Broussard was called upon to give a demonstration of the new features the world's police were being called upon to pay for. This demonstration went far better than the two in Kulsaka, Zambezi.

Secretary General Herriot-Dupont had already forgiven Broussard for his less-than-perfect performances in Kulsaka and during the system collapse a few days after their return from Africa. Secretary General Herriot-Dupont had apparently remembered just how important Monsieur Broussard was to the organisation, and to the Secretary General personally.

"An award-winning member of my staff, gentlemen," DHD had said before Broussard stood up to go to the boardroom podium. "Instrumental in improving on X-24GT, vis-à-vis the original design."

The American EC delegate, Steve Bradwell, a US Postal Inspection Service man from San Francisco, shifted ostentatiously in his seat. He said nothing.

"What was the award, my friend?" Dragusha had asked through his hangover. "Something very good maybe, ha! Ha!"

"A car," Broussard had said quickly, before Milonakis could catch his eye. "And a component that was cash."

Watanabe said, "This organisation is giving autos away as prizes?"

The American said, "Nice."

"Not a prize, Yoko," DHD said. "An award for outstanding service to global law enforcement. Access to an Interpol vehicle. A leased vehicle, of course."

"This man needs an auto for his official work?" Watanabe said, writing something in her Japan National Police Agency detective's notebook.

"Gilles, we're getting a little behind schedule here now, so could you please begin your presentation for us?" Milonakis said.

"Yes, let us by all means not be late for our appointment with Mr Paul Bocuse for dinner!" Dragusha said merrily. "And Mr Brou Zard, award winner, can you come to my hotel room possibly before we go tonight, yes? To rectify a small problem I am having with my computer. A movie I was watching last night is frozen on my screen. Most embarrassing, yes? Something you, a winner of awards, will find too simple to fix for me, I think."

Gilles Broussard, at home with his wife at last after a very trying day, had indeed been somewhat embarrassed by what was frozen on the computer screen belonging to the EC delegate from Serbania. He had found the entire day extremely trying, only to have been confronted by that particular image on the laptop screen at the Hotel Grande Bretagne.

The previous few weeks had all, in fact, been extremely trying. Highly confidential meetings with the Secretary General, lunch alongside the Secretary General's wife, travel to exotic locales, significant changes in diet and climate, long hours of work in difficult circumstances, private meetings with Secretary General's wife, presentations to large groups of foreigners, presentations to the EC, summonses to hotel rooms of Eastern European policemen.

And that image frozen on Monsieur Dragusha's laptop screen. Was it even legal in France to download such images to a computer, in any case? Was the girl even of legal age?

"I am much in demand these days, *ma chère*," Broussard said to his wife as they sat watching a musical variety show on their TV.

Madame Broussard was exceptionally proud of her husband's recent career successes. She did not fully understand the tension this entailed. And she did not understand why a man of such value to the world's largest international police organisation, a winner of major awards, had not been invited, along with his spouse, to the official dinner at Restaurant Paul Bocuse.

Monsieur Broussard promised that he would take her *chez* Bocuse at some later date. He had explained that Interpol general staff did not usually receive invitations to dine with the EC. He did not explain to her how upset he had been after his encounter with Valon Dragusha in the Hotel Grande Bretagne, how much he simply wanted to come home to his little house. He had never seen images like that, quite like that, in all of his years in law enforcement circles. And he liked to think that he was a man not easily surprised or shocked.

"Perhaps you should have insisted a little more to be included among those going tonight to Paul Bocuse," his wife said quietly. "A man of your stature in the organisation."

Madame Broussard was a woman of traditional (some might say dated) tastes in restaurants. France had moved substantially beyond Bocuse in its culinary accomplishments. But she – and, it seemed, the sampling of the world's police attending Executive Committee meetings in Lyon – still liked their official dinners old-fashioned and overpriced.

"Perhaps next time, *ma chouette*," Broussard said.

Secretary General Herriot-Dupont had always argued, when critics raised unfair allegations about cost and appearances, that the official dinners and lunches enjoyed by EC delegates were worth every euro spent. Much important police work was accomplished over foie gras and beef bourguignon and well-cellared Cotes du Rhone wine. Important bonds were established between police forces. Where else could a respected senior member of Japan's NPA get to exchange information in a very relaxed atmosphere about police matters with, for example, a respected senior member of Serbania's esteemed State Police?

When EC members went home happy, their important work done, important bonds and relationships having been formed, this was all to the benefit of international law enforcement, *non?*

True, in this case, at this particular EC meeting, there had been no real agreement, and in fact some rather lively discussion of Interpol's ever-increasing budget, its ever-expanding activities and projects and scope of work. True, Yoko Watanabe of Japan had clashed – one could justifiably use that word – repeatedly with the Serbanian delegate, and with the Sudanese chairman and others. The Japanese police were, it seemed, somewhat out of sorts these days. Freiderikos Milonakis had already been assigned to smooth those waters, post-EC and before the General Assembly in Munich.

But now, with the day's important deliberations done, Herriot-Dupont was delighted that Watanabe and Dragusha were seated together and bonding even further. DHD had himself taken charge of seating arrangements for the dinner, dismissing suggestions from his Chief of Staff and Events Manager and others as to where certain delegates should be placed in relation to each other.

"See how well Madame Watanabe and Dragusha are getting along now in this convivial atmosphere," DHD whispered to Milonakis as the night progressed.

Dragusha was extremely drunk, and trying his best to bring Watanabe along on that journey with him. The Japanese policewoman, a very precise user of alcohol, showed no outward signs of intoxication. She just stared straight ahead and nodded curtly and rapidly in response to everything Dragusha shouted in her ear.

"Death penalty, death penalty, Yoko," Dragusha shouted. "Our countries are in full agreement, yes, about this very effective law enforcement method! Here we drink to the solidarity between the policemen of the great nations of Serbania and Japan." He leaped to his feet, a tumbler of costly red wine gripped unsteadily in his puffy right hand. "I propose a toast to the death penalty, and to the important work of Interpol, both at the same time," he shouted.

All members of the EC rose to make this toast. Interpol's President, Jafar Kheir El-Mowab of Sudan, a good sport despite his strict views on alcohol use, clutched a crystal glass of mineral water. He, and the Sudanese police, would certainly never miss an opportunity to endorse effective law enforcement techniques such as hanging or firing squads. Steve Bradwell of the USA joined in enthusiastically, of course.

"To the heroes of international police cooperation!" Herriot-Dupont then proclaimed, himself uncharacteristically merry. "Wherever they may be!"

SEVEN

The pressures of the Executive Committee meeting behind him, and with a very small breathing space ahead before he had to turn his full attention to the General Assembly with all of its attendant problems, Secretary General Didier Herriot-Dupont quite understandably wanted sex. With his wife if possible, or with one or more of his mistresses if necessary, or, ideally, with all of the above in rapid succession, depending on Lyon traffic. The rigours of international police work, or, to be precise, the politics thereof, regularly worked up for DHD a mighty carnal appetite.

Julia Smith was, for some reason in recent days, denying the Secretary General his conjugal rights. So his expectations were not high when, after a strenuous post-EC kendo practice session in the living room of his official apartment, DHD, quite understandably, entered the official bedroom with thoughts of an official post-kendo coupling. He was wearing his kimono, not a policeman's uniform, but even the wonderfully embroidered black and red Japanese number did nothing for Madame DHD's libido.

"But my darling woman, is it something I have said or done?" DHD asked his clearly disgruntled wife.

Julia was reading Dostoyevsky in bed. *Crime and Punishment.* She looked over her American academic-issue wire-rimmed glasses at her kimono-clad crime-fighter husband and said tartly, "Not a good moment, Didier. I'm reading."

The Secretary General pondered this for hidden meanings, nuances. What was his crime, he wondered, to be dismissed so brusquely in this way? Why this punishment? Julia had simply not been the same since coming back to Lyon from the US. Her mood was dark. There was the nasty incident with the confiscated gun, yes, but she had become even more dark since her return from Africa. As it were. And what of that troubling incident of Madame DHD and Gilles Broussard being discovered together in the hotel room in Kulsaka?

Could she and the Assistant Manager of Interpol's computer department actually be having an *affair*? Julia, with a reedy little *fonctionnaire* in a ratty cardigan? No, Herriot-Dupont thought, this is impossible. This would be a bit much. That would really and truly be too much.

Still, Julia's recent resistance to the Secretary General's manly charms was evidence of something gone badly awry. It did not take the leader of the world's largest international police organisation long to deduce that. Professional women, students, chambermaids throughout France, and indeed the world, could be brought forward to attest to DHD's sexual athleticism and his attractiveness generally speaking.

"*Eh, bien,*" Herriot-Dupont said to his bibliophile wife. "I will not disturb you, my darling. I have some important reading of my own to do before bed."

DHD beat as dignified retreat as he could, under the circumstances. He stopped by his dressing room on the way out, gathered up various items of clothing, – black in colour and expensive in cut – and dressed himself in his office beside his giant official desk. He summoned his car, with his ever-so-discreet night driver at the wheel, and within minutes was letting himself into the small but elegant apartment of the lovely Evangeline on the Quai Saint-Antoine. The lovely and talented Evangeline, never unhappy to be distracted from her university studies late at night, always exceedingly grateful for the rent-free accommodation that can be so helpful to any struggling student, always more than happy to assist the Secretary General in any way.

Frank Franklin, as much to his own surprise as anyone else's, had managed to persuade CNN to send a crew to Lyon to do up a piece about Interpol. Or so the story would go. In fact, when the telephone in his small office rang one morning shortly after the Executive Committee meeting, the CNN woman on the line, of the brassy Yank-journo-in-London variety, was someone he had not been in contact with at all. She professed to be unaware of Franklin's repeated requests that CNN do a story about Interpol.

"No one said anything about that to me," she said sharply. "What department?"

"I was just calling the general number on the news desk," Franklin said. His international news contacts were occasionally reduced to this.

"That's no use," CNN woman said. She had not yet introduced herself. "Those guys get hundreds of pitch calls all the live-long day."

"Well, that's OK," Franklin said in his best Canadian deferential tone. "At least we're in touch now. I'm glad CNN is interested in Interpol."

"Oh, we're interested alright," CNN said.

"What unit are you with?" Franklin said, assuming his Chief Press Officer role with a little bit more style. "And what's your name?"

"Oh, we're the investi…the, ah, features unit. Long features unit. In-depth stuff. I'm Sally Birchgrove. A producer."

"Great. Well, I told your news desk I'd be happy to open some doors down here for your people if they came. Arrange a few interviews. You can have the Secretary General. Exclusive."

"That's what I like to hear," Sally Birchgrove said.

"Great. When? And who's coming? You?"

"Nah. Not me. I'm sending one of our best guys. Rob Henderson. He's a pro. Been around for years. Knows his way around a story. Ex-foreign correspondent. Used to anchor for a while in Atlanta. Kinda reports on what interests him now. What captures his attention. He's an older guy."

"I haven't seen his stuff," Franklin said. "But our monitoring might miss that sometimes."

"Oh, he doesn't file too often. He kinda comes to me when he's got a bee in his bonnet about something."

"He's got a bee in his bonnet about Interpol?" Franklin asked, his worry antennae rising.

"No, no, just a figure of speech. I'm from Minnesota originally."

Mortman had just been released from hospital again. Acute stomach pains. Again. Two nights' observation, but then even the French healthcare system decided he did not need to stay in any longer than that. He needed a bit of good news, however, on his return to work. That CNN was coming was good news.

"Well done, Franklin," Mortman said, chewing an antacid tablet. "Very well done. Thank heavens for these small mercies."

"Thanks," Franklin said. "It's a guy named Rob Henderson."

Mortman blanched. "The investigative reporter?"

"Long features, the producer said. I've never seen his stuff."

"Sweet Jesus," Mortman said, reaching for another antacid. "When is he coming? Does Milonakis know?"

"He arrives tomorrow," Franklin said. "He's hot to trot, apparently. Is there a problem?"

Rob Henderson was everything US commercial television could produce and a whole lot more. He and his crew rolled up to the Interpol main gate the next day in a giant rented people-mover packed to the roofline with black and silver equipment boxes, leather cases, booms, lights, reflectors, briefcases and discarded Styrofoam coffee cups. Henderson bounded out of the still idling vehicle to shake Franklin's hand. The Interpol press officer had been waiting for them at the gate.

"You Franklin?" Henderson shouted as if from under the rotors of an Apache attack helicopter. He was wearing CNN-issue tan chinos, a navy blazer with gold buttons, and a pair of oxblood penny loafers. Grey hair, expensively cut. Classic crinkles around the eyes. Brilliant white caps on all visible teeth. "You know my stuff?" he shouted.

"Hello, Rob," Franklin said. "Well, I – we monitor everything we can but a lot of stuff gets sent to me and I can't really watch everything I get all the time…"

"Fine, fine, hey, that's OK, Frankie. I've been around a bit, I don't take it personally. Been in the field for thirty-five years. Seen a few things. Dodged a few bullets."

"Your producer was saying."

"Yeah, Sally loves me to death."

"Well, I'm here to help you with your piece. At your service."

"Great, Frankie, great. Let's get this shit through Interpol's world famous building security and get started. I'll do a promo and my stand-up first, I think. Then we can do some interviews, maybe."

"You want to do your stand-up first?"

"Always, Frankie. That's how it's done." Henderson called out to his crew. "Come on in, guys. Welcome to Copville!" To Franklin he said, "Jacoby over there is my cameraman. He's a conflict zone sort of guy. Been everywhere. Doesn't take any shit from security people. The other guy getting the stuff out of the truck is the sound man. He doesn't say much."

It took an extremely long time to get the CNN gear through Interpol security. Interpol's security guards did not get much exciting work to do most days, and they were certainly not going to let all this interesting equipment pass through their lines of defence without a thorough look. And it would be fodder for lunchtime conversations for some weeks to come.

When Henderson and Company were finally allowed to enter the five-storey, light-filled atrium in the main Interpol lobby, Jacoby whistled in appreciation.

"Pretty pictures, Robbie," he said. "Check out that giant Interpol mosaic on the floor."

"Yup, I'll do my stand-up there," Henderson said. "You get up onto that second-floor balcony for a wide shot, then come in close and get me with the logo."

Jacoby and Sound Man headed immediately for one of the glass-sided elevators. Franklin called out after them.

"Hey guys, you have to wear these security passes. And you can't go up there without an escort. That's an operational area on the second floor."

"Fuck that," Jacoby said.

From the second floor, Jacoby planted his chunky Sony camera on a tree-sized tripod and peered expertly through the viewfinder, flipping his ponytail out away from his shoulders. Sound Man, his New York Yankees baseball cap on backwards and bulky recording apparatus slung across his chest, peered down at pulsating VU meters and status lights. He blew a small bubble with his glistening pink chewing gum.

"Recording," he said, snapping the gum bubble.

"Go!" Jacoby shouted.

Standing resolute on the Interpol mosaic below, Henderson brushed his temples, thrust out his chin, grasped a cordless FM microphone and roared to an imagined worldwide audience of millions, "Tuesday night, on *INSIDE EDITION!* We take you INSIDE INTERPOL! Join us for this exclusive glimpse into the innermost secrets of the world's most secretive police organisation. Tuesday! Only on CNN!"

"Again," Jacoby shouted down two floors. "Pump it up!"

"Tuesday night, on *INSIDE EDITION!* We take you INSIDE INTERPOL…"

"Fuck," Franklin said softly from the corner where he had taken cover. He dialled Mortman's number on his mobile phone.

From the interior balcony on the fifth floor, Chief of Staff Freiderikos Milonakis watched the CNN action in the atrium with a frown. Mortman had called him on his mobile phone immediately after

Franklin had called on his. An individual in a blue blazer was shouting up to someone on the second floor. A small crowd of Interpol staff had gathered to watch on their way into the dining room.

Somewhat alarming that CNN had sent a so-called investigative journalist to Interpol, but nothing to panic about so far, Milonakis thought. The Secretary General was a master with the media. The interview with Herriot-Dupont would be the key, Milonakis thought. Nothing to panic about, so far.

He retreated to his office to resume his usual plotting and scheming.

Franklin, on the other hand, was fighting off panic. Henderson had given him a handwritten list of interviews he wanted, and shots his crew would need to take. The list was scrawled on Hotel Grande Bretagne stationary.

"You've already checked in? I thought you guys came straight from the airport," Franklin said.

"No, no, we've been around for a couple of days already, Frankie," Henderson said, smoothing hair against his temples after the rigours of the stand-up shoot. "You know, getting a feel for the place, sniffing around, talking to the locals."

"The locals?"

"Yeah."

"Staff?"

"Hey, Frankie, relax. What's up? I'm just doing my job. That's what I do, buddy. Go places, talk to a few people, take pretty pictures, file a piece. Real TV work is easy, it's a very simple matter."

Franklin looked forlornly at Henderson's list:

Must-have shots:

- *Command Centre, lots of screens, blinking lights, world maps, wanted crims mug shots if possible. Cops looking serious, peering at stuff, breaking cases. Arrests, if possible. Cops at work. Blah blah blah.*
- *The armoury. Guns on racks, Pistols and ammo. Patrol cars. Interpol logo on car doors.*

- *Building. All kinds of shots inside and outside, wide/narrow. Basement. Condition of building. The Interpol sign, close-ups. (Ladder or cherry-picker needed.) The gardens, garden beds. French cop car parked outside.*
- *Staff dining room. The staff bar: doors leading in, closed. Shots inside without people. Is there a staff gym? Staff shots. Arriving for work keen/going home tired out.*

Must-have interviews:
- *Building maintenance guy.*
- *Building security guy. Plus health and safety rep?*
- *Head of the computer department. Some X-24GT people. Troubleshooters.*
- *The operational guy, Moulin?*
- *Budget people. Audit chief.*
- *Staff union rep, staff association rep.*

Franklin looked up from the page.

"The Secretary General isn't on this list. You don't want to interview the Secretary General?" he asked.

"Sure," Henderson said. "If he's got a minute, why not? Busy guy, probably."

"Why do you need the building maintenance person?"

"I have found you can learn a lot about a place by talking to people who work in the bowels of a headquarters building. They know where all the bodies are buried, right! Get it?"

Jacoby, standing nearby, snorted loudly. Sound Man snapped a gum bubble.

"And you want to talk to the staff association?" Franklin said.

"Yeah. Get a real feel for what's it's like in the world's largest international police organisation. Ordinary people, rank-and-file crime-fighters, that sort of thing. Toiling away. Making the world a safer place and all that. How are things going with staff around here anyway, Frankie? Pretty tough, I would imagine – all these temperamental Frenchies jammed in together with cops from all over, in the same place. Sort of a, whatchacallit, a pressure cooker kind of environment, right? Bubble, bubble, toil and trouble… Kaboom!"

"Why do you need shots of the staff bar?"

"It's where people used to go, right?"

"Used to go?"

"Closed down, right? So I hear."

"Temporarily. How'd you hear that?"

"What's up? Morale OK? Troubles?"

"No, no. It's just a temporary closure."

"The French like their vino after work, right?"

"Like everybody, I guess," Franklin said.

"You got that right," Henderson said cheerily. "Jacoby and I put back a few last night at the hotel."

Henderson leaned closer to Franklin, suddenly conspiratorial: "Not our sound guy, though. He's on medication for something. Depression, I think it was."

Franklin studied the list again. "You want Moulin?"

"I hear he's pretty good. A cop's cop."

"He's very experienced. From a sort of European perspective. The Secretary General, though…"

"I'm told Moulin is great TV talent. A very good speaker."

"Who said that?"

"You saying he's no good?"

"I'll just have to clear the interview requests with the higher-ups," Franklin said. "And see when the Secretary General is available for you."

"Oh look, if he's busy busting bad guys we can just lift some of his quotes off the speeches on your website."

"You don't need an interview?"

"Well, if he's got a minute, why not?"

Franklin put the list in the pocket of his corduroy jacket. "There's no armoury here. No guns," he said. "Interpol guys don't carry guns and they don't make arrests. National police forces make arrests, with our help. Journalists often get that wrong."

"No guns. You gotta be joking," Henderson said. "You hear

that, Jacoby? These Interpol guys are running around the world with no guns."

"Unfuckingbelievable," Jacoby said.

"Any pets allowed in the building these days?" Henderson asked suddenly. "Any animals? You got police dogs in here? The SG got any pets upstairs?"

"Pets?" Franklin said.

"Yeah. Animals of any kind."

Chief of Staff Milonakis had, very unusually, come down to the fourth floor to the Communications and Publications Office to interrogate Mortman and Franklin about the CNN situation. Mortman had called him again on his mobile phone.

"If that reporter exits this building without interviewing the Secretary General, you are both dead," Milonakis hissed. "You know that, don't you? And I will be dead too. The Secretary General will kill me immediately after I have killed you."

Mortman looked like he had been dead for several days already. He was ashen-faced, chewing antacid tablets forlornly as he listened from a guest chair. Milonakis always took over an officer's desk and chair when he visited subordinates. Franklin stood beside Mortman, CNN list in hand.

"He can't have Moulin," Milonakis said. "Impossible."

"It was a specific request," Franklin said. "He wants an operational guy. A senior cop."

Milonakis regarded Franklin as if here were a naughty, intellectually handicapped schoolboy.

"The Secretary General is what you Americans call an operational guy, Franklin. He is our most senior operational guy. He was one of the most senior officials in the French national police. Why does CNN want Moulin when they can have the Secretary General?"

"Not sure," Franklin said. "It was a specific request."

"Impossible. The Secretary General will kill both of you and then he will kill me. Then he will kill Moulin."

Milonakis chose not to share with his communications department colleagues at this stage his fears about Moulin's reaction when told he would not be speaking at the General Assembly. He was going to be very disappointed indeed. Moulin was a lot of things, Milonakis reassured himself, but he was not disloyal. Disappointed, but not disloyal. And Moulin would leak things to *Le Monde* if he was upset, or Euronews. Not CNN, surely.

"And why does Henderson want to talk to budget people?" Mortman managed to say.

"Not sure," Franklin said.

"Someone has been talking to him," Milonakis said.

"He's been in town a couple of days already. Staying at the Grande Bretagne."

"Can CNN afford the Grande Bretagne?" Milonakis asked.

"It's where we put the EC members, Fred," Mortman said sadly.

"I know exactly where we put the EC members, Alf," Milonakis said.

"Maybe he's talked to Yoko Watanabe," Franklin said.

"Watanabe is back in Tokyo," Milonakis said. "Days ago."

"That doesn't mean anything these days," Franklin said. "If Watanabe's got a bee in her bonnet about the budget."

"A bee in her bonnet?" Milonakis said.

"It's an American expression."

The trio sat in silence for a moment, pondering scenarios.

"And the staff association? And his question about pets in the building? Who has Henderson been talking to?" Milonakis said eventually.

"It could be any number of people, Fred," Mortman said sadly. "To be truthful with you."

"That is not what I need when I come to this office, Alf," Milonakis said. "You know that perfectly well."

"Let's say we have a leak," Franklin said.

"Leaks," Mortman said. "We seem to have a lot of leaks."

"Where is CNN now?" Milonakis said.

"We left them in the dining room, for coffee," Franklin said.

"Who's with them?" Milonakis said.

Mortman and Franklin looked at each other in alarm. Milonakis stood up suddenly.

"After them!" he shouted.

Franklin rushed out of the room. Milonakis gave Mortman a very dark look; then followed Franklin out at a more dignified pace.

When Milonakis had gone, Mortman turned up Vivaldi a little louder on his CD player. He listened wistfully for few moments, seeking comfort, peace; a state of grace.

Milonakis took the long way back to his office, first descending in a glass-sided elevator to the atrium floor on ground level. When things got complicated and he needed to think, he would occasionally make a grand tour of the building, eyes truly open, ears truly attuned to the words and tones of voice around him, seeking intelligence.

He walked by the Command Centre, where Interpol officers fielded calls and electronic messages from the world's police, and sent them information they required. He saw the electronic world map lighting up reassuringly in parts of the world where calls originated and where police data were being exchanged. He climbed the stairs to Level 1 and walked through the fingerprint division. Diligent technicians pored over computer screens showing giant blow-ups of prints, all whorls and swirls and mysterious, otherworldly patterns in black and white. He went into the counterfeit banknotes lab. Here again, technicians were hard at work, studying bogus bills sent in from around the globe. All appeared to be well.

In other offices on other floors, police; Interpol staff – many of them, anyway, at least some – were actually going about their police business and getting hungry for lunch. He recalled Moulin's mantra. Real police work is easy; it's a very simple matter. It is to find and apprehend wrongdoers.

Why does it always have to be so complicated here? Milonakis asked himself sadly. Then his mobile phone rang. He looked at the name that flashed up on the little screen. It was the Secretary General.

Interpol Secretary General Didier Herriot-Dupont was alone in his office on the fifth floor. He sensed something was amiss. He had a sense of foreboding. His well-honed powers of observation, the skills that had led him nearly to the top of French policing and right to the top of international law enforcement, could not be ignored.

His Chief of Staff seemed inordinately troubled these days. Milonakis was absent from his office too often, absent from the fifth floor, the very nerve centre of world policing. Milonakis, his most senior and loyal lieutenant, his eyes and ears in the Interpol headquarters and beyond, seemed inordinately troubled.

Dark forces were at work. His own wife was possibly among the schemers, armed and possibly dangerous. His most senior operational man, some technical people, perhaps, and various members of the Executive Committee. Plotting against him – the evidence was becoming clear.

The Secretary General ran his fingers through the mane of wavy hair that had helped him conquer so many women over the years, that had made him look so, well, leonine in various official photos. He was weary, troubled, alone with his worries. It was, as all great leaders come to realise, lonely at the top.

He wandered out onto his spacious balcony under the brilliant Southern French sun. The flawless blue sky sprawled magnificently up and eastward all the way to the distant foothills of the Alps beyond. All should be right with the world. Here at the very pinnacle of the world's largest international police organisation. And yet, alas, it was not.

He cast his weary gaze downward. In the forecourt below, just inside the security gates, he saw a magnificent gunmetal grey BMW automobile moving slowly forward and then come to stop. His driver and bodyguard got out proudly, leaving the doors open. A small crowd of security guards and police and civilian staff immediately gathered around. It was the Secretary General's brand new custom-built, armour-plated car, the best and biggest that money, an extremely large sum of money, could buy. Delivered to headquarters that very day.

Suddenly, in another part of the forecourt, the Secretary General saw a TV crew interviewing a member of Interpol staff. He couldn't quite make out which one. Was it Cholet, perhaps? Buisson? A young man with a ponytail peered into his camera. A technician in a baseball cap stood beside him and fiddled with controls on a piece of equipment slung across his chest. In giant letters on the back of his T-shirt was emblazoned *CNN*. A tall man in a blue blazer stood resolutely in the sun, microphone thrust forward to his interview subject.

Behind them, a ladder had been propped up against the wall, beside the reinstalled Interpol sign. Two Interpol building maintenance men in blue overalls loitered near the ladder, smoking cigarettes. One of them held what looked to Herriot-Dupont like a TV light and reflector.

The CNN crew had by now seen the magnificent car roll to a stop nearby. The interview ended abruptly. Cameraman and sound technician rushed toward the gleaming vehicle. The blazer-clad reporter followed more sedately behind.

"*Merde!*" DHD shouted. "The Japanese must not see this! *Mais non, c'est impossible!*"

He gesticulated wildly from the terrace. He reached for his mobile phone. As he frantically punched in a number, he saw Jean-Marc Moulin walking swiftly from inside the building toward the car and the camera crew, a frown on his face. Moulin did not like journalists. Events Manager Antonio de Caldevilla trotted close behind, frowning also. He did not like journalists either.

Opposite the building, across the forecourt, through the staff pedestrian gate to the street, DHD then saw his own wife, Julia Smith, coming into the Interpol compound. Behind her trailed Gilles Broussard, a cardigan slung stylishly over his shoulders.

They too headed toward the growing commotion around the shiny new car.

"*Merde alors!*" DHD shouted again, louder still, as he waited for his call to go through. He gave a petulant stamp of his short, flannel-clad legs. The double tassels on his Gucci loafers flip-flopped wildly. "Where is my Chief of Staff? Where is my Chief of Communications? Where are my press office staff? Must I always do everything myself?"

EIGHT

Milonakis was paid quite handsomely to worry about things. Essentially, this was his job. He was the official worrier for the world's largest police organisation, and, more specifically, for its Secretary General. He worried quite elegantly, it is true, with few apparent signs of unease when situations got complicated or risky or out of control. In the present circumstances, however, even a professional worrier of Milonakis' calibre could be forgiven for feeling somewhat overwhelmed.

Problems and failures and threats were mounting up, on various fronts. That was something he could deal with. Except, possibly, the CNN problem. However, his biggest worry at the moment, he thought as he sat quietly and alone in his office, was the increasingly puzzling situation with Gilles Broussard. The computer technician was becoming more and more popular with every passing day; more in demand, it seemed, with key people in the organisation. Milonakis still could not understand why.

Secretary General Herriot-Dupont had had another private meeting with Broussard in his office. Milonakis had not been invited to attend. In fact, Milonakis had found out about it only when one of his most astute informants and allies, the Secretary General's senior appointments secretary, had let him know the meeting was actually underway.

"They have been in there for twenty minutes already," Madame Poirier had whispered to him over the phone. "The meeting was requested by the Secretary General himself. No discussion topics were provided. I was not asked to assemble any documents."

"Thank you very much, Madame Poirier," Milonakis had said, genuinely grateful for this intelligence. He had cultivated his sources in the building very carefully, and they now routinely paid off in this way. "You have done the correct thing and I very much appreciate your professionalism and your judgment."

He scratched a note to himself on a lined pad: *Flowers for Madame Poirier. Theatre tickets?*

Milonakis was reluctant to interrupt the meeting, as he had done some days previously when a similar secret assignation was underway. It would not look good to appear too concerned at this stage. It might drive the situation further underground, and this would be even worse.

"What are those two up to?" he asked himself. "And what is Madame DHD up to? Why does she lunch with this man? Why does she summon this little technician to her hotel? Why does Valon Dragusha summon this little technician to his hotel? Why would anyone summon this little man anywhere?"

Milonakis tapped his fingers distractedly on his desk. The X-24GT system failure: could this be somehow connected to these meetings with Broussard? Milonakis thought not.

His telephone rang. It was Madame Poirier's line. He picked it up.

"The Secretary General has ordered coffee for two persons," his informant whispered. "And some cakes."

Inside the Secretary General's office, the meeting was at a delicate stage. DHD had attempted to put Gilles Broussard very much at ease. Some friendly preliminary conversation had taken place. DHD had enquired after Broussard's wife and children. They had discussed the Lyon weather; unseasonably warm for this time of the year. They had discussed the unusually successful season being enjoyed by Olympique Lyonnais on the soccer fields of Europe. Coffee and cakes had been ordered. Broussard had politely declined the offer of wine.

"Never before noon, *monsieur*," Broussard had said. "It is my unshakable rule in life."

"I admire discipline in a man," DHD had said. "It inspires confidence."

"Thank you, *monsieur*," Broussard said, beaming happily.

"You do have my complete confidence, Gilles," DHD said. "You know that, don't you? I need to have good men around me on whom I can rely fully, with whom I can discuss sensitive matters very frankly."

"*Je vous en prie, Monsieur le Secrétaire Général,*" Broussard said, looking as though he might actually burst with pride, right there on the black leather sofa.

DHD paused. "There is in fact a rather sensitive matter which I need to discuss with you today, my friend," he said.

"I am at your service, *monsieur*," Broussard said.

"Of course all of this must be utterly confidential," DHD said. "This conversation must be shared with no one. Absolutely no one."

"Not even my manager Monsieur Cholet?"

"No, I'm afraid not, Gilles. Not even Cholet."

Broussard looked deeply troubled.

"Sometimes," DHD said, "at the most senior levels of organisations such as ours, Gilles, the burdens can be heavy. But this is the price we pay when confronted with situations of a delicate nature, the law enforcement implications of which can be profound."

"I understand," Broussard said gravely. "I am at your service."

DHD paused again. He stared down at his loafers for a moment.

"Gilles, you and I have already discussed in this office my concerns about the General Assembly in Munich. We have discussed the computer systems that will be place for that meeting, and in particular the electronic voting system which will be in place. You will recall our conversation on this matter, of course."

"Of course, *monsieur*."

"On that occasion you assured me that you thought tampering was most unlikely, but you did not entirely rule this out. Did I understand you correctly at that time, Gilles?"

"Well…" Broussard said.

"You did not rule this out," DHD said.

"It is true, I did not," Broussard said, somewhat uneasy now.

"The Munich meeting is crucially important, as you know," the Secretary General said. "For world law enforcement."

"*Absolument*," Broussard said. "I agree with you on this point."

"I have a question for you, therefore, Gilles," the Secretary General said, leaning over and lowering his voice conspiratorially. "A hypothetical question, but one that is nonetheless crucially important."

Broussard sat up straighter in his seat. "I am ready, *monsieur*," he said.

"If you, as the man in charge of computer systems at the Munich General Assembly, were to discover something unusual going on with the systems on that day, if you were to discover an attempt was being made to interfere in some way with proceedings generally, or the voting procedures in particular, what would you do?"

"Do?" Broussard said.

"Yes. What would your reaction be?"

"Well, I would be, of course, extremely, ah, concerned."

"Yes, Gilles, but what would you do?"

"Well, I would of course inform someone. My superiors."

The Secretary General looked pained. "Your superiors?" he said.

"Well, yes."

"Who, exactly?"

Was this a trick question? Broussard was not sure.

"Well, you, of course, *monsieur*."

"And if I were unavailable? Otherwise engaged, shall we say? On the official podium, for example? Not immediately available."

"Well, the Chief of Staff, I would say, *non?* Monsieur Milonakis, I would say, at that point."

"Very good," DHD said. "But discreetly, discreetly, you would agree?"

"*Absolument, monsieur*," Broussard said.

"And tell me this, Gilles. Here is another crucially important hypothetical question for you, on which the future of global law enforcement could quite possibly depend. If you were to discover that something was being planned, in an effort to, for reasons I am not at liberty to share with you at this time, spoil the outcome of this crucially important meeting in Munich, what would you do? If you could see that something evil was being planned, if you could see something was coming, if you were to see beforehand, or on the day itself, that a situation or an outcome was to be manipulated so outrageously and so obviously that something quite simply had to be done, are you a man who could intervene in the correct way and actually *prevent* an outrage from occurring?"

"Well, I…" Broussard said.

"If someone were to attempt to manipulate the results of the vote to re-elect the Secretary General, for example?"

"This would, of course, never happen," Broussard said.

"But if you were to see evidence that it *was* happening, Gilles. On the floor of the General Assembly. If saboteurs had somehow managed, despite your best efforts, to manipulate things electronically or otherwise so that the result of that crucially important vote were so obviously wrong, so clearly falsified, so impossibly incorrect, would you take steps to *prevent* this outrage from occurring? From being seen to occur?"

"Well, I, of course would want…" Broussard said.

"Do you expect me to win the vote at the General Assembly in Munich, Gilles? Do you genuinely expect me to win a resounding, perhaps even a unanimous, second mandate to steer this organisation forward? Speak very frankly. I invite you to do so."

Panic was in Broussard's eyes. Sweat appeared on his ageing brow.

"You are a very effective *Secrétaire Général, monsieur*. On this all are agreed."

"All?" DHD asked. "You think such feelings are unanimously shared? Unanimously? You think it likely that these feelings will be reflected in the vote in Munich? Do I take it that you would find it unusual, a matter of suspicion, if the result of that crucially important vote for some mysterious reason, some nefarious reason, did not on the day reflect this unanimous good feeling you have so clearly identified? You would take, be willing to take, steps to actually *prevent* something from affecting the outcome of the vote on that important day and plunging Interpol into scandal and disrepute? Are you the man for that job, my friend?"

Earlier, Franklin had eventually been able to restore some semblance of order on the CNN front. He had been rushing frantically around the building in search of the errant TV crew when he got a call from a furious Chief of Staff, who had got one himself from a furious Secretary General.

"They're in the forecourt, Franklin," Milonakis had hissed, "interviewing anybody they please and taking shots of the Secretary General's new car. He's watching it all from his terrace and he is going to kill us both. Find out who they have been interviewing. Find out what people are saying to them. Get out there right now and supervise that TV crew or the Secretary General says he will come down and do it himself."

The thought of an angry Herriot-Dupont in direct contact with an international television network crew filled Franklin with a profound, end-of-the-world dread. He rushed outside to perform some crisis communication work, his speciality.

"Guys, guys, guys, you really need to let me know what you're doing when you're in the building," he called out to Henderson, who was watching happily as Jacoby and Sound Man took shots of the interior of the armoured BMW. "It's a high-security building."

Henderson looked over with a smile and said nothing. Moulin and Caldevilla were standing to one side, talking in whispers between themselves. A couple of security staff were smoking cigarettes nearby.

"Guys, guys, that's it for now, OK? You've got your shots, let's go inside and regroup," Franklin said.

Moulin called out to him, "I tried to stop them."

Henderson said, "Yeah, Officer Moulin over there was making federal case of it. Said we couldn't shoot the car, we couldn't interview anybody without clearance. And he says we can't interview him at all. What's his problem?"

"I am a police officer, that's the problem," Moulin called out.

Jacoby, climbing out of the car, snorted and flicked his ponytail. "Cops," he said disdainfully.

"Hey," Franklin said.

"*Oui, monsieur*, I am a cop, yes, a cop," Moulin shouted. "Twenty-seven years with the Belgian Federal Police. And so?"

"Jean-Marc, Jean-Marc, easy does it. I'll take care of this, OK?" Franklin said.

Moulin was an ally of his, most of the time, despite Franklin being a journalist by trade. They were combat buddies, both being in the Secretary General's line of fire every day.

"About time, Frank Franklin," Caldevilla said.

"What's the problem here, Frankie?" Henderson said. "Why is everyone so keyed up all of a sudden? Everybody we talk to seems kinda tense around here. What's up, buddy?"

"Who have you been interviewing?" Franklin asked.

"Oh, a bunch of people. You know, rank-and-file guys. And your building guy."

"When, today?"

"Yeah. And we got some people yesterday."

"Not in here."

"Nah. Outside."

"Where?"

"Frankie, we're journalists. We move around. We know how to gather information. Simple as that. We're going to need the security guy next, the head security guy."

"I'll have to check that out first, Rob," Frankie said. "Get clearance."

"Fuck that," Jacoby said.

"Hey you!" Moulin called out. "Have you ever been arrested, my friend? Frank, can you please control these journalists?"

"You guys can't arrest me," Jacoby said. "You can't arrest anyone, for fuck's sake. Interpol man."

"Easy, easy, easy, everybody," Franklin said. "Jean-Marc, I'll take care of this, OK? Come on, guys, let's go inside and have a coffee and re-group."

"They are not to go into the Command Centre," Moulin said.

"Hey, that's where we can get the best pictures," Henderson said.

"Let's just go inside and talk things over, shall we?" Franklin said.

Moulin walked back into the building in disgust. Caldevilla looked triumphant. He followed Moulin in. A small crowd of curious Interpol support staff lingered, engrossed in the show.

"Interpol man," Jacoby said again. "I'm shaking in my fuckin' boots."

Henderson, even over coffee and croissants in a quiet meeting room, would not tell Franklin who had been interviewed already and what they had said.

"You can't be serious, Frankie. That's not how it works, buddy," he said. "You said we could come down here to do a story and that's what we're doing. We don't have to tell you what we're doing every second we're on the job."

"It's a police thing, Rob, we need to make sure that operational stuff—"

"Come off it, Frankie. Operational stuff. Give me a break. I've been in the field for thirty-five years. I know how to deal with operational stuff. I know how to put a little police story together."

"What angle are you guys actually after?" Franklin asked.

"What makes Interpol tick," said Henderson. "Take our viewers inside Interpol. Simple."

"But there's a whole lot of ways to do that, Rob. I need to know where you're headed with this. So I can help you out."

"We'll muddle through, Frankie. Really. It's cool. So get on board, or get out of the way. Right?" Henderson said with a chuckle. "Right, boys?"

"All aboard!" Jacoby shouted. "Choo-choo. Choo-choo."

"Can I see the footage you've got already?" Franklin asked.

"You can't be serious, Frankie. That's not how it works."

"It's Interpol, Rob. It's different. We can't just let people—"

"Get on board, Interpol man," Jacoby said. "Whoo-whoo!"

"I'll need a list of questions you're going to ask the Secretary General, though, Rob. Seriously," Franklin said.

"Really, Frankie, I'm not sure we're going to need the guy. We get the security man, and we get an operational guy or two and that should do us. Some exterior shots and we can get on a plane."

"You don't want the Secretary General?"

"He's a pretty busy guy, I would imagine."

"He'd be happy to talk to you."

"Let's see how we go for time," Henderson said.

Franklin had a very bad feeling about where the CNN story was going. He wanted badly to talk things over with Mortman, but Mortman had gone home with chest pains. He installed CNN in the meeting room with some sandwiches and one of his junior press officers, Phoebe, an impossibly young former and extremely serious civilian media staffer with the Royal Canadian Mounted Police who had not yet quite gotten used to Interpol's idiosyncratic ways.

"Stay with them, Phoebe. Don't let them out of there until I get back," he had said.

"What if they want to go out?" Phoebe asked. "I can't keep them prisoners in here, Frank."

"Just keep them in there until I get back."

"What if they insist?"

"Phoebe, for Christ's sake."

"I'll do what I can," she said.

"They don't seem to want to interview him," Franklin told Milonakis on his mobile. He was standing in the atrium, talking low.

"They don't want the Secretary General?" Milonakis said.

"Doesn't look like it," Franklin said sadly.

"Well, it's your job to make them want the Secretary General," Milonakis said.

"I can't force them, Fred."

"Of course you can."

"No, Fred. I can't."

"This is a disaster."

"TV's tricky," Franklin said. "They need a fresh angle. And pictures that go with it."

"Tell them about his Arabic lessons."

"His what?"

"His Arabic lessons. The Secretary General is learning Arabic. To deal more effectively with Arabic police, and Middle East issues, and things like that. In a post-9/11 world. What about that?"

Since when is he learning Arabic?" Franklin asked.

"Since yesterday."

"Yesterday."

"Yes. He said CNN would be welcome to film him in a lesson with his Arabic tutor, with some Arabic writing on a whiteboard. Something like that. Good pictures. And the tutor is a nice-looking woman. She wears a headscarf."

"Well…" Franklin said.

"That's a fresh angle, isn't it?" Milonakis said. "How many heads of Interpol ever knew how to speak Arabic?"

"We can't tell them he speaks Arabic, Fred."

"He's learning, Frank. He's making the effort. Tell them that."

When Franklin got back to the meeting room, Phoebe was standing alone beside the table. She was punching a number into her mobile phone.

"I was trying to reach you, Frank. They took off."

"What?"

"They wouldn't stay."

"Why didn't you go with them?"

"The cameraman started filming me when I got mad. Then he just rushed off with the reporter. I thought I'd call you first to see what you thought I should do."

"Phoebe…"

"He swears a lot. He's aggressive."

"Where are they?"

"I don't know."

"Phoebe, for Christ's sake."

"Don't raise your voice to me, Frank. I'm feeling really nervous about this already."

"I am nervous at this stage also, Phoebe. Really fucking nervous."

"Please don't swear," Phoebe said. "You're as bad as that cameraman."

The CNN crew had somehow managed to talk their way into the Command Centre. When Franklin arrived, Jacoby was filming over the shoulder of a young police officer sitting at an X-24GT screen. Moulin arrived just as Franklin did.

"Hey, hey there," Moulin called out. "You can't take photos of the police information on that screen."

Jacoby did not even look up. He continued to film. Moulin moved closer.

"Young gentleman, I'm talking to you," Moulin said.

Jacoby stood straighter, turned, and trained the camera directly onto Moulin. Moulin put his hand over the lens.

"You're not allowed to film in here. This is a restricted operational area," he shouted.

"Jacoby, come on now, you really shouldn't be in here," Franklin said. "Easy, Jean-Marc. Easy."

"I want these people out of here," Moulin said. "They're not allowed to shoot in here."

"You getting this, Jacoby?" Henderson called out.

"Rolling," Jacoby said, peering intently through the eyepiece.

"Sound?" Henderson said.

"Rolling," Sound Man said.

Moulin said to the Command Centre's officer in charge, "Get security up here."

"Great stuff," Henderson said.

"Rolling," Jacoby said.

Franklin had never seen Moulin as angry. When the security detail arrived on the second floor, he had ordered them to escort the TV crew immediately from the building. He would not listen to Franklin's protests.

"They are out," Moulin had said. "Now."

"They're not finished with their work," Franklin said.

"Yes they are," Moulin said.

The TV crew stood in the hallway, talking in whispers amongst themselves.

"I'll need to talk to the Chief of Staff, I think, Jean-Marc. The Secretary General wanted—"

"I'll deal with the Secretary General on this. And the Chief of Staff. It's an operational matter. It's a security matter. This is a police operation we run here, Frank, not a TV show."

Moulin would not be dissuaded. He accompanied the security guards and the TV crew right down to the forecourt and waited while their van was brought up from the garage. Franklin waited nervously with him. CNN was somewhat subdued.

"Hey, Rob, look, I—" Franklin said.

"Sorry it's turned out this way, Frankie," Henderson said. "We're just trying to do our job."

"I'll call you," Franklin said. "I'll see if I can arrange the Secretary General and some other stuff for you to get over the phone."

"It's TV, Frankie," Henderson said.

"I'll call you, when you get to London."

"We're not going to London, Frankie boy," Henderson said. "We're going to Serbania first. Got to do another shoot there first."

"Serbania?!" Franklin said. "What are you doing over there?"

"TV, Frankie," Henderson said with a wink. "You know, radio with pictures."

Sound Man took the wheel of the van. Henderson climbed in front, then Jacoby in back via the sliding door.

"*Ciao*. It's been a slice," Henderson said.

Jacoby lowered a window and began filming from inside.

"Hey, you, no more pictures," Moulin shouted.

The van pulled slowly off, with Jacoby taking a last few long shots.

"You can't use those pictures!" Moulin shouted after them.

"You getting this? Henderson asked.

"Rolling," Jacoby said.

The post-CNN post-mortem was a sombre affair. Director of Interpol Legal Services Cynthia Payne had, unusually, been invited to attend. She sat alongside Milonakis, Moulin and Franklin at a boardroom table, directly facing the Secretary General. Mortman was in the hospital and could not attend.

"No, Secretary General," Payne was saying in the super-calm tone she adopted when someone was about to make a very rash move, against all professional advice. "With respect, I have to say again that there are no grounds whatsoever to seek an injunction at this time."

"Of course there are grounds," Herriot-Dupont growled. "There must be grounds. We can see what they are trying to do. They are trying to ruin this institution."

"We can't be sure of that, sir," Payne said steadily. "With respect. We have no grounds to try to prevent broadcast at this moment in time."

"When does this report go to air, Franklin?" asked Herriot-Dupont. "This piece of *merde*?"

"I don't know the answer to that, Secretary General. They didn't say."

"Did you ask them?"

"Not directly, no."

"So we can expect it to go to air soon. Before the General Assembly."

"Possibly," Franklin said. "But they said they were going to Serbania first."

"Serbania?" Milonakis exclaimed.

"Serbania?" the Secretary General exclaimed.

"To do what?" Milonakis asked.

"To do what?" the Secretary General shouted.

"They didn't say. Some other story, possibly," Franklin said.

"Unlikely," Milonakis said. "That's very unlikely."

"Dragusha!" the Secretary General growled. "*Merde!* I knew he would be involved. He's a destroyer."

"We don't know he is involved in anything at this stage, sir," Payne said quietly.

Herriot-Dupont looked at his chief legal counsel with pity, as if at a pedestrian who had just been struck by a large car.

"Cynthia, you surprise me," DHD said. "You are naïve."

"I'm a lawyer, sir," Payne said testily. "A naïve lawyer is an oxymoron. In Scotland, in any case."

Moulin had been silent throughout the meeting. Now he spoke up.

"The journalists were not adequately supervised," he said. "In a police operational setting. In my view. Frank, I'm sorry to have to say this. They were inadequately supervised. We have police work to do here. We are not actors in some cheap television programme."

"I'm sorry too, Jean-Marc," DHD said. "Sorry to have this utterly useless Canadian on my staff. Franklin, if I didn't need you for the General Assembly and if that imbecile Mortman, that Alf Mortman, were not at this moment lying in hospital, you would be on the first plane to Toronto. If any airline flies to that godforsaken city. You would be terminated."

"The man has a contractual arrangement with Interpol, sir," Payne said.

"Thanks, Cynthia," Franklin said.

"Not for long," DHD hissed.

*

Secretary General Herriot-Dupont sat alone at his enormous desk, weighed down by the demands of international law enforcement in a post-9/11 world. The sky over Lyon was growing dark. It was the time of day when self-doubt could grip even the most visionary leader. It was lonely at the top of the world's largest international police organisation.

DHD picked up his office phone and dialled a number.

"Gilles," he said. "It's Didier." He paused. "Didier Herriot-Dupont. The Secretary General. Yes. I'm sorry to disturb you at home."

Another pause.

"Well, we have a problem of the sort you and I spoke about in my office, Gilles. I'm sorry to say. Yes, yes… Yes, a great shame. Tonight, I need to know that you have understood clearly what we are up against, Gilles. I need your assurance that you are committed to work with me to ensure that everything will go according to plan in Munich. I need that very much tonight, Gilles."

It was very, very lonely at the top. DHD listened intently, gripping the telephone receiver tightly. He twirled his fountain pen on the desk as he listened.

"Thank you, Gilles. Thank you very much," the Secretary General said. "Now, perhaps, I may be able to get some rest."

He put the phone down, and twirled his fountain pen some more. Then he picked up the phone and dialled another number.

"Evangeline, *ma chouette*, it's Didier here," he said very softly. "I can't sleep. Didier is very lonely tonight, *chouette*. Could I perhaps give you some assistance with your homework, my dear?"

In the Secretary General's apartment, criminologist Julia Smith – Madame DHD – very quietly replaced the telephone receiver. The red light for the Secretary General's private office line went out. She sat for a moment in her armchair, considering carefully the conversations she had just overheard, and others like them in recent days. She gazed silently at the collection of rifles and shotguns mounted on all available walls.

NINE

Interpol Secretary General Didier Herriot-Dupont badly needed a crisis in world law enforcement around now; a nice little terrorist attack somewhere, perhaps, with not too many dead; or maybe a thriving child pornography ring, preferably somewhere in Europe, involving a senior politician or two. Something along those lines. Then he could order an Interpol Incident Response Team aboard a plane to elbow its way into some positive media coverage and some shared glory, whether an Interpol IRT was to be welcomed by local police authorities or not.

True, recent Interpol experience with IRTs had not been good. There had been some embarrassing failures, in which local police had, for reasons that were obscure to Herriot-Dupont, resisted having Interpol personnel pile off aircraft and barge their way into the local response to a major incident. An unfortunate situation in Lebanon came to mind, in which the police there had rudely refused Interpol's kind offer of assistance and packed the IRT back onto their plane in the days following that nasty political assassination. And there was the incident with the Indonesian authorities, so ungracious in the days following the tsunami disaster, when Interpol had so kindly offered assistance with victim identification, and, of course, some highly photogenic people to front international TV crews swarming around at the scene.

The Indonesians had resisted, inexplicably, receiving a team of eager Interpol agents whom the Secretary General had dispatched immediately after his own post-tsunami news conference in Lyon

– and well attended it was by world media – in which he had shed tears on camera and pledged all of Interpol's resources at no matter what the cost to the organisation. Only the churlish would think the dispatching of IRTs a crass publicity stunt, or that their sudden and uninvited appearance at a world crisis somewhere would not be immediately useful to harried local authorities.

Herriot-Dupont would not be deterred. The world's police needed Interpol and its Incident Response Teams, whether the world's police knew it or not. And Interpol very much needed some positive media coverage around now. The very real prospect of a disastrous CNN report about Interpol loomed on the horizon, and decisive diversionary action was required.

The Secretary General pondered these matters alone in his office. He had considered, then rejected, the idea of a pre-emptive strike on another world TV network or in a major newspaper. He had considered attempting to generate a positive item on, say, BBC TV or in the *New York Times*. He had considered trying again to generate the sort of 'Interpol-making-the-world-a-safer place' story that he had so much hoped CNN would produce. Then he thought of his communications team; he thought of Mortman and he thought of Franklin, and he abandoned the idea altogether.

So now he gazed at the giant world map that took up much of one wall of his office. He stood before it, pondering the grand scheme of world law enforcement. Where, in an ideal world, would the next crime crisis or major disaster strike?

Asia would be just right. He very much needed a boost in Japan, and TV footage of an IRT hard at work in Japan (ideally!) or perhaps Thailand would be very useful indeed. Maybe a big drug bust in the Golden Triangle? That would be good. But the major players in Southeast Asian drugs enforcement weren't sharing much with Interpol just now. Alas.

Africa, maybe. No, he thought, not after the Zambezi experience. No, too soon for another Interpol expedition to Africa.

North America? No, not in the US in any case. His detractors were too numerous there. To snare a bit of good publicity about Interpol in the US would require respect and cooperation from the FBI or Homeland Security, and too many of their officers had been through Interpol secondments and gone home with stories to tell. No, not the United States; sad though this was.

Canada? No. Nothing really bad ever happened in Canada, and the Royal Canadian Mounted Police didn't wear their scarlet tunics and shiny brown riding boots anymore, except on ceremonial occasions, so where were the good pictures in that? No, Canada was too boring for Didier Herriot-Dupont's public relations needs at the present time.

He cast his eyes, therefore, to Latin America. Hmm. Yes. Latin America. Drugs, drug barons, high-level corruption, prostitution, human trafficking, intellectual property crime, counterfeiting of all kinds… Very positive indeed. A little law enforcement crisis of some kind in Latin America, a well selected Incident Response Team, some preparatory phone calls to world media outlets, a carefully orchestrated press conference, and presto: an Interpol success story.

Herriot-Dupont picked up his phone. Interpol's best were about to be ordered into action. Or forced into action. Whatever was necessary with media storm clouds and a General Assembly looming on the horizon.

Before him, looking extremely apprehensive, were his Chief of Staff, as one would expect in such a strategy meeting, along with Jean-Marc Moulin; Interpol's chief legal counsel, Cynthia Payne; and, unfortunately but necessarily, Frank Franklin. Mortman was still on sick leave. DHD wasn't sure whether this was a problem or a bit of good luck.

"Franklin," DHD began, "you are extremely fortunate to still be employed by Interpol. It is too difficult right now to find another Chief Press Officer and so you will assist us with these matters until I have had a chance to think about your future."

"Um, I—" Franklin said.

"Cynthia, among many other things you will be doing in the days ahead is to look closely at Franklin's contract and give me a briefing on the organisation's room for manoeuvre in this," Herriot-Dupont said.

He looked imperiously at Franklin, and then over at the Chief of Staff. Milonakis knew, however, that Franklin's days were almost certainly *not* numbered, not with a General Assembly only weeks away. But he knew also that DHD wanted to make the Canadian as fearful and unhappy as humanly possible.

"Cynthia," DHD continued, "what is your professional opinion as to our chances of getting an injunction that would prevent CNN from broadcasting that report about Interpol?"

"Zero," Payne said immediately. "Zero chance."

"Zero?" DHD repeated.

"What grounds would we have for seeking an injunction?" Payne asked. "We've discussed this before."

"They are going attack this organisation and they are going to attack me," DHD growled.

"How do we know that, sir?" Payne asked.

"It is obvious that they came here with an agenda," DHD said. "They had been briefed somehow beforehand. Leaked information, whispered accusations and allegations. Am I right, Fred?"

The Chief of Staff looked up from his notebook.

"Most likely, Secretary General," he said quietly.

"Well, um, I don't think we can say for sure the piece will be all negative," Franklin ventured.

"Precisely," Payne said. "No grounds for injunctive relief at this stage, in my view."

Herriot-Dupont turned theatrically in his seat to face Franklin more directly. "You are surely not the person best placed to make that sort of judgment, Franklin," he said. "You are the cause of this problem. In *my* view. You could not control those journalists."

"Controlling journalists is…" Franklin stammered.

"…like herding cats," Payne offered.

DHD glared at them both. "We will have to assume the worst," he said. "And as you are no help to me, Cynthia, with a lawyer's ideas as to how we might get an injunction against the network, we must now do something that will counter the negative effects of that story when it is aired on television. I have, therefore, a plan."

Milonakis blanched visibly. A DHD plan usually involved life-shortening stress levels, exorbitant costs to the organisation and diplomatic fallout throughout the world policing community.

"We will send an Incident Response Team to Venezquay, tomorrow. We will announce that Interpol is throwing all of its best resources at intellectual property crime and product counterfeiting as a source of terrorist financing. In particular, the sale of fake cigarettes financing terrorism plots. We will hold a news conference there. The IRT will not return to Lyon until major arrests are announced, or major coverage eventuates on world television. Fred, tell our colleagues in Venezquay the team will be on the way within hours. I will handle the Interior Minister. Tell Argentina and Brazil as well. Tell them to send some senior officers to Asuntiago for a press conference on Thursday. Franklin, get all major media to attend the press conference. I myself may come down to Asuntiago to attend that. We are going to break this neglected area of international crime wide open."

DHD sat back in his chair, running a hand through his mane of salt-and-pepper hair.

"Questions or comments?" he said.

Moulin, stony-faced, said, "It's still not proven that counterfeit goods are a major source of terrorist financing, Secretary General. Counterfeit cigarettes, for example, are not directly—"

"We sent out a circular about that last year," DHD shouted.

"We were repeating what some police thought might be happening on a small scale in certain places. For cigarettes, perhaps Northern Ireland, for a time, but before the peace agreement. A few other suggestions—"

"Suggestions only. Hypotheses," Milonakis said.

"Interpol's position is that counterfeit goods, especially cigarettes, *can* be a source of terrorist financing, no?" DHD said.

"Well, as I have tried to—" Moulin said.

"Not especially cigarettes," Milonakis said.

"Did Interpol make statements about terror financing in the past or not, *oui ou non?*" DHD said.

"Well, yes, but in a context that was—"

"Is the tri-border area of Venezquay, Argentina and Brazil a hotbed of intellectual property crime and product counterfeiting or not?"

"Well, yes, it is," Moulin said. "But—"

"Are there counterfeit cigarettes produced there, or not?"

"Well, yes."

"Is terrorism not a major world public security concern? Does terrorism not need vast amounts of illicit funding to do its evil work? Is Interpol to ignore this area of international policing because you all lack imagination and determination?"

Moulin was already worn down by the relentless assault. He went silent. He wrote things in his notebook.

"The IRT leaves tomorrow," the Secretary General said. "Let Venezquay know, and the other countries. Pick a team that has gender balance and be sure to take along that very good-looking Spanish woman who works in the intellectual property crime unit. The redhead from Barcelona. Fred, you will go. And Franklin. This may be your chance to redeem yourself. Let's get some new IRT vests and baseball caps made up. And we must choose a new name and acronym for the operation. Operation Snuff Out, perhaps? Would this work? Smoke Out Terrorists? Butt Out Terrorism? BOT, Operation BOT? Fred, what is your view? Operation SOT, or BOT?"

When his officials had retreated, Herriot-Dupont picked up the phone.

"Francine," he said curtly, "get me the Interior Minister of Venezquay."

Madame Tremblay was exceptionally efficient, always. Within

minutes, Venezquay's estimable Interior Minister Oscar Fuentes was in contact.

"*Hola*, Oscar, *hola*, are you well?" the Secretary General shouted down the line. "How goes the battle to make the world a safer place?" He waited. "Oscar, my friend, how would Venezquay like to have a representative on the Interpol Executive Committee?" he said. "Your Chief of Police, perhaps?"

An extremely pretty, very young and very well-dressed woman eased herself out of a taxi at the Interpol gates in the bright afternoon sunshine. She was perhaps even a trifle over-dressed for the time of day, in fact, in a short, figure-hugging black cocktail frock and with diamonds dangling from her ears. She was a feast for the eyes of Interpol's ever-alert security staff. Even the sleepy French police officers lounging in their tiny patrol car sat up and took notice.

She was French, and local, it seemed, and in a very excited state of mind. She was, she insisted loudly, a good friend of the Secretary General. She must see him right away on an urgent personal matter. She did not have an invitation and her name did not appear on the day's list of expected visitors. That the Secretary General was at the moment en route to South America seemed to distress young Evangeline even more.

Interpol's Chief of Security, Bernard LeBlanc, had been summoned to the gatehouse when the situation seemed to be getting out of hand. Young Evangeline had started to shriek threats and accusations at the guards, and had flung her briefcase at them, scattering University of Lyon books and papers over a wide area. She tottered dangerously atop her spiked heels.

"It was my birthday last night!" she shrieked.

"*Mademoiselle, Mademoiselle, du calme, s'il vous plait*," LeBlanc said repeatedly. He reached out to touch the young woman reassuringly on her very fetching bare shoulder. Other security guards had attempted this calming manoeuvre as well, without success.

Evangeline batted LeBlanc's proffered hand away, gripped her long auburn hair with both of her fists and bellowed, "If you put your hand on me again I will call the police!"

"But we are the police, *mademoiselle*," LeBlanc intoned. "This is Interpol."

Evangeline shrieked again and again, "I want to see the Secretary General! I want to see him right now! You must let me in! I demand to be let inside!" Tears streamed down the young woman's face.

"But we of course cannot allow you inside without authorisation," LeBlanc said. "That is impossible."

The situation was getting out of control. The French police opened the doors of their car and got out. A crowd of curious Interpol staffers was forming outside the guardhouse. The entry of other bemused official visitors was being delayed. LeBlanc did what he thought was best in the circumstances. The Secretary General was on an aircraft. So was the Chief of Staff. Jean-Marc Moulin had also left Lyon hours before. A young woman was having a *crise veritable* at Interpol's front gates. LeBlanc therefore felt he had no option but to call the Secretary General's wife, Julia Smith, and asked her to come down from the apartment to help out. A woman's touch was perhaps in order, *non?*

It was relatively calm aboard Air France Flight 454; Paris to São Paulo, Brazil. An elegant hush lay about the cabin as business-class passengers sipped champagne and nibbled at dainties from small ceramic offertories. Among the fortunate few enjoying expense account peace and quiet were one Didier Herriot-Dupont, Secretary General of the world's largest international police organisation, and his trusted and unflappable chief of staff, Freiderikos Milonakis.

They were still some hours away from São Paulo and the connecting flight that would take them on urgent law enforcement business to Asuntiago, Venezquay. Combating cross-border criminality did not stop for champagne and nibblies, however. The two men were hard at work in the business-class dimness, locked in a grave, even somewhat heated, discussion.

"Fenstermacher said what?" the Secretary General hissed, disturbing the late-night calm ever so slightly. "He said what?"

Milonakis, ever reluctant but ever able to deliver bad news when necessary to a powerful superior, remained, as it were, unflapped.

"He said the request had come from Valon Dragusha himself," Milonakis said gravely. "The call came from Virana. Dragusha was not at that point in Munich."

"*Mon dieu*, it has come to this, Fred. Dragusha now makes his moves in the open. He makes no attempt to hide what he is doing even from the German organisers themselves!"

"We're still not sure what he is doing, Secretary General," Milonakis said.

"Something bad, clearly. Something nefarious, clearly," DHD snarled.

"The Germans would not be able to understand what he is up to," Milonakis said. "For them, at this stage, it was a simple but somewhat unusual request from a member of the Executive Committee. They're now standing by for our instructions. Fenstermacher was quite professional about it on the telephone with me."

The bad news being broken mid-flight was this: Interpol Executive Committee member Valon Dragusha had startled the German head of the General Assembly organising team by requesting access to the conference venue. Dragusha, according to Fenstermacher, had asked to review all aspects of the preparations and inspect the main hall and office spaces and computer facilities and other areas and equipment set aside for the Interpol senior staff. Three weeks before the General Assembly was set to begin, and as soon as the Germans could make necessary arrangements for his visit. Would this be alright; was this to be officially and formally authorised, Fenstermacher had very Germanically wanted to know?

"Of course it is not alright!" the Secretary General shouted. A flight attendant rushed over to his seat to see if all was well. DHD waved her away. "Of course it is not alright."

"What grounds do we have to refuse him?" Milonakis said.

"We risk alienating him. There is that risk. He may, in fact, just be curious. He may just be looking at ways to maximise his own media coverage in Serbania."

Milonakis did not appear truly convinced by his own suggestions. The Secretary General was not at all convinced.

"He is plotting against me, Fred. We know this. Perhaps he will bring CNN with him."

"We don't even know CNN has been in contact with him at all."

"You delude yourself, Fred. Or you are naïve. It concerns me that my Chief of Staff can be so naïve."

The two sat in silence, ten kilometres above the wine-dark Atlantic Ocean, pondering scenarios, trying to untangle possible plots.

"What harm can it do to let him tour the facilities, have a little look around?" Milonakis said eventually. "Better to say yes than to upset him with a refusal."

DHD looked over at his Chief of Staff. "Escorted at all times," he said.

"Of course."

"By one of our people also. Not just the Germans."

"Agreed."

"But who?"

Milonakis paused, considered. "Mortman? He is back at work. Franklin is already in Asuntiago."

"No."

"Moulin?"

"Moulin is waiting for us in Asuntiago."

"LeBlanc?"

"No, not LeBlanc. Of course not LeBlanc."

"Who then?" Milonakis asked.

"Why does he want to look at the computer facilities, Fred?" the Secretary General asked suddenly.

"No idea. He wants to see all aspects of the preparations. He has in fact asked that we send Broussard to Munich for his tour."

"Broussard?!" the Secretary General shouted.

"Perhaps Broussard could be Dragusha's Interpol escort."

"Why does Dragusha ask for him?"

"Perhaps we need to find out."

"Broussard," the Secretary General said darkly.

"Yes, why not? He is loyal."

"Can we be sure of this?" DHD said. "And he's too junior to be our only man in Munich with Dragusha. He is too naïve. He's the nervous sort. He's not even a police officer."

"He can keep an eye on Dragusha," Milonakis said. "It's a simple enough mission if we instruct him correctly. He'll do this for you as a special service."

"Or we will take away the car," the Secretary General said.

Milonakis nodded gravely in agreement.

"We must make clear to him how crucial this assignment is."

"I'll see to that," Milonakis said.

Franklin had already redeemed himself somewhat in Asuntiago. Or, more accurately perhaps, Venezquay's Interior Minister Oscar Fuentes had helped Franklin to redeem himself. Shortly after landing, along with a very jet lagged Jean-Marc Moulin, Franklin had sat looking across a gigantic desk at Fuentes in the Minister's office, seeking assistance.

"And do you think we can expect some journalists to attend, Señor Fuentes?" Franklin asked. "This is very important."

Fuentes, with the requisite Latin American strongman's handlebar moustache and profusely oiled hair, scattered cigar ash as he waved his hands at the young Interpol representative.

"In my country, young man, when the Interior Minister instructs *periodistas* to attend a press conference, they will attend!" he said. "*Periodistas* must do exactly as they are told. I learned this many years ago when I was still in the police force. It should be this way in your country, France."

"I'm Canadian, *señor*," Franklin said.

"In Canada too!" Fuentes shouted. "Am I right, Moulin?

Everywhere we must make these *periodista* dogs understand who is holding the leash!"

Moulin smiled weakly at his fellow policeman, despite his fatigue.

"International media, too?" Franklin asked hopefully. "The wire services? BBC?"

"All, all, all," Fuentes said. "They will come!"

In some ways, one could describe the Interpol event in Asuntiago as a major success. It could, from a certain perspective, even be described as Frank Franklin's finest hour.

The photogenic and gender-balanced Interpol Incident Response Team was filmed by a battery of TV and newspaper cameramen getting off the plane at the airport. The arrival story led the local television and radio news. *Crisis in counterfeiting! Terror attacks financed by counterfeit proceeds! Fake cigarettes fuel global assassination plots! Interpol pledges unlimited resources to smash criminal gangs!*

The press conference the next day in an elegant function room at the Granados Park Hotel was well attended, as Señor Fuentes had correctly predicted. And yes, there amongst the local scribes were in fact certain members of the international media. They, and their local colleagues, scribbled dutifully in notebooks as first the Interior Minister, then representatives of the police services of Venezquay, Argentina and Brazil took to the microphones to describe new efforts to stamp out intellectual property crime in the tri-border area. Interpol Secretary General Didier Herriot-Dupont, sitting quietly to Fuentes' right hand, had graciously eschewed the opportunity to speak, preferring, ever the diplomat, not to deflect limelight away from his Latin American colleagues.

Crime-fighting efforts in the region were to be redoubled. The full weight of Interpol's mighty databases and technical expertise and dedicated specialist officers would now come crashing down on offenders. Effects would be immediate. Arrests in large numbers would certainly follow. The tri-border area, and indeed the world, would be a safer place.

The BBC correspondent in Asuntiago, a sallow, prematurely bald young man in a crumpled white suit, was first to raise his hand in question time, after the formal statements had been delivered.

Franklin, at the podium, was moderating. "Yes," he said. "In the third row?"

"Sebastian Wilson-Smith, BBC," the reporter said in a reedy, though elegantly inflected, voice. "A question, if I may, for Secretary General Herriot-Dupont."

"Sir?" Franklin said, looking along the line of seated spokesmen toward DHD.

"If my colleagues will permit?" DHD said, looking modestly over at fearsome array of South American cops to his left. "This is their press conference, not mine."

"Go!" Fuentes said. "*Sì, sì, por favor.* The Secretary General has flown all the way from France to be with us today! He should speak, yes, yes."

Fuentes glared down at the local press corps. Some applauded. Others scribbled even more furiously in their notebooks.

"Why now? Why here?" Wilson-Smith asked. "Why the sudden interest from Interpol in this area of crime? Why suddenly, now, did you decide to throw significant new resources at this? And forgive my confusion, Secretary General, but can you explain for me please the link between fake cigarettes and the financing of terrorism? It escapes me."

Oscar Fuentes leapt to his feet. *Periodista* pens paused in mid-scribble.

"Money, money, money, money, money!" Fuentes thundered at the BBC reporter. "This is the link. You see, BBC? Forgive me, Secretary General, forgive me this interruption. But the BBC man is for some reason unable to see this very obvious link. I can assist him to understand. It is simple. My officers battle this reality every day. My Argentinian brothers and my brothers in Brazil do the same. We are in a crisis. Interpol is, therefore, here to assist. Arrests must therefore follow. It is very clear, no? Why does this BBC man lose his way in the small details? What more is there to explain? Excuse me this interruption, Señor Dupont."

Secretary General Didier Herriot-Dupont smiled graciously at his Venezquayan colleague. Freiderikos Milonakis, seated in the audience, front row, smiled graciously at their Venezquayan colleague. Interior Minister Oscar Fuentes switched off his frown, shifted his gaze away from the offending *periodista*, and sat down. A rare smile escaped from beneath his glistening moustache. Venezquay's spot on the Interpol Executive Committee was assured.

"Next question," Franklin said curtly from the podium.

Chief of Staff Milonakis was relaxing the next morning in his suite at the Granados Park Hotel. Another sort of man would be extremely pleased at how things had gone; would be resting on his laurels. As promised, Señor Fuentes had delivered uniformly positive coverage in the Latin American media and on the Spanish-language news wires. Much of that coverage, thanks to the voracious and uncritical appetites of other segments of the global news machine, had been routinely translated and uncritically regurgitated over an even wider area in English and French. Asian media were now beginning to pick up the story. Success.

But Chief of Staff Milonakis was nonetheless engaged in some heavy worrying as he waited in his room for the car that would take him and the Secretary General to the airport.

He had worried for only a moment about the very minor incident that somewhat marred the post-news conference exit of the Interpol delegation, followed by TV cameras as they strode out of the hotel onto the street in Asuntiago's grimy core. None of the stations had used any footage of the small crowd of young men trying to sell an array of counterfeit watches and designer-label shirts and movie DVDs to the departing Interpol officers. Señor Fuentes, a most reliable and effective colleague, had apparently seen to that.

No, Milonakis was worrying instead about other weighty matters. Among these, and in no particular order: Julia Smith, an excitable young woman named Evangeline, Valon Dragusha of Serbania, the preparations for the General Assembly in Munich, an otherwise forgettable French computer technician named Gilles Broussard, and the global TV news network CNN. Among other matters.

Security Chief Bernard LeBlanc had briefed Milonakis the evening before on the telephone about the unfortunate scene in Lyon with DHD's mistress – one of them – and the subsequent role of Julia Smith in that drama. LeBlanc has taken his long-distance verbal thrashing from Milonakis without complaint or excuse, though there could be no excuse whatsoever for his having involved Madame DHD in such a situation. Julia Smith, it seemed, had graciously invited young Evangeline up to the Secretary General's office for tea and Valium, and a nice long chat. Milonakis could only guess what might have been said, and what toxic fallout would now eventuate. He was mulling over when to inform DHD.

Valon Dragusha had been high on Milonakis' list of worries for quite some time. That the oleaginous Serbanian policeman was probably now, at this very moment, poking around in the preparations for General Assembly in Munich was only the latest in a series of troubling developments. Dragusha was clearly making a move, or moves, of some sort and Milonakis became very nervous indeed when he could not see, at a minimum, several moves ahead of any opponent. The situation would have to be handled very carefully indeed.

And there was Broussard. Had DHD unwittingly created a little French monster in Broussard? The man had had contact with Dragusha in Lyon. Dragusha had now requested his services in Munich. Broussard had had lunch with the Secretary General's wife. He had been found in the Secretary General's hotel room with Julia in Kulsaka. The Secretary General himself had spent too much time and lavished altogether too much attention on this heretofore inconsequential clerk. Why was Broussard so important in this increasingly complicated game?

Milonakis had taken the liberty of obtaining from LeBlanc records of all of Broussard's recent telephone calls; dialled and received, via mobile or landline, at home or at Interpol. The results would make any Chief of Staff, anywhere, in any organisation, indulge in some industrial-strength worrying.

There were calls to and from Dragusha. There were calls to and from Julia Smith. Some rather late at night. And there were calls to and from the Secretary General himself. This was all, Milonakis mused, highly irregular. It was something he must understand far better, and as soon as possible.

And then there was CNN. That a televised catastrophe, a pre-General Assembly catastrophe, was in the wind was beyond reasonable doubt. If it could not be headed off, the consequences must be minimised, absolutely. Milonakis hoped the Latin America mission would do the trick.

In the interim he would try one last pre-emptive move. He looked at his watch, and summoned Franklin to his room.

Franklin was exceptionally hung over when the call came from Milonakis. Truth be told, Franklin was still sound asleep in his giant Granados Park Hotel bed when the phone jangled so intemperately at mid-morning. With all drapes tightly drawn, Franklin thought it was the middle of the night. In fact, in the middle of the previous night Franklin had been dancing wildly in a very unsavoury salsa club with a fetching young female constable recently assigned to media and public affairs work for the Venezquayan National Police. What had subsequently become of her was no longer clear.

Despite his condition, Franklin managed to get dressed, chew half a dozen breath mints and drag himself to the Chief of Staff's room within half an hour. Milonakis did not proffer any critical remarks about the appearance of Interpol's Chief Press Officer. He merely barked orders and instructions.

"Franklin," Milonakis said, "I want you to get on the phone to CNN and get them to hold that report until after the General Assembly. Or get that crew back to Lyon for more interviews. We will give them the Secretary General."

"What, now?" Franklin said. "Call them now?"

"Yes. Use that phone there."

"Now?"

"Yes."

"What time is it in London?"

"I don't care what time it is in London," Milonakis said.

Franklin stood blinking and licking his parched lips. He reached for a breath mint. "Um…" he said.

"Call," Milonakis said. "Use the speaker. I'll listen in."

Franklin fumbled with his BlackBerry, looking for numbers. A sheen of sweat, with a dangerously high alcohol content, formed on his brow. He poked unsteadily at the white phone beside the Chief of Staff's bed. They both stood listening as the call went through to London.

"News desk, Johnson," a baritone American voice said.

"Um, may I please speak to Rob Henderson?" Franklin said, nodding hopefully at Milonakis.

"Who?" the baritone said.

"Rob Henderson. He's one of your TV reporters."

"He's on assignment. Gotta go."

"Wait, wait," Franklin said. "Where on assignment?"

"No idea. Busy here. Got a newscast coming up. Gotta go."

"No, wait. Is Sally Birchgrove there?"

"Who is this?"

"Frank Franklin. From Interpol."

"Interpol? Bullshit."

"No bullshit. I need to speak to Rob Henderson or Sally Birchgrove urgently."

"Hold on."

The line went silent. Again, Franklin looked over at Milonakis. The Chief of Staff said nothing. He was stony-faced. Then Birchgrove came on the line.

"Yes?" she said. "Birchgrove."

"Sally, it's Frank Franklin. From Interpol."

"OK. What's up? Busy here."

"Well, Sally, look," Franklin said. "The fact is, we're a little concerned about the piece Rob Henderson is doing up. We feel he's not got the full story because he didn't have access to all the people he, um, needed. The Secretary General, for example."

"Rob knows what he's doing. He's a pro."

"Yeah, but we think he should come back down to Lyon and, you know, gather a bit more stuff."

"Talk to Rob. It's his deal."

"Where is he?"

"I dunno. Eastern Europe somewhere, I think. Or Munich, maybe. Not sure."

"What's he doing in Eastern Europe?"

"Frank, what's up? I'm busy."

"Well, it's just that, we all feel that maybe—"

"Maybe you won't like the piece."

"Well, it's just that we all feel kind of—"

"Welcome to TV, Frank," Birchgrove said. "You're worried about something, call the reporter."

"I don't have his mobile number."

"Rob didn't give it to you?"

"No."

"I can't give it out then. No can do."

"I really need to talk to him."

"Sorry, buddy. Gotta go."

"Sally—"

"Welcome to TV."

Milonakis stepped forward and whispered, "Tell her we'll seek an injunction."

"What's that?" Birchgrove asked.

"Nothing, nothing. Just someone here with me."

"What's the guy saying? An injunction?" Birchgrove asked. "Gee whiz, you guys must be pretty damned nervous. That's a nice little angle. I'll let Rob know. OK? Gotta go."

"No, wait," Franklin called out. "When is the piece going to air?"

The line went dead.

"Franklin, Franklin, Franklin," the Chief of Staff said gravely, shaking his head. "Tell me something: is that really the very best you can do?"

TEN

Here is Julia Smith in the spacious living room of the official apartment at Interpol headquarters. The evening light outside is fading as she awaits the Secretary General's return from Venezquay. She is in a pensive mood, as befits the wife of a serial womaniser, the wife once more betrayed. She stands looking intently at her husband's collection of lethal weapons hanging on the walls: rifles and shotguns of all descriptions, firepower enough to start a revolution, in the unlikely event that Lyon, France were ever to be the epicentre of some violent upheaval.

Betrayal is nothing new to Julia Smith. She was well aware of her husband's extramarital penchants and peccadilloes. She had entered the marriage knowing DHD's reputation, having been forewarned. She entered it with her eyes wide open and willing, as an ambitious young criminologist, to go along for the career-enhancing ride as wife of the head of the world's largest international police organisation.

This did not mean, however, that she would be deceived and humiliated and ignored forever. No indeed. But Julia was one of those who knew that revenge is a dish best served cold. She had always known there would eventually be a day for revenge and an end to marital charades. She had known before making this latest journey from Washington to France that the time was fast approaching. And now, a conversation with the lovely and talented Evangeline all too fresh in her memory, she knew the time was nigh.

She pondered all of this, as she waited quietly for the Secretary General's return.

Didier Herriot-Dupont was somewhat taken aback as he opened the door to his apartment. There, standing in the dimness and holding a hefty Beretta AR70/90 assault rifle casually by her side, was his wife. For an instant, fear was upon him. But then reason prevailed. Surely Julia was not about to do him harm? And reassuring to him at this slightly awkward moment was the thought that none of his collection of guns was ever loaded, and that proper cartridges for most of them would be very hard to obtain.

DHD set his small suitcase down, ever so slightly tentative. He had been briefed by his Chief of Staff, of course, about the Evangeline incident. He sensed, though wished he did not, that his wife's sudden interest in beautifully crafted Italian military weapons might have something to do with that. He very much hoped his intuition was not correct.

"My dear woman, why are you standing there all by yourself in the dark?" he asked with a thick layer of warmth and concern in his voice. "And, ha ha, my dear, why so heavily armed?"

Julia did not answer. She looked steadily at her husband for a moment, saying nothing. Then she slowly placed the Beretta back on its wall rack. DHD decided that this was the appropriate moment to move forward and proffer a returning husband's kiss. Madame DHD received said kiss without enthusiasm.

"Why the long face, my dear?" he asked. "Are you unwell? Is something on your mind?"

He believed, with his wife now unarmed, that he should get to the heart of the matter immediately, the better to spark another angry quarrel, the better to defuse the situation as quickly as possible; moving expertly through the accusation and recrimination and denial stages to the inevitable reconciliation, with a view, as always, to some bittersweet post-conflict coitus.

Julia still said nothing. DHD made another attempt at ignition.

"What is your news? Did anything interesting happen while I was away?"

"No," Julia said eventually. "Not really. Nothing significant."

"Nothing at all?"

"Not unless you count that intern, Evangeline."

DHD stiffened, as it were. "Evangeline," he said reflectively, stroking his chin. "Intern."

"Former intern, apparently," Julia said. "A very attractive young woman. Well dressed. Long, dark hair. From Lyon."

"Hm. Ah yes, yes. Evangeline," DHD said. "An intern. Of course. From last year. In the human trafficking department, if I recall. Yes. She was very good."

"She speaks extremely highly of you, Didier. In glowing terms."

"How nice. But when did she say this? You met her?"

"She came here. To see you."

"Me?"

"Yes."

"Whatever for?"

"She was upset. Very upset."

"What about?"

"She said you had forgotten her birthday. Isn't that the oddest thing?"

"Her birthday?"

"That's right."

"What an odd thing for her to say."

DHD and his wife eyed each other steadily across the demilitarised zone. Would it soon echo with gunfire, real or metaphorical? Would Julia fire the first shot?

Julia said nothing. DHD felt he had no choice but to break the silence.

"Surely I can't be expected to remember the birthdays of each of the Interpol interns," he said. "That would be unreasonable."

"Evangeline was in a very unreasonable state of mind when she came up here for a cup of tea. Out of control. Raving, in fact. Saying all sorts of crazy things."

"How unfortunate you had to deal with that," DHD said.

159

"Yes," Julia said. "Very unfortunate."

Any connoisseur of battle scenes would know that this was the moment for the first shot to be fired, the first explosion to sound. DHD braced himself, donned his marital flak jacket and helmet, and sought metaphorical cover.

To his surprise, Julia merely locked eyes with him. It was a death stare. She said nothing. This was a chilling new tactic on her part. DHD shivered, but not with relief. This did not bode well. He knew that the battle was not over. It was far from over.

She is up to something, he thought. She's going to make me pay some other way. Revenge, as the Anglo-Saxons say, is a dish best served cold.

The Assistant Manager of Interpol's computer department was, to the practised eye of the organisation's Chief of Staff, becoming intoxicated by power; his own and his proximity to the power of others. The spies whom Freiderikos Milonakis had scattered so liberally throughout the headquarters building were consistently reporting worrying signs. Gilles Broussard had become uncharacteristically assertive, even aggressive, in his relations with other staff. He was coming in to work later in the day, taking longer lunch breaks, occasionally going home early. He was seen talking on his mobile telephone for long periods during work hours.

Perhaps even more telling in the case of a minor bureaucrat in a France-based organisation, Broussard had changed his eyeglasses. He now sported a very modern pair of red and white frames, the latest Parisian style and likely the most expensive the Interpol health fund would approve of. He had also changed his hairstyle, from a standard-issue minor bureaucrat's windswept look to a sculpted confection, heavily gelled. But to Milonakis' practised eye, the most striking outward change for a man of this sort was Broussard's new cardigan sweater. Gone was the ratty brown number he had worn for all of his years at Interpol. In was a new yellow mohair creation; tighter, shorter and far more fashionable than the previous.

Broussard was sporting his new eyeglasses, hairdo and sweater when he answered the Chief of Staff's summons for a private meeting on the fifth floor. The summons had clearly added to his growing self-esteem. He strode purposefully into Milonakis' office and sat down, beaming happily.

"How can I be of service, *monsieur?*" Broussard asked brightly, adjusting his new red and white frames with his left hand.

Was that an expensive new watch on his wrist, Milonakis wondered? Can a lowly computer man really afford a TAG Heuer Carerra?

"You are looking exceptionally well these days, Gilles. Very prosperous indeed," the Chief of Staff said.

"*En forme,*" Broussard said. "I am very well at the present moment."

"I am hearing positive reports as to your performance these days, Gilles. From various quarters. It seems you have become a very popular man, since your award."

"*Je vous en prie, monsieur,*" Broussard said. "I try to serve this organisation to the best of my ability."

"Serve a wide range of people in the organisation, I am told."

Broussard showed none of his usual diffidence. "Yes, that has been my privilege in recent weeks," he said.

"The Secretary General, Madame DHD, our Serbanian colleague Dragusha. Are there others I should know about, Gilles?"

"I try my best to meet all requests that come my way, *monsieur.*"

"All requests?"

"Within reason of course."

"Precisely," Milonakis said. "Yes, exactly. May I ask, therefore, if you have lately had any requests that you and I, or the Secretary General, would find unreasonable, Gilles? From anyone at all?"

This question appeared to dent Broussard's newfound confidence ever so slightly. He hesitated for a moment before answering.

"I'm not sure I understand you," he said.

Milonakis sensed an opportunity, but thought Broussard had not yet been sufficiently cowed.

"Let me phrase the question another way," he said, standing up and coming round to the other side of the desk in order to assert his power in the most basic, zoological way possible. Milonakis stood silently beside Broussard for a moment, very close, the better to spray the scent of genuine power all over his now slightly apprehensive adversary. Broussard removed his splendid new eyeglasses in order to focus more clearly on the Chief of Staff standing just inches away.

"Let me ask you this, Gilles. When requests for your services come your way, in what way do you prioritise your possible responses?"

"I do not follow you, *monsieur*."

"Who is your boss, Gilles? Let me phrase it that way."

"Well, my manager, Pierre Cholet."

"Really? Are you sure?"

"Well, of course, yes, I see – well it is you, *monsieur*. And the Secretary General, of course. Yes."

"Very good. So when you receive requests or instructions from others which may be confusing to you, or unusual, or, dare I say it, perhaps not in the best interests of the Secretary General, what should your reaction be in such a situation?"

"Well," Broussard said hesitantly, his eyes shifting this way and that, "I would say that in certain circumstances it would be justified if I came to you for a discussion."

"In certain circumstances?"

"Well, all circumstances of concern, *monsieur*."

Milonakis was not yet satisfied. This was still not the deferential Broussard of old.

"Our Serbanian colleague Valon Dragusha has requested that you travel to Munich to meet him there and explain the technical facilities to which Executive Committee members will have access during the General Assembly," he said.

"I am aware of this, *monsieur*," Broussard said.

"I see," Milonakis said. "And how were you made aware of this?"

"Monsieur Dragusha telephoned me to say."

"He telephoned you?"

"Yes."

"Does this happen often, Gilles?"

"From time to time," Broussard said proudly. "Since I assisted him when he was last in Lyon."

Milonakis studied the computer technician intently. "And you also assist the Secretary General's wife?"

"When requested, *monsieur*."

"What sort of requests does Madame make of you, Gilles?"

"Oh, these are matters of a, shall we say, technical nature. She asks me to explain how things work."

"She does?"

"*Oui, monsieur.*"

"Does that not strike you as odd?"

"*Non, monsieur*. I see nothing odd in this. She is an intelligent woman, curious…"

"Curious?" Milonakis said.

"About technical matters, I would say yes."

"Gilles," Milonakis said, "do you like your work?"

"Yes, very much."

"You would like to continue? In your present position?"

"Why, of course. Unless I should be so lucky as to one day receive a promotion."

Milonakis studied Broussard very closely.

"Your manager is not going anywhere, I would say," Milonakis said.

"For the moment," Broussard said.

"I see," Milonakis said. "Yes, of course."

Broussard put his new spectacles back onto his tiny nose.

"Be very, very careful, Gilles," Milonakis said suddenly. "In Munich. And generally speaking. Do you understand me?"

"I think so, *monsieur*."

"We rely on you, the Secretary General and I. There is a bond of trust. We would be extremely disappointed if you were to break that bond."

"I understand."

"You have been well rewarded for your services of late. Gilles. Remember that. Your performance has been recognised. Some travel, some new responsibilities. There was the award. And the new car."

"Ah, well, to be truthful with you, *monsieur*, my wife and I have lately been finding that car to be very small," Broussard said, picking at the sleeve of his splendid yellow sweater. "For our purposes. If you get my meaning. The car is unfortunately rather small."

Franklin and Mortman were in the Communication Chief's office, taking stock. Mortman, just out of hospital and back at work for one day, was already looking like another collapse was imminent. Franklin had been filling him in on various communication issues. Mortman was sipping a restorative Cotes du Rhone from his favourite NYPD coffee mug, a gift from his counterpart in the New York police.

"So now Milonakis has decided he wants to go up to Munich," Franklin said. "And he wants me to go along with him. To inspect installations, check out all the preparations, and think again about media requirements."

"The Germans will have everything in hand, as always," Mortman said dolefully.

"He still wants to go. Broussard from the computer department is going too. He's already on his way."

"Broussard? Why Broussard?"

"Not sure," Franklin said. "He came down to Zambezi with us too."

"Broussard?" Mortman said again.

"Yup."

"When do you go?"

"Tonight. The Lufthansa flight at eight o'clock. Travelling with Milonakis."

"I'll be alone here," said Mortman, much like someone who has been asked to sleep overnight in a haunted house.

"You'll be alright, Alf."

"What if someone calls?" Mortman said. "What if a reporter wants something?"

"Leave it for the press officers."

"What if the CNN report goes to air tonight?"

"Ah," Franklin said. "Yes."

"That's why you're going away, Frank. Isn't it? I know it. Be honest with me." Mortman's face was very red. He did not look well at all.

Franklin reached across the desk and patted the Chief of Communication's hand with filial affection. "Be strong, Alf."

It was very late when Franklin and Milonakis rolled up to Munich's InterContinental Hotel in a gleaming Mercedes taxi. The driver had muttered bitterly the whole way in from the airport about Turkish guest workers staining the fabric of German society. Milonakis had ignored him completely. Franklin the Canadian, sitting in front, had listened politely and murmured sympathetically from time to time. The driver took this politesse for vigorous agreement.

"There's one of them now," he snarled, and pointed as Franklin paid the fare.

Bounding out of the InterContinental lobby, despite the late hour, was Valon Dragusha, a picture of vigorous Serbanian manhood in his chalk-striped burgundy suit.

"Taxi, taxi, taxi!" Dragusha shouted, not yet recognising his Interpol colleagues.

The driver raced off at top speed.

"He's Serbanian!" Franklin called out after the car, to no avail. The driver did not stop.

"Frank Franklin, my dear boy," Dragusha shouted. "And Mr Chief of Staff Freddie Milonakis, the Greek stallion. Into a taxi, quick, quick. Tonight we will find the real Munich."

Dragusha crushed Franklin in a bear hug, exhaling wafts of highly alcoholic fumes. Milonakis fended off an embrace.

"Not tonight, Valon, thanks," Milonakis said, though Franklin looked distinctly interested at the prospect of seedy Munich girlie bars at Interpol expense. "Breakfast tomorrow instead. I'm interested in your impressions of the preparations."

"Who knows where I will be at breakfast tomorrow, my dear friends and colleagues?" Dragusha roared. "A man can get lost in a city like Munich." He slapped Milonakis energetically on the back. "But Franklin, you will accompany me, yes?" he said.

Franklin looked briefly over at the Chief of Staff. "Perhaps not, Valon," he said sadly. "We have an early start tomorrow."

"Bah, you Canadians. Bah," Dragusha said in disgust.

"Where is our friend Broussard?" Milonakis asked.

"Ah, that man has been very, very helpful to me today," Dragusha said. "But I think I may have tired him out at dinner. He has had a sort of collapse. When he stood up at the table. The hotel security man and I put him to bed in his room. He will be fine by morning. Not accustomed to Serbanian rakia, he says. It is a very potent drink. He has broken his eyeglasses."

Another taxi rolled up under the hotel's glass awning. A valet opened the door for the sweating Serbanian policeman. Dragusha got inside.

"Are you certain you will not accompany me, gentlemen?" he said, with an exaggerated wink. "I know some very special places. Exclusive places. We will be well looked after, the three of us."

"Not tonight," Milonakis said.

"Don't get arrested, Valon," Franklin said brightly.

"Ah, handcuffs, Franklin, yes," Dragusha shouted as the taxi pulled off. "Excellent idea!"

Franklin and Milonakis had almost finished their breakfast when Broussard appeared, looking very poorly indeed. Layers of masking tape held one arm of his new glasses in place, but they now sat askew on his nose. He had a deathly pallor and was wearing no cardigan at all, despite the air-conditioned chill of the InterContinental dining room. Milonakis beckoned him over.

"You're not well, Gilles," he said.

Broussard sat down heavily. He spilled some of the coffee he had obtained from the buffet, and took a tentative sip.

"It is a flu, I think, *monsieur*. A fever."

"That's not what we heard," Franklin said. "Dragusha said you had a big-time dinner with him last night."

Broussard was too hung over to be alarmed, or to try to explain. He just sipped more coffee and said nothing. There was still no sign of the Serbanian.

"I will need a briefing as to what you and Mr Dragusha accomplished together here yesterday," Milonakis said. "A full briefing. But first we have our meeting with the Germans. Drink that coffee and come with us."

"I have some aspirin, Gilles," Franklin said. "I always carry it."

"It's very cold in here," Broussard said miserably. "My sweater is lost."

The problem with all of the cultural generalisations and stereotyping about German precision and efficiency and authoritarianism is that most of them are based in fact; most of them are accurate. Even the most politically correct visitor to Germany will come away mightily impressed with Germanic planning and design and attention to detail. And the German federal police team organising the Interpol General Assembly in Munich had no intention whatsoever of being the exception to the rule.

Interpol member countries take turns hosting the annual General Assembly, and each does its very best. But to compare a General Assembly staged in, say, Lima, or Manila, or even Madrid, with one staged in a German city would be most unfair. That every fifth year the General Assembly is also the occasion when Secretaries General are elected or re-elected was an extra reason why the Munich organisers had thrown the full weight of Germanic efficiency at the project.

In charge, very much in charge, was Dr Adolph Fenstermacher, a thirty-year veteran of the *Bundeskriminalamt*. No cloud had ever cast a shadow over Dr Fenstermacher's police career, no law enforcement assignment had ever been fumbled. He was determined that the BKA would stage the best and most impressive General Assembly in Interpol's ninety-year history. He intended to let nothing stand in his way.

This was despite his extremely negative view of Interpol as an institution, and of its staff and its current Secretary General in particular. Fenstermacher's first allegiance was to the German Federal Criminal Police, followed by the German state police, the *Landeskriminalamt*. If he and his senior colleagues were ever to risk sharing police information with other law enforcement agencies, they very much preferred to use Europol, of course. Staffed as it was entirely by Europeans, with not an African or Asian or American police officer in sight. And run far, far differently than Interpol under the command of one Didier Herriot-Dupont. A mere French showman of dubious credentials and reputation, in Fenstermacher's view; a careerist, a law enforcement dilettante at best.

Nonetheless, Fenstermacher had been given his assignment and he intended to make the General Assembly a resounding success. The Germans had spared no effort, no expense. They had booked the cavernous main ballroom of the InterContinental, large enough to hold some six hundred delegates with ease. The main stage, raised high above the delegates' area, was dominated by a massive table set up to seat thirty dignitaries in one long row, each with their own microphone.

To the left of that table was a majestic podium worthy of a Third Reich rally. It was festooned with BKA and Interpol insignia. Behind that were two digital screens so large that they would have made Albert Speer weep with joy. On these screens would be projected, in real time, video images of keynote speakers, cutaway shots of delegates at work, important announcements and the results of various votes.

Interpol officials, including Chief of Staff Milonakis – of the Hellenic Police, of all things – had already visited far too often in

Fenstermacher's view, and put their noses where they didn't belong. So he was in no mood for Interpol nonsense when Milonakis and his media man walked into the hall that morning, carrying notebooks. He tried his best to completely ignore the loathsome French bureaucrat who trailed behind them, the same little man who, the day before, along with that equally loathsome Serbian policeman, had pestered Fenstermacher's staff with a series of inane technical questions and requests.

Fenstermacher actually snapped his heels together as he greeted the latest Interpol visitors. His handshake was firm; his gaze steely, police-like. He was not in uniform, however. He wore the well-cut navy blue suit favoured by all BKA detectives and senior officials.

"I am at your service, gentlemen," Fenstermacher said. "Though I can assure you that all is going exceptionally well here. There are no problems of any kind. My team is working ahead of schedule and under budget."

"We would just like to have a final look around, Dr Fenstermacher," Milonakis said. "I always do this in any country where there is a General Assembly."

"Germany is not just any country, Mr Milonakis," Fenstermacher said.

"Indeed," Milonakis said.

"As you can see, the main hall is virtually ready," Fenstermacher said, waving his arm widely.

"Big," Franklin said.

Fenstermacher examined Franklin as an entomologist would examine a not-particularly-interesting insect.

"Looking good," Franklin said.

Fenstermacher walked them all around the vast, high-ceilinged hall, then up onto the stage where they could admire the installations. Workmen and BKA staff were still bustling around. A technician was taping wires inside the speaker's podium. Both Franklin and Milonakis simultaneously wrote the word *podium* in their notebooks. They exchanged knowing looks.

"Um," Franklin said.

"Yes?" Fenstermacher said.

"Well…" Franklin said.

"The podium is too high, I'm afraid," Milonakis said.

"Too high? It is standard height. Always podiums are of this height."

"Too high," Milonakis said.

Franklin stood behind it and pointed to television camera area many metres away at the back of the room. "The line of sight doesn't work," he said. "The stage is high and the podium is high. He'll disappear behind this thing."

"Who will disappear?" Fenstermacher said.

Franklin looked at Milonakis. Milonakis looked at Fenstermacher.

"The Secretary General," Milonakis said.

"He's, um, not very tall," Franklin said.

"That is the European standard podium height, EU standard," Fenstermacher said. "It was designed especially for this event. It cost thousands of euros. It is wired for electronics and recording and has a speech-prompting computer screen built in. It is too late to replace this extremely complicated equipment."

Fenstermacher snapped his fingers at a workman and growled, "Get me a tape measure, *schnell!*"

"Perhaps a little platform, a riser," Franklin said quietly. "You have carpenters here. We can get one built for the Secretary General's speech. Someone can quickly take it away afterwards."

"In front of six hundred police delegates?" Fenstermacher barked.

"We also have a question about the honour guard and the Secretary General's security detail," Milonakis said.

"Yes, what about them?" Fenstermacher said irritably.

"How tall are they?" Milonakis said. "Are they tall men, or average height?"

Fenstermacher looked as if he were facing aliens from another planet.

"We're thinking about the official photographs and the TV shots,"

Franklin said helpfully. "You know. How the shots will look. If the guys were to be, um, you know, a whole lot taller than our guy."

Fenstermacher reluctantly agreed to see to the construction of a small platform to add six inches to the Secretary General's height. A reliable BKA man would be assigned to discreetly slip it in and out of place during proceedings.

"How this will be done in front of the delegates I do not yet know," Fenstermacher growled.

He also promised he would look into the pressing issue of whether any tall people would appear alongside the Secretary General during proceedings and for official photos. Then he then took his visitors on a tour of the rest of the installations: the private office for Herriot-Dupont, another one for Milonakis, a room for Franklin and the Interpol and BKA press officers, an elaborately equipped press conference room, a workroom for journalists, a lounge room-cum-office for Executive Committee members, and a technical area for computer and audiovisual work.

"All is in order," Fenstermacher said proudly. "All is exactly as you have requested."

Milonakis was examining the computer servers and terminals. "Gilles, you checked all of this yesterday?"

"All is in order," Fenstermacher said before Broussard could speak. "Your man agreed with me on this yesterday when they inspected it."

"Gilles?" Milonakis said again.

"*Oui, monsieur*, all appeared to be in order," Broussard said. His hangover was lifting slightly, it seemed. "We tested the voting system as well."

"We?" Milonakis said.

"Monsieur Dragusha was inspecting it with me yesterday," Broussard said.

"We will discuss that later, Gilles," Milonakis said curtly.

"There was no need to bring the Interpol voting equipment," Fenstermacher said. "We agreed to provide all technical equipment required. Your system is very old, it is old-fashioned."

"It has served us very well for many General Assemblies, Dr Fenstermacher," Milonakis said. "We know the equipment well. It is ours and we know it well. Correct, Gilles?"

"*Absolument, monsieur,*" Broussard said. "I have operated this system many times, in many places. And I have replaced the batteries in all of the voting units as I always do. One device can now be distributed to each national delegation."

He held up an aging grey remote control unit with its green and red buttons and an infrared eye.

"Any garage doors that may fly open unexpectedly around here?" Franklin asked cheerily. "When everyone's punching buttons and voting on the day?"

"There are better systems available," Fenstermacher insisted.

Milonakis sent Franklin off in search of Dragusha and sat alone in the press room with Broussard. Fenstermacher had gone grumpily back into the main hall to resume his supervision of the final preparations.

"And so, Gilles, tell me," Milonakis said. "What is there to report about your time yesterday with our Serbanian colleague?"

"He insisted that I join him in too many toasts, *monsieur.* I am sorry," Broussard said.

"I don't care how much you drank at dinner. I want to know what went on in your tour of the facilities."

"Oh, well, I see. Therefore, I can say there was nothing exceptional, *monsieur.* We walked through the various areas, much as today, and the Germans were there to answer our questions."

"What questions did Mr Dragusha have, Gilles?"

"Oh, well, some minor questions of a logistical or technical nature."

"Such as?"

"Well, where the Serbanian police delegation would sit. Where the TV cameras would be placed. When he could get the video record of the event for use on the Serbanian police website. When the voting would take place. How that would be carried out in practice. He was very concerned that this all go correctly."

"Correctly?"

"I mean, without any difficulties of a technical nature. He said it would be terrible if there was some computer malfunction. He asked me to show him all aspects of how these things would work. We discussed this."

Milonakis observed that Broussard was becoming very uneasy. A bead of sweat appeared on the Frenchman's brow.

"Do you have anything else to report to me about that, Gilles? Be very, very careful not to omit anything important."

Broussard shifted nervously in his seat. He wiped his brow, removed his damaged eyeglasses; rubbed his eyes.

"Are you ill?" Milonakis asked.

"A flu is coming, *monsieur*."

It was late, after midnight. The InterContinental was wrapped in the elegant quiet of a five-star hotel at such an hour. As he always did before important international gatherings, Chief of Staff Milonakis wanted to take one last walk-through of the conference venue, without distractions. He called Franklin on the media man's mobile and insisted that he come along for a final stroll and to help think of any possible requirements that had been overlooked; any possible difficulties that might arise.

Franklin was at approximately 8.5 on the Richter scale of intoxication by that hour, after a long session in the hotel cocktail lounge and another, more private, one using up the supplies in his room's mini-bar. But he was nonetheless able to make his way successfully to the deserted lobby to meet the Chief of Staff.

"Were you able to locate Dragusha?" Milonakis said.

"Not for the whole day," Franklin said, chewing on a mouthful of mints. "The chambermaid said his bed had not been slept in last night."

"Has he checked out?"

"No. Apparently not."

"Damn," Milonakis said.

They walked together through the main hall, imagining possible disasters together. Franklin, after four years at Interpol, was very good at this sort of work, and Milonakis was a master. They found very little to worry about, with the Germans being in charge of preparations.

They had a last look at the Interpol offices and the press room. Then, at the end of a hallway, they saw a light on in the computer room.

"That's weird," Franklin said.

They walked into the room and there, by himself at a terminal, sat Gilles Broussard. He had found his yellow cardigan. He leapt to his feet when he heard his colleagues enter.

"*Mon dieu, mon dieu*, you frightened me, *mes amis!*" he said. "What are you doing here at this late hour?"

"What are *you* doing here at this late hour, Gilles?" Milonakis said.

"I couldn't sleep and I came, therefore, to make some last-minute checks, *monsieur*. To ensure that all goes perfectly on the day."

"Hey, that's what we like to hear," Franklin said.

"Commendable," Milonakis said with suspicion. "Carry on, carry on, please."

Broussard sat down again. His computer screen showed that for some reason he was linked to Interpol's Red Notice pages, with their grim mug shots of the world's wanted criminals. He tapped a few keys and then his screen displayed the image that would be projected onto the main hall's giant TVs showing General Assembly voting results on any subject of deliberation. No values had yet been entered. Broussard tapped a few more keys and sample numerical results, along with a pie chart showing the graphical percentage breakdown, appeared in green and red, for and against.

"Neat," Franklin said.

"It is easy," Broussard said. "For the voting I will, of course, install myself in the main hall with this equipment."

Then Broussard's mobile rang. It was sitting beside his keyboard. He looked down at it as if it were a rodent. He looked up at Milonakis and Franklin and back down at the phone. On its little screen appeared the words: *Incoming Call. Madame Julia.*

Broussard looked up again with a sheepish smile and shrugged his small shoulders.

"Answer it," Milonakis said.

ELEVEN

Unusually, the Secretary General was in the Chief of Staff's office. He sat in Milonakis' chair behind the desk and Milonakis sat in one of the guest chairs. This seating arrangement put Herriot-Dupont face-to-face with the framed picture of Niccolò Machiavelli on the Chief of Staff's desk. He picked it up.

"Why do you feel it necessary to have a picture of this man on your desk?" DHD asked.

"We have had this discussion before, Secretary General," Milonakis said politely. "It is, let's say, a little indulgence of mine."

"But a philosopher, in a frame," DHD said. "Why not children, a wife?"

"Which wife would I choose, *monsieur?*" Milonakis said with a wry smile.

"The current one, perhaps," the Secretary General said.

"I am between wives at the moment, as you know."

"Yes, yes, I know. A pity. The complications of married life."

The two men gazed at each other in silence. A dignified silence was the only appropriate response. Then Herriot-Dupont laughed bitterly. He was in a remarkably sanguine mood, Milonakis thought, despite the mounting troubles, despite the briefing he had just been given about the Munich trip. Was it a mood of quiet resignation? No, this would be out of character. The calm before a storm, perhaps.

"And so," Milonakis said, getting back to business. It was his office after all. "Dragusha."

"We simply have no choice but to continue to watch him very

closely, Fred. That is all we can do at this stage. He is an Executive Committee member."

"I feel we must get more information about his strategy," the Chief of Staff said.

"Broussard has told you what happened in Munich."

"But all?"

"Broussard is our man, not Dragusha's," DHD said. "I feel confident of this again."

"I wish I could be sure," Milonakis said.

"Trust me on this, Fred. He is ours. Dragusha is our problem, not Broussard."

"Broussard is changing."

"I'll speak with him privately. I'll ensure he is loyal."

"He's more demanding."

"In what way?"

"He seems unhappy suddenly with his car, for example."

"Get him another one," Herriot-Dupont said.

Milonakis was incredulous. "The staff will be enraged," he said. "People are already speaking against him. So my informants tell me."

"Keep Broussard happy, Fred. Until after the General Assembly. He's important to us. Get him the car he wants."

"Secretary General, did you give him a watch?" Milonakis asked suddenly. "As a gift?"

Herriot-Dupont stopped spinning a pen. "No. Why? Does Broussard want a new watch too?"

"He's wearing an expensive TAG Heuer these days."

"They're not so expensive. Some of them."

"He's a Level 7 pay grade, a technician. Those people don't wear watches like that."

"Is it genuine?"

"I would think so."

"Perhaps he bought it in Venezquay."

"He wasn't with us in Venezquay."

"A gift from someone, then. Not from me."

177

This thought troubled them both.

"Dragusha?" the Chief of Staff said.

"Let's hope not," the Secretary General said.

Milonakis hesitated. The subject matter was becoming extremely delicate. Herriot-Dupont saw where the conversation was heading.

"My wife does not give watches as gifts to just any man, Fred. Of this you can be sure."

Milonakis was not at all sure. "He has been doing things for her," he said.

"Banal things."

"She called him after midnight on his mobile phone. In Munich."

"You said he told you she had a technical question. A computer malfunction."

"At midnight?"

"I work late into the night, Fred."

"Does she?"

"Apparently," DHD said.

"And so she calls Broussard."

"Alright, I will ask him about this again. In private," Herriot-Dupont said. "But he is our man, Freiderikos. Of this you can be sure. What else do you have for me?"

"Your General Assembly speech. Mortman has finished a draft for you to look at."

"It will be rubbish. I will write that speech."

Milonakis adopted his most soothing tone. "Better to have input and suggestions from a range of people, sir. I plan to have a look at it—"

"I know what needs to be said. Visionary things. Inspirational things. I will need pictures and graphics. The future of international police cooperation."

"All the speakers will be focusing on that."

"We will have fewer speakers, then. Moulin is out this year, as I have told you."

"I'm still not sure this is a good idea, sir. With respect."

"I will deliver the main message on behalf of Interpol this time, Fred."

"Moulin is very popular among the delegates, Secretary General. And among his own team and most of the other Interpol staff. They will think it strange that the Director of Operational Police support doesn't speak."

"I will handle Jean-Marc," DHD said. "I'll explain my strategy personally."

"Alright," Milonakis said reluctantly, jotting something in his notebook.

"And Fred, note that I've decided we will be reopening the staff bar as soon as possible."

"But you said the closure would be permanent. You told staff it was permanent."

"Did I?"

"Yes."

"A misunderstanding. Poor translation. Have Franklin draft an appropriate notice for all staff. He's a fool but he is a good writer, no? He's writing fiction in his spare time, I'm told. He's just the man for this job."

"Well…" Milonakis said.

"And, as I am a good writer as well, I will make sure no one in Munich ever forgets my speech."

"I—"

"I will make several important announcements," Herriot-Dupont said.

The Chief of Staff hated surprises. The Secretary General's policy surprises were legendary and usually very expensive.

"Such as?" Milonakis said warily.

"For one, Interpol's new sponsorship arrangements," DHD said triumphantly.

"Sponsorship?"

"Yes. I have been developing this idea for some time. I will announce an exciting new way of doing police business. We will engage directly with the business community. They will fund a number of important new projects."

"Sponsorship," Milonakis said again.

"Correct. I am in the final stages of discussion with the big tobacco companies, for example. They are happy to provide millions of euros to combat the illicit trade in cigarettes. We will expand our team. Have a conference somewhere. Publish brochures. Tell the world's media."

"I wasn't aware."

"I'm telling you now."

Milonakis felt a rare stab of anger at the lack of consultation.

"We should discuss this, I think, Secretary General," he said. "It's a major departure for the organisation. Some police will surely think that corporate sponsorship of law enforcement activity is—"

"I don't care what police think. I am the Secretary General of Interpol."

"The media, then. Tobacco companies are, as you know—"

"It's decided, Fred. I will announce the new programme in Munich. In my speech. Get Franklin to draft a press release to have ready. As he is our fancy writing specialist."

"A fiction writer," Milonakis said.

The Chief of Staff sat alone in his office for a long time after the Secretary General left. He consulted his leather-bound enemies and problems lists, bringing them up to date and shifting some entries higher. No entries ever seemed to drop off his lists anymore. And several items were crowding for space at the top.

Julia Smith, sad though this was, had to be moved from the 'possibles' area near the bottom of the list to a spot quite near the top. Sad but true. Milonakis wrote down Gilles Broussard's name, but with a question mark. He also put down Jean-Marc Moulin's name, with two question marks. He put two asterisks beside Valon Dragusha's name.

On the problems list he now put *CNN report* at the top. He

inscribed an asterisk beside Adolph Fenstermacher's name. He moved *Interpol budget approval by Japan* nearer to the top. He added a new entry: *World anti-smoking campaigners' reaction to sponsorship.* He added *Zimwabse honorary Interpol president/media/European delegates* to his problems list, along with *Stolen banknote specimens.*

These last two items he had not raised with the Secretary General in the meeting just ended. Milonakis was not sure if this was because he truly wanted more time to address them before alarming the Secretary General unduly, or if it was that he simply couldn't face the stress of any such discussions that afternoon. I am tired, he thought ruefully. I am very, very tired.

The Zimwabse situation was deteriorating. European media coverage, especially from London, of Interpol having the loathed chief of Zimwabse's police as an honorary president had started to ring alarm bells in European political and law enforcement circles. There were rumours now of a possible boycott of the General Assembly by a number of police chiefs (Europol lackeys!) if Commissioner Josiah Matonga were allowed to come to Munich. There was talk of a visa being denied by the Germans, and of his being turned back at the airport by immigration officials if he tried to attend.

And now there was the unfortunate matter of the stolen banknotes. Interpol was the repository of the world's largest collection of specimen notes from central banks, and of a vast collection of counterfeit bills from dozens of countries. For collectors, a pristine new-design US $100 note, for example, with all the zeroes as a serial number, or a newly released edition of a Belixican 50 peso note with the world *sample* emblazoned across it, or a rejected design for an Indian 10,000 rupee note would be very valuable indeed, and all but impossible to obtain.

That someone inside Interpol had apparently been regularly pilfering a sample banknote or two over recent months and selling them for extraordinary prices to a grateful numismatic dealer in Antwerp was hardly news Milonakis had needed to hear. Belgian police had told him in recent days that they were coming ever closer to making an arrest. Milonakis prayed that this would occur after the General Assembly. He had put off informing Herriot-Dupont and the media office of another impending storm until the security system for storing the banknotes at Interpol was reviewed and rectified, and until he had all the facts. What can possibly go wrong next? he thought wearily.

Machiavelli spoke to him from an undisclosed retirement location: *Before all else, be armed.*

Secretary General Didier Herriot-Dupont was making a rare walking tour of the Interpol headquarters. He was almost never seen in the building's hallways or offices or operations rooms. He usually entered and exited the building via his private elevator to the garage. Those he needed to meet came to him on the fifth floor.

Today he startled police and support staff by making an unheralded progress through various corners of his personal fiefdom. He walked alone. He was in a pensive, though expansive, mood; exuding the preternatural calm and goodwill of the powerful man securely in charge. He dispensed warm smiles and regal hand gestures to his people. He gave no outward sign of the heavy burdens of office.

He stopped first at the Interpol bar. Through the glass doors he saw cleaners and other workers preparing the space for its imminent reopening. Tables were being wiped down, bar shelves restocked. Ice was being delivered. His people would be very pleased.

Then he walked into the Interpol dining room. He walked in through the main doors just as any other staff member would. He walked past people pushing their trays of subsidised lunch along racks toward the cash register. He nodded to André Julien, the head chef and cafeteria manager, who was at that moment preparing fluffy omelettes to order for the child pornography team. He walked into the main seating area, amidst the hubbub of happy employees eating hearty, well-deserved meals and exchanging views on a range of global law enforcement matters.

The hubbub stopped abruptly, completely. All eyes turned to the Secretary General. His all but unprecedented appearance here had caught everyone completely off guard. Glasses of wine were hurriedly placed back on tables. A few French *fonctionnaires* stood up respectfully in their places.

"*Bon appétit, mes chers collègues!*" Herriot-Dupont called out, beaming an incandescent smile. He raised his right hand in a gesture of greeting and affection.

One or two French staffers called out, "*Mais merci, Monsieur le Secrétaire Général! Merci!*" Other staff members were silent; perhaps too overwhelmed by the occasion to respond.

DHD turned, and was gone as quickly as he had arrived.

His next stop was the Command Centre, the pulsating heart of international law enforcement and cross-border police cooperation. His actual destination was Jean-Marc Moulin's office nearby, but he wanted on this day to admire the blinking lights on the electronic map of the world, lights which showed the global flow of crucially important police information. Technicians and analysts hard at work at their terminals spied the Secretary General gazing in at them through the plate glass. Word quickly spread that DHD was outside.

Alerted by his staff, Moulin materialised at DHD's side in the hallway.

"There, Jean-Marc, on that electronic screen in there is the reason you and I, and all who labour so diligently here to make the world a safer place, get out of bed each morning," the Secretary General said.

Moulin appeared somewhat taken aback by the Secretary General's unusually philosophical, even, one might say, elegiac frame of mind.

"I suppose you could say that, yes," he said, gazing through the glass alongside his boss.

"How is the data traffic this afternoon, Jean-Marc?" DHD asked.

Moulin looked slightly uncomfortable with the question. "The volume is, I would say, it is…"

"Increasing always?"

"Well…"

"That is our objective, Jean-Marc. Yours and mine in particular."

"*Absolument, monsieur,*" Moulin said. "Some member countries, however—"

"We must get a photographer to capture images of this Command Centre working at full capacity, Jean-Marc. For use during my speech in Munich. What do you think? I will arrange this."

"An interesting idea," Moulin said. "But the photographer will have to be careful not to show any confidential information from the screens. Photographers are not normally allowed in there."

"The pictures will only be shown to General Assembly delegates, of course," DHD said.

Moulin looked even more uncomfortable.

"Our trusted colleagues," DHD said. "Everyone in the Interpol brotherhood shares the same objectives, no?"

"I would say, well, one would of course wish…" Moulin ventured.

"Jean-Marc, it is actually about the Munich meeting that I came down here to see you today," DHD said. "My speech. What I will say to the delegates."

"I am flattered that you wish to consult me, *monsieur,*" Moulin said, apprehension in his voice.

"Perhaps we could go into your office for a little chat?" DHD said.

Secretary General Herriot-Dupont stopped at the door to Milonakis' office on the way back to his own. The Chief of Staff looked up from his work.

"I've had a meeting with Moulin," DHD said, standing in the doorway. "Just now."

"How did it go?" Milonakis asked.

Herriot-Dupont waited for a moment before answering.

"Moulin is a hard man to read," he said eventually.

"Angry?"

"No. Not angry."

"Disappointed."

"I think you could say that. But he is a police officer. A professional. He sees what is good for global law enforcement and he goes on about his duties. Interpol is bigger than both of us, no? All is well."

"Are you sure?"

"I suggested he could go on a fact-finding mission somewhere soon, if he wished. Jamaica, for example. Thailand. Somewhere sunny with drug crime. Bring his wife, and stay afterward for a little holiday."

"How did he react to that?"

"He said he would think about it."

After the Secretary General had left, Milonakis dialled one of his informants in the Command Centre, Javier Herrera, an ambitious young criminal analyst from Argentina. Milonakis asked if there was news.

"The Secretary General came for a visit today," Herrera said. "Without warning. Then he and Mr Moulin went for a private meeting."

"Interesting," Milonakis said.

"Twenty minutes, more or less," Herrera said.

"I see."

"Some of us heard shouting."

"From inside Mr Moulin's office?"

"Yes, sir."

"Whose voice? Both?"

"It sounded like the Secretary General, people said."

"Hm," Milonakis said.

"Someone heard breaking glass," Herrera said.

"In the meeting?" Milonakis asked with dread.

"No, after."

"What do you mean?"

"We think Mr Moulin might have broken something in his office."

"After the meeting. Not during the meeting?"

"Correct. Then he went home for the day," Herrera said.

"At what time?"

"Three o'clock. More or less. He usually stays until late."

After he had hung up, Milonakis opened his leather-bound notebook to the enemies list. With a sigh he picked up his pen and crossed out the question marks he had just a short time earlier entered beside Jean-Marc Moulin's name.

Here is Julia Smith, at the Lyon shooting range of the French National Police. The Secretary General's bemused driver and bodyguard, plain-clothes French police officers on long-term secondment to Interpol, stand behind her. She has persuaded them to bring her here for an afternoon practice session, assuring them it is with the Secretary General's blessing.

She wears protective glasses, ear coverings and a Washington Redskins baseball cap. She sights confidently down the short barrel of a Sig Sauer Pro .357 semi-automatic pistol, an official side-arm of the French police. She fires four rapid shots – bam, bam, bam, bam – and her wrist and hand recoil sharply after each blast. A police instructor hits a switch and the man-shaped paper target whizzes toward them on a steel cable.

Julia is no expert, but all three policemen on the range with her nod and murmur appreciatively. All shots have hit the body outline of the target in the chest area. Only one is substantially off centre.

"You have fired pistols many times before today, *madame*," the instructor says with a smile, handing her the paper target for a souvenir, and hanging up a fresh one for another attempt.

"Only for sport," the Secretary General's wife says. "Never in anger."

Two days later and Frank Franklin was exceptionally, exquisitely drunk. There is no polite way of putting it. Dead drunk, in his office, in the middle of the afternoon. The CNN report had gone to air the night before, and in Franklin's view there was no other way to respond to something like that than by consuming excessive quantities, end-of-the-world quantities, of alcohol.

He had decided to drink as much as he could before facing colleagues at the reopening of the Interpol bar, scheduled for later in the day.

The CNN feature was a disaster, a catastrophe, worse than anyone had even imagined. It had now been broadcast and re-broadcast by the network around the world for hours. In his stupor, as he sat wringing his hands and fighting off panic in his office, the evil words and pictures cascaded around in Franklin's head like some hideous horror-movie kaleidoscope, like that very bad acid trip from his University of Toronto days. No amount of booze was able to silence the demon voices or make the scary pictures go away.

Here is CNN's Rob Henderson standing tall in his chinos and blazer. "Tonight we're taking you INSIDE INTERPOL! It's an exclusive glimpse into the innermost secrets of the world's most secretive police organisation!" Now here's a Henderson voiceover, against wide shots of the glass-enclosed headquarters, with people moving in and out: "The good ship *Interpol* is dangerously off course, steaming unsteadily into stormy waters. What about the man ostensibly at the helm? Can the world risk ongoing turmoil in the world's largest…? In a post-9/11 world… As world policing becomes…"

More Henderson, then interviews, more horror-movie pictures, all spinning around unceasingly in Franklin's head! More, more, more…

Excessive spending on new projects of questionable law enforcement value… Abrupt changes in strategy… Debate over the organisation's ballooning budget… The recent catastrophic failure of the costly X-24GT communications system… Grumbling among the world's police at the new direction Interpol is taking… Database issues, member countries not sharing enough data… A downbeat regional police conference in Africa… Staff morale at an all-time low… Stress leave, resignations, anger in the ranks… French police officers assaulted by frustrated staff outside headquarters building… A popular staff bar closed as punishment, no more place for employees to unwind… Repeated security breaches and incidents at the building entrance… Building in disrepair… Europol liaison officer narrowly escapes serious injury in her crumbling office… Belarusian officials in a near miss with falling Interpol sign…

Here is Henderson standing beside workmen as they try to hoist the giant sign back in place. He turns to the camera, microphone in hand, asking TV viewers, "Is this a symbol of the grave problems facing this once-proud institution?"

More Henderson voiceover! "The Secretary General, Didier Herriot-Dupont of France, meanwhile, lives a lavish lifestyle at the expense of member countries… Palatial penthouse apartment, large personal staff, unlimited expenses, jet-setting around the world… Takes private language lessons in work hours… Takes delivery of a shiny new BMW while things crumbles around him…"

Here is Jean-Marc Moulin shouting directly into the camera: "You are forbidden to shoot pictures of that car!" Here are pictures of the Secretary General getting out of said car and going into Le Passage restaurant in the company of an unidentified young woman in a stylish black cocktail dress.

Bizarre late night rituals! Buried animals in the Interpol garden! Skeletons recently uncovered! What happens when police from seventy countries congregate far from their homes? What traditions and superstitions do they bring with them?

Here is Jean-Marc Moulin again, shouting directly into the camera and putting his hand over the lens. "I want these people out of here. They are not allowed to shoot in here. Get security up here!" Now Henderson: "In the midst of all this controversy, Interpol refused to allow CNN access to the Command Centre, where crucial international police work is supposed to get done. What are Interpol's most senior officers trying to hide? Secretary General Herriot-Dupont did not make himself available for comment on any of the problems…"

More, more, more! "Well-placed police sources from Eastern Europe have told CNN there is growing unease at the Executive

Committee level about the current situation. Asian police are also said to be gravely concerned."

Here is a burly, unidentified police official in an ill-fitting suit, voice electronically distorted, face blurred and backlit, speaking anonymously to CNN! "Does Monsieur Herriot-Dupont have the confidence any longer of the Executive Committee? I do not know. Does he deserve that confidence? Are the world's police truly behind him? My friend, I cannot anymore say."

Here is Rob Henderson on a hill across the river from Interpol, doing a final stand-up with the headquarters building shimmering far away in the heat haze behind him. "How this will all play out at the Interpol General Assembly in Munich in one week's time is anybody's guess. Secretary General Herriot-Dupont is up for re-election there for another five-year term. Can he weather the current storm and hang onto his job? Can Interpol ever be put back on course? Those are the questions on everybody's lips… This is Rob Henderson, reporting exclusively for CNN *Inside Edition*, from Lyon, France!"

The official reopening of the Interpol bar was, on the other hand, a resounding success. When Franklin finally managed to get away from the telephone ringing incessantly in his office, when he had managed to stagger at last through the double doors of the bar, the festivities, one might say, were in full swing. It seemed as if just about every employee had decided to attend. Except, of course, for Secretary General Didier Herriot-Dupont and the Chief of Staff.

A tsunami of sound – music, clinking glasses, shouted conversations in many languages – washed over Franklin. He headed directly up to the crowded bar. It had been at least thirty minutes since his last drink. He stood there unsteadily, waiting his turn.

Alf Mortman gripped his arm fiercely. The Estonian was swaying and reeking of schnapps.

"What are you doing here, Alf?" Franklin said. "I thought you'd gone to the hospital."

"I did. They told me to rest and relax. I have rested and I've come back in here to relax," Mortman said. "Allow me to buy you a drink."

"Whisky," Franklin said. "Double."

"Double, double, double," Mortman said. He ordered the drink and began humming quietly to himself.

"We are dead men, Alf," Franklin said.

"I was dead before," Mortman said. "I am just a little extra dead now."

"Maybe they won't kill us until after the General Assembly."

"Would that necessarily be a good thing, Franklin, Franklin, dear Franklin?"

"Good point. To your health."

"*Skol.*"

Franklin turned around to face the room, leaning up against the bar. Throngs of police and civilian staff stood in little groups or crowded on chairs around small tables full of glasses and bottles. The No Smoking regulations were being utterly ignored. A miasma of cigarette and cigar and pipe smoke enveloped everything. Far from grieving about the profound implications of what had gone to air that day on television, the gathering looked for all the world like a celebration. How could that be?

People had come to the bar whom Franklin had never seen there in the past. Behold, for example, standing among his Command Centre team, Jean-Marc Moulin, a man who drank very little and never, ever with Interpol subordinates. Tonight, his face was flushed, his tie loosened. Nodding and smiling, he leaned over to hear what an earnest young analyst was telling him over the din. Moulin was clutching a bottle of notoriously strong Belgian beer.

Moulin noticed Franklin watching him from across the room. He raised his beer bottle in Franklin's direction, holding it very high, and nodded slowly. A toast. But a toast to what?

And there was Interpol's Events Manager, Antonio de Caldevilla, holding court with various attractive young secretaries and assistants. He was smoking a very large cigar and gesticulating wildly as he regaled his all-female audience with a long story of some kind. They listened politely, with looks of barely disguised apprehension on their faces, as if they expected Caldevilla to suddenly drop his pretext at social skills and lunge at them murderously with a knife.

Who else? Why, Marianna Ozols, Europol liaison officer, recently back from sick leave and none the worse for wear after a piece of ceiling had fallen on her head. She was dancing energetically with Bruce Mackenzie, the notorious Australian police officer who worked in the stolen passports division. Mackenzie was one of the Interpol officers who had so offended the French police keeping watch from inside their very small car outside the building, the gang whose actions had prompted the bar's closure in the first place. Franklin very much hoped that the Australian and his wild cronies would leave the French cops alone at closing time.

Over there was the lovely and talented Cynthia Payne, the Chief Legal Counsel. What was she doing here? Franklin had never seen her in the bar before. There was André Julien, still in his white chef's smock. And, there, LeBlanc and Buisson, heads of building maintenance and building security, both indirect targets of CNN's attack last night. Hosting large glasses of red wine and laughing uproariously over some shared pleasantry. Did they not realise the very future of the organisation and the career of the Secretary General were now at stake?

"My God!" Franklin said suddenly.

"What, Franklin, what?" Mortman said, his humming and his private reveries rudely interrupted.

"Julia Smith. Over there. Look. With Gilles Broussard."

It was true. There was the Secretary General's wife, wearing a baseball cap, sitting nonchalantly with Broussard and other members of the computer team. All of them were drinking shots of vodka from small glasses. A bottle of the best Serbanian rakia stood in the middle of the table. Ashtrays overflowed with squashed cigarettes. Broussard's yellow cardigan had been slung carelessly over the back of his chair. Julia Smith was shouting something into his ear.

Then the sound in the bar changed abruptly; the volume started to fall. One by one, the standing and seated groups of revellers fell silent. All eyes were now trained on the door. There, in a splendid Italian suit, stood Chief of Staff Freiderikos Milonakis himself. Many cigarettes were hurriedly extinguished. Glasses and bottles were placed gently on tables and bar.

Milonakis had in the past only occasionally come into the staff bar, and only when he needed to gather intelligence. His pattern was to order a glass of mineral water with ice and lime, and discreetly circulate from table to table for perhaps thirty minutes, before elegantly making his exit. Tonight, Milonakis was making what could only be called a grand entrance.

"Colleagues, colleagues," he called out as he stood in the doorway. "Please. I want all of you to carry on enjoying yourselves exactly as before!"

Milonakis called out to the harried chief bartender. "Nicolas! A fresh drink for everyone. I will sign."

There was a collective gasp from the gathered staff, and then a hearty cheer. The waiters bustled around, pouring and shaking and opening things. The noise level immediately surged back to where it had been. Milonakis looked over at Franklin and Mortman, and walked toward them at the bar. Franklin's heart sank.

"Please, no," he whispered.

Mortman's humming stopped. Franklin had had a number of heated conversations with Milonakis since the CNN report went to air. They had been in constant telephone contact. But the Secretary General, Milonakis had informed key colleagues, was still making up his mind about how to respond. For the moment, Didier Herriot-Dupont was speaking only to Milonakis. He had not emerged from his office.

Milonakis stood between Franklin and Mortman at the bar. He seemed remarkably calm, giving off the aura of a man resigned, a man at peace.

"I think, gentlemen, that it's time for me to have a drink," he said.

Milonakis ordered an ouzo. Not mineral water. A startled barman brought it immediately.

The Chief of Staff was in a very strange mood. He lit a cigarette, took a puff, inhaled deeply. He raised his glass to Franklin and Mortman.

"I would like to propose a toast," he said quietly.

Franklin raised his whisky. Mortman raised his glass of schnapps.

"A toast," Milonakis said. "Before all else, be armed…"

TWELVE

When Secretary General Herriot-Dupont emerged from seclusion, his first action was to call an emergency meeting of all senior staff, an emergency SSM. Those invited to attend trudged apprehensively into the Interpol boardroom, expecting the meeting to be even more S&M than usual. It was the day after the reopening of the staff bar, and all were hung over to varying degrees. They resembled participants in some highly questionable medical experiment examining the effects of alcohol on the human body and mind.

The agenda, which had arrived that morning in everyone's email inbox, was unusually short – ominously short. Herriot-Dupont's agendas for senior staff meetings often ran to two pages or more. This one simply said:

1. *Interpol response to CNN report.*
2. *Preparations for General Assembly.*

Meeting participants looked at each other uneasily. An agenda this short meant there was no place to hide. Coffees and other restoratives were sipped cautiously, mints and antacid tablets chewed meditatively.

Around the table were Milonakis, sitting as always to the Secretary General's right hand, Chief Legal Counsel Cynthia Payne, Jean-Marc Moulin, Mortman, Franklin, Events Manager Antonio de Caldevilla and Security Chief Bernard LeBlanc. The Secretary General, at the head of the table, was wearing a black suit: a very bad sign indeed.

At first, DHD said nothing. He merely looked slowly around the table, meeting the gaze of each member of his senior staff in turn. He came to Franklin last. He locked eyes with the Assistant Director of Media Relations. It was a death stare. Still he said nothing. Franklin stopped chewing his breath mint. He appeared to stop breathing. If the wordless encounter had been filmed, it would be of incalculable value for zoological researchers everywhere.

Finally, Herriot-Dupont broke the silence.

"Who would want to wreck Interpol?" he asked in a loud voice.

No one answered.

"Who are my enemies?"

There was an embarrassed silence. Where to start? No one around the table dared speak.

"You are my senior advisors," DHD said. "How have things been allowed to deteriorate in this way?"

Still no one spoke.

"Cynthia," the Secretary General said finally. "What are our legal options?"

"About the CNN report?" Payne said.

"Yes, yes, of course about the CNN report," DHD barked.

"We would have a very hard time making a case for defamation, sir, I regret to say. This is a very tricky area of the law, especially in France."

"My allegedly lavish lifestyle? Jet-setting around the world? Bizarre late-night rituals? My projects of allegedly questionable law enforcement value?"

"The reporter cited sources inside the organisation, sir. A judge would almost certainly see this as fair comment on a matter of public interest."

"Fair comment?!" DHD shouted.

"In law, of course. In law. Interpol is a well-known institution. You are a public figure. The test for defamation is quite rigorous in such cases."

"You disappoint me, Cynthia," the Secretary General said.

Mortman, extremely red in the face and sweating alarmingly, said quietly, "Pursuing them would just add fuel to the fire, sir. Draw more attention to the report. In my humble opinion."

"I agree with Alf," Payne said.

"Um, me too," Franklin said.

"You disappoint me, Alf," DHD said. "You all disappoint me. And you, Franklin, you disappoint me most of all. How could this disaster have been allowed to happen? You're a journalist, you were assigned to generate a positive story about Interpol."

"That's hard to do sometimes," Franklin said weakly. "Especially for TV. That guy Henderson was tough. He knew what he wanted before he even got here."

"Agreed," Mortman said.

"Franklin, we are one week away from the General Assembly. I unfortunately still need your services at this point. And I cannot afford another negative story in the press if I fire you. So until further notice you are still my Assistant Director for Media Relations. Then we shall see. Until then, it is your task, and Mortman's, and that of all of your staff, to make sure all coverage of this organisation, in all countries, is positive at all times. And all coverage of the General Assembly is to be positive. Do you understand?"

"Bravo!" Caldevilla said. "Bravo, Secretary General!"

"Yes, sir," Franklin said.

Mortman nodded sadly.

"That's a pretty tall order for these people, Secretary General," Payne said. "In my humble opinion."

Herriot-Dupont locked eyes with his Chief Legal Counsel, but she did not flinch. Cynthia Payne was eminently employable elsewhere, and knew it.

"So how are we to respond?" DHD asked the room. "Are we to just do nothing at all?"

"That's what I would recommend," Mortman said.

"Me too," Franklin said. "Say no to all interview requests. We should just say you're not going to be available."

"Have there been interview requests?" the Secretary General asked. "Since the CNN report?"

"About a dozen so far," Franklin said.

"From around the world," Mortman said.

Chief of Staff Milonakis had so far been unusually silent. He had watched the scene unfold before him with an air of detachment, or resignation. This was not like him at all.

"I can call key members of the Executive Committee," Milonakis now said. "I'll explain that the TV story is inaccurate. Bad journalism. If they've seen it at all."

"They will have seen it, Freiderikos," DHD said.

"Possibly," Milonakis said.

"You can't call all delegates to the General Assembly," DHD said. "EC members maybe, but not delegates."

"I can call some of the key delegations," Milonakis said.

This seemed to soothe the Secretary General somewhat.

"We will need success stories," he said. "Now more than ever."

"Agreed," Milonakis said.

"Jean-Marc," DHD said, "where are my law enforcement success stories? For the General Assembly."

Moulin, too, had an air of weary resignation about him. "We are doing our best, sir. Police work is—"

"I know all there is to know about police work, Jean-Marc," DHD shouted.

Moulin said nothing.

"You have nothing to report? What about my terrorism watch lists?"

"The numbers are growing slowly."

"Too slowly, Jean-Marc. And what about X-24GT? Are all countries now connected?"

"Not yet, sir. We still have problems in Africa. And in some Latin American countries."

"Not good enough! Not good enough! I need to announce in Munich that everyone is connected to our improved communications system!"

Moulin was again silent. He sat stony-faced, clearly trying to contain his anger.

"And are you still against me on the sponsorship programme, Jean-Marc?"

"I am, sir, yes," Moulin said. "Police won't like that idea. They won't understand how companies can sponsor police work."

"I agree," said Cynthia Payne. "They can understand new things like the new bioterrorism project, maybe. Just maybe."

"I'm not even sure of that, Cynthia," Moulin said.

"The what?" DHD said.

"Your bioterrorism training project," Payne said.

"Oh, I've dropped that. Weeks ago," the Secretary General said. "That's been dropped."

"I wasn't aware," Payne said.

"Nor I," Milonakis said.

"I wasn't either," Moulin said.

"We've been doing up publicity materials and a training video for police," Mortman said. "Things are almost finished."

"Dropped," DHD said. "That programme has been dropped."

Milonakis wrote something in his notebook. Moulin did as well.

"The General Assembly preparations?" DHD said. "What are the remaining issues?"

"All is very good," Events Manager Caldevilla sang out. "The German police band has been given the Interpol anthem to practise. The police honour guard has been selected. All is extremely excellent."

Herriot-Dupont looked over at Milonakis. "Have they, ah, been checked?" he asked.

"Checked?" Caldevilla asked. "For what?"

"Yes, all checked, Secretary General," Milonakis said.

"There is Zimwabse, sir," Payne said. "That's getting complicated."

"Yes," Milonakis said.

"Some of the European member countries say they really can't attend if the Zimwabse police chief attends," Payne said. "The

European Union sanctions against Zimwabse are—"

"They will attend," DHD said. "They're bluffing."

"I'm not sure they will, sir," Milonakis said.

"The Germans may not even grant Commissioner Matonga a visa," Payne said. "I very much doubt they will."

"That is undemocratic," DHD said. "Interpol is apolitical. Everyone knows that. Josiah Matonga is Zimwabse's most senior police officer, with every right to attend an international conference. I won't hear of any such interference in Interpol's internal affairs. It's an outrage to the African delegates. They'll be highly offended. We must stand on principle. It's a matter of principle."

"That's not quite how the Europeans see it, where Zimwabse is concerned," Payne said.

"That's not how the *Tempo of London* newspaper sees it," Franklin said. "They're still on the warpath. You've seen their stories in the press digest."

"Is the *Tempo* attending the General Assembly?" DHD asked.

"Two of their guys are accredited already. Their Munich guy and their senior political reporter from London."

"Will CNN be there?"

"Absolutely," Franklin said.

Herriot-Dupont looked over at his Chief of Staff.

"I can make a call to Matonga," Milonakis said.

"Try to explain the situation to him," DHD said. "I can speak to him if that will help. I hope he hasn't already bought his plane ticket."

As punishment, Frank Franklin was assigned by Milonakis the impossible task of editing and shortening and polishing and making sense of the Secretary General's keynote speech for Munich. Milonakis handed him the latest draft after the senior staff meeting, saying only, "Fix this. By tomorrow."

Both knew that the Secretary General was sure to be outraged and offended by any changes made, and that the changes would never be used in any case. Herriot-Dupont had taken Alf Mortman's first draft and altered it unrecognisably. It now ran to roughly one hour and fifteen minutes. The Secretary General's speaking slot at the Munich Assembly was to be twenty minutes.

The text was now an unfettered ramble through the history of international police cooperation, the origins of Interpol in the 1920s, the Secretary General's boyhood in bucolic Normandy and his determination to have a law enforcement career, his early years in the French police, and his eventual triumph in the election as Interpol head five years ago.

Then the speech lurched into a self-congratulatory listing of Interpol's many new ventures and alleged achievements under Herriot-Dupont. In the section entitled *Latest success stories*, however, were only the words: *To come ASAP, via Press Office and Moulin*. There was much on the new sponsorship idea, and much about terrorism watch lists. But the Secretary General had forgotten to delete paragraphs about the now-aborted bioterrorism project. This yielded Franklin's first, relatively simple, edit.

The rest of the job would take hours. And the Secretary General had ordered up dozens of costly news agency photos and video clips illustrating the crime and terrorism problems plaguing the globe. Only one or two of these, if any, would ever actually be used for the speech. Sourcing the images would be another onerous task. Franklin knew he would not be sleeping that night. He opened a bottle of excellent Burgundy and in a cupboard found his lucky wine glass, without which he could never work on a Herriot-Dupont speech. He sat alone at his desk in his small office, gazing wistfully from time to time out over the Rhone.

Mortman came in, clutching the latest press digest.

"Is it bad?" Franklin asked.

"*Le Monde* has now picked up the CNN story. And the Lyon paper. It's still getting picked up in a lot of other countries. But it's not as bad as yesterday," Mortman said.

"Thank God."

"There is no God, Franklin."

"Steady, Alf. Don't let things get to you. Your doctor said to take it easy."

Mortman appeared to brighten up slightly. "The doctor says now that I shouldn't go to Munich. He's given me a letter."

"Alf, you're joking."

"I'm sorry, Franklin. The doctor says my heart can't take the stress of a General Assembly."

"*This* General Assembly."

"Any General Assembly."

"I can't do it alone, Alf. The reporters will eat me up and spit me out."

"Take a couple of extra press officers. You should take Phoebe. She would be happy to go."

"Phoebe's not very tough, Alf."

"She's smart."

"I don't think she could take the stress. Look how she operated when CNN was here. When that cameraman said boo she just caved in. She's not experienced enough for this sort of stuff. I need you up there with me."

"I'm sorry, my friend. Doctor's orders."

"This is going to kill me, Alf."

"Yes," Mortman said. "Probably."

Milonakis was pacing around in his office, plotting and scheming. His main concern now was to head off catastrophe in Munich. But he knew that the main battlefront was Serbania, followed by the DHD marital front.

What is that shifty Serbanian reprobate really up to? Milonakis thought over and over again. What's his real game? Is it just to keep the Secretary General off guard in Munich, to stop him from looking good in front of delegates? To pave the way for a real challenge next time around? Or was Dragusha actually planning to spark some sort of floor challenge to DHD's re-election itself?

There were a number of ways that Dragusha could be stopped.

But they were not without risk. Especially in Germany. Having him arrested in the hotel for storing child pornography on his computer, for example, could quite likely be arranged. Broussard, a naïve fool, could quite likely be enlisted to help with that. But the German police would take such a matter perhaps a little too seriously, and the world media covering the General Assembly would almost certainly get wind of it. *Interpol Executive Committee Member Arrested Over Child Porn.* No, maybe not.

Maybe a prostitute discovered in Dragusha's room, then? Better still, an underage prostitute, say one from the Philippines, or Turkey. That would take virtually no arranging at all, given Dragusha's record at past Interpol gatherings. A discreet call to the BKA was all it would take. A quick vice squad raid, Dragusha detained – probably not charged, simply deported. Yes? But what about the media? That risk remained.

Illness? Hmm. Yes, perhaps illness. A police officer of Dragusha's age could surely not be expected to attend the General Assembly sessions if he was not well. Nothing serious, of course. A nasty little stomach bug, yes? Food poisoning, what a shame. Surely just something he ate or drank, no doubt. Rest in bed, drink fluids, stay near the toilet. Hmm. Milonakis was no doctor. But surely something like this could be arranged? Those damn Germans, however, were far too fastidious, and Germany was far too hygienic a place for this to be easy. How would one get a little faecal contamination into the Serbanian's food at the InterContinental Hotel in Munich? Difficult.

Milonakis consulted a small notebook, looked at his watch; then picked up the phone. He dialled Dragusha's office in Virana.

"Valon? Valon, it's Freiderikos Milonakis… Yes, fine, I'm fine, thanks… Look, Valon, I'm just checking in before the General Assembly. As I normally would… Yes. But also in this case to ask if you've seen that foul, despicable CNN report. You have? And? Your thoughts on this?"

Milonakis drummed his fingers on his desk and rolled his eyes as he listened to the Serbanian profess dismay at the other end.

"Agreed. Agreed," Milonakis said. "And we are trying to limit the damage, of course, at my end. My press team is on this as a matter of urgency."

Milonakis listened again, then said, "Valon, tell me something. You are a man whose finger is on the pulse of your region. So tell me. Who do you think that unidentified source from Eastern Europe was in the CNN report, the one who spoke with his face blocked out and his voice distorted? Any idea who that might have been, Valon?"

Listening. Then: "No idea at all? That's too bad. Because, as you know, the Secretary General values the loyalty of his colleagues above all else. He values loyalty, and he rewards it. As I do also. But you know that already, don't you, Valon? I hardly need to tell you this, correct?"

Milonakis shifted the telephone receiver to his other ear.

"The person responsible for that anonymous comment will of course know that also, wouldn't you say, Valon? Given the Secretary General's reputation, and mine. We will of course find out eventually who made those comments and we will, how shall I put it, come crashing down on the offender. We will ruin him, Valon. We will crush him absolutely. We will do whatever it takes. I will make it my mission in life to crush him. Do you follow me? I hope the person responsible knows how very, very angry the Secretary General and I are about this, Valon. Do you think the person would know that?"

Listening. Then: "Well, do call me if you have any questions or issues whatsoever in the next few days, in the run-up to Munich. Anything whatsoever, alright? And tell me, Valon, what day are you planning to arrive at the hotel? What time, approximately? And are you bringing your wife?"

Milonakis sat quietly for a moment after the phone call ended, drumming his fingers on the desk. He pressed his other hand, clenched into a fist, up against his lips and nose. He was the picture of malevolent concentration. He once again consulted his notebook, looked at his watch and dialled another number.

"Yoko Watanabe, please," he said. "This is a call from Interpol headquarters."

He was made to wait only a moment.

"Yoko? Fred Milonakis here… How is the weather in Tokyo? How is your husband? How are all the little Watanabes?"

The Secretary General, too, had been sitting at his desk that morning, plotting and scheming. Now, however, he was worrying. His bodyguard had just informed him that dear Julia was taking a sudden interest in target shooting. That she had insisted on being driven to the police shooting range for a practice session, using a .357 calibre Sig. Even allowing for the fact that his wife was American, or perhaps because of the fact she was American, this had to be seen as significant news.

"She is a very good shot, *monsieur*," Francois had said. "The instructor was quite impressed. I was also. And Serge, the driver."

"You should have reported this to me first, Francois," DHD said. "Before you went. Not after."

"Madame Julia insisted, *monsieur*," Francois said. "She told us you had approved this. I'm sorry, *monsieur*. Next time I will—"

"There will be no next time, Francois. Do you understand?"

"*Oui, monsieur*. Understood."

Herriot-Dupont sat for a long time, lost in thought. Things were deteriorating, this much was clear. The question was, how had things been allowed to get to this state? Who was to blame? Whom could he blame? Who could be punished, humiliated, flayed alive, executed, made an example of?

With the General Assembly now just days away, DHD felt the cold dread of someone no longer in absolute control. Who was still to be trusted? Who could still make sure he was unanimously re-elected?

He consulted a little notebook, looked at his watch, then picked up the phone. He dialled a number.

"Gilles? Hello, it's Didier," he said cheerily. "Are you well, my friend? Yes? Very good. Good. And tell me, Gilles, how are you enjoying the car? Is this one large enough for your needs? Your wife is pleased with it, I hope…"

*

The Secretary General of Interpol cannot be expected to work all the time. Even the Secretary General of the world's largest international police organisation needs rest and recreation from time to time. After his session of plotting and scheming and worrying and phoning, Herriot-Dupont's thoughts turned to relaxation.

He thought, of course, of young Evangeline. But Evangeline, unfortunately, would be in a classroom at Université de Lyon at this hour, or hurrying to her class clutching books and papers so sweetly against her lovely little breasts. No, there could be no consolations of that sort just now. Perhaps a little kendo instead to help him unwind? Yes, why not?

He went from his office to his apartment through the door behind his desk. It was quiet inside, safe; a private haven. He changed into a black silk kimono and went out into the living room to select a gun from the wall racks. Today, he thought, a rifle might be the thing, not a shotgun.

He selected a nice example of the Mauser 66 7x57, the rare commemorative edition given to him by a grateful Interior Minister of Kazakhstan for services rendered. He stroked its glowing wood and perfect barrel bluing. This one did not have the usual bulky telescopic sight attached, so it made a perfect substitute for the *shinai* sword. DHD was already starting to feel himself relax.

As always, for those very few who had ever seen him practise, the visual effect of a stocky, silver-maned Normand peasant dressed in a kimono and swinging a rifle in graceful kendo arcs, was, to say the least, memorable. Herriot-Dupont was the picture of concentration, his years of diligent practice immediately apparent as he went through his routines in front of the floor-to-ceiling mirror. Troubles and the burdens of high law enforcement office were, for the moment, forgotten.

Suddenly, the tranquillity was shattered. The door to the private elevator opened and into the room strode Julia Smith. She was as startled as her husband, and both froze. But the Secretary General, on this occasion, was the one who was armed. Madame DHD looked apprehensively at the menacing Mauser brandished before her by a sweating man in a silk kimono.

"Julia, my dear, how good to see you," Herriot-Dupont said. "Don't be alarmed, this isn't loaded, ha ha. But it is a lovely weapon, wouldn't you say?"

"I'd forgotten how you like to do your kendo with a gun instead of sword, Didier. I just forgot, that's all."

They stood silently facing each other across a carpeted no man's land. It was another in their recent series of awkward marital moments. Herriot-Dupont dismissed the fleeting thought that his wife was about to lunge at the wall racks and grab a rifle or shotgun of her own. Nonsense, he chided himself. And nothing's loaded in here anyway.

"François tells me you have been to the shooting range, my dear," DHD said. "So you can't be that nervous around guns, I would say. And there was that lovely gun you brought me from Washington as a little gift. My first handgun. Very thoughtful."

"I told François you wouldn't mind, Didier," Julia said. "I hope he's not in any trouble."

"No, no, not at all. He was just surprised by your request. As was I."

"Oh, I just find it fun to shoot once in a while. It's relaxing in a way. You know. Takes your mind off things."

"I see."

"It's kind of how we Americans relax, I guess you could say."

Husband and wife eyed each other silently; then each laughed nervously.

"And why are you using the elevator to the garage, my dear?" asked Herriot-Dupont, a man given increasingly to paranoia. "Were you at the shooting range again this afternoon? Or on some other top secret mission elsewhere, perhaps?"

Frank Franklin took a little walk. He had writer's block. He went up to Jean-Marc Moulin's office on the fourth floor. He could arrive unannounced at the office of the Director of Operational Police

Support because they were friends and allies. Despite occasional professional disagreements. Franklin would visit Moulin from time to time and they could commiserate, even though Franklin was not a policeman.

"I'm not surprised to see you up here," Moulin said. "I've been expecting you."

Moulin's office was filled with memorabilia, just as one would expect for a policeman with thirty-seven years' experience. Police badges and pennants from many countries, ball caps received as gifts, a set of handcuffs in a frame, operational photos, conference photos, trophies, award plaques. He watched as Franklin made his usual inspection of the items on walls and shelves. He looked as morose as Franklin on this occasion.

"If you were a policeman instead of a slippery little journalist you might have interesting souvenirs too, Frank," Moulin said.

"I'm no journalist anymore, Jean-Marc," Franklin said. "I'm the Secretary General's hired gun. His fiction man."

"As I am, unfortunately," Moulin said.

"I'm working on his General Assembly speech. I don't know what to write."

"He won't use your speech anyway, Frank. Don't waste your time."

"I have to write something."

"Make something up."

They both laughed ruefully.

"I hear you're not speaking this time, Jean-Marc."

"That is correct."

"Why not?"

"Ask the Secretary General."

"You pissed off?"

Moulin raised an eyebrow. "No comment. That's what I was trained to say to journalists in Belgium when I was just starting out."

"That's not quite how it came out on CNN the other night, Jean-Marc. Not quite."

They both laughed ruefully again.

"I liked the bit where you put your hand over the lens," Franklin said. "That was the best bit. Is that what they trained you to do in Belgium also?"

"Please," Moulin said.

"Jean-Marc, you've got to help me out. Seriously. I've got to write something. Maybe we can talk the Secretary General into saying something in his speech that won't make things worse. If he can say something sensible. And keep it short."

"Good luck, my friend."

"What were you going to say in your speech, Jean-Marc?"

"No comment."

"Come on. Help me out."

Moulin stood up suddenly behind his desk. "Ladies and gentlemen, thank you all for being here today in Munich," he said in his best public speaking voice. "Ahem. Real police work is a very simple matter. It is to find and apprehend wrongdoers. That is all."

Moulin sat down again.

"Can I quote you on that?" Franklin said.

"It's your career, my friend."

The Assistant Director of Interpol's computer department rolled up to the gates of the world's largest international police organisation in grand style. It was a brilliant blue-sky Southern France afternoon. Broussard was at the wheel of a magnificent jet black Citroen C6, a very large sedan with delusions of limousine. He looked a picture of health and confidence, with his modern new hairstyle and his chic new eyeglasses – repaired since the little incident at the InterContinental in Munich – and his fetching yellow cardigan.

Each and every member of the Interpol front gate security detail rushed out of the squat reception building to admire their colleague's new automobile, and of course to perform the requisite checks for explosives, weapons and contraband.

"*Mon dieu*, Gilles, what has happened to your little Renault Clio?"

Security Chief Bernard LeBlanc called out. "It is all grown up now. An adult car, no longer a baby!"

Broussard climbed out while guards shoved mirrors under the vehicle and opened hood and trunk to look inside. Another guard sat behind the wheel and turned up the radio very high. He beeped the horn a few times. A small crowd of Interpol staffers returning from lunchtime strolls began to gather around.

"*Mes chers amis, chers amis*, please, it is just a car. Please," Broussard said proudly. "I was the first winner of the Interpol staff excellence award, as you all know. Please. Please."

"But Gilles, that award was a little Clio, no?" LeBlanc said. "Not a Citroen C6."

The crowd murmured.

"My wife Claudette and I found that the Clio did not meet our needs," Broussard said. "*Monsieur le Secrétaire Général* kindly agreed that it could be replaced."

"*Eh bien, mon dieu,*" LeBlanc said.

The crowd murmured. Someone called out, "And so are you running now for the post of Secretary General, Gilles? Will that be next? You could take that car with you up to Munich."

The crowd guffawed. Broussard dismissed such wild speculation with a good-natured wave of his hand. At that moment, two of Milonakis' spies peeled off from the crowd, independently and simultaneously. Data compiler Chantalle Duquesne and criminal analyst Javier Herrera both hurriedly dialled numbers on their mobile phones. Both stood waiting in the sunshine, looking up to the windows on the Interpol headquarters' fifth floor.

THIRTEEN

For many of the world's most senior police officials, and particularly those from developing nations, an Interpol General Assembly is their annual opportunity to enjoy business-class flights to an attractive capital city somewhere, stay in a five-star hotel on a generous expense account, meet cop colleagues from dozens of nations, sample the local night life, do some extravagant shopping and, almost as an afterthought, debate a range of weighty law enforcement issues. Every fifth year, the festivities take on an even more exciting aura, as this is when a sitting Secretary General is up for re-election or a new one will be selected.

The excitement is increased further, some years, in some host countries, when elaborate corporate sales stands are erected in a massive venue near the conference hotel by multinational companies peddling expensive toys for the police. In Munich, the toy show was in a congress centre a short distance away from the InterContinental. Manufacturers of pistols and rifles and bullets, stun guns, handcuffs, tear gas, police boots, badges, batons, stab vests, sirens, spotlights, walkie-talkies, eavesdropping equipment, water cannon, patrol cars, even armoured personnel carriers – anything on a police officer's wish list – had set up shop and would watch in delight as chiefs and officials from around the globe placed large orders for the necessities of law enforcement life.

Not surprisingly, then, many national delegations arrived early for General Assemblies. And many delegations included, in addition to chiefs and commissioners and commanders, an array of wives, mistresses, powerful or deserving government types, and various other flunkies and hangers-on. Some delegations, on the other hand, were quite small; just two or three people, depending on the country in question, the level of police or government corruption, and the seriousness with which the local cops took their financial and law enforcement responsibilities.

Munich was no exception. Several days before the General Assembly was to begin, national delegations began to roll up to the hotel in gleaming black vans dispatched to the airport by the German federal police. Some of the African countries were well represented among the early arrivals – Ngheria, for example – and some from Latin America. Kazakhstan was usually among the first to arrive at any General Assembly, and Belarus, two countries with a particular reputations for big spending on entertainment, and on semi-automatic weapons or other thoughtful gifts for their riot squads.

The Belixicans also arrived early in Munich. A large rented truck rolled up to the hotel behind the German police van. The Commander of the *Polícia Federal* himself, Alonso Gomez, in uniform, supervised the unloading of dozens of cardboard cartons from the truck. Rumour had it that these boxes contained handsome gifts and favours for every delegation, to be distributed over the next several days. Rumour also had it that Commander Gomez would in Munich well and truly launch his bid for a seat on the Interpol Executive Committee.

And of course, this year the Serbanians arrived early. Valon Dragusha, as always wearing his favourite burgundy suit (he would only wear his splendid lanyard-encrusted police uniform once a General Assembly was formally underway) bounded out of his van followed by a relatively small entourage: a Deputy Chief of Police, two saturnine Interior Ministry officials and their wives, a burly, unidentified gentleman sporting very dark Ray-Ban Wayfarer sunglasses, and a willowy young woman. This was Dragusha's personal assistant, said to be a former Miss Serbania.

Interpol Chief of Staff Freiderikos Milonakis had stationed himself under the hotel's lofty driveway awning to greet his Serbanian colleague. He stepped forward to grasp Dragusha's hand and shake it vigorously.

"Valon, my friend, welcome to Munich," Milonakis said warmly. "We have some very important police business to attend to over the next few days."

"Agreed, agreed, Freddie, yes!" Dragusha shouted.

"You are well, I hope?" Milonakis said.

"I am. I am fighting fit, as my lovely assistant will attest," Dragusha said. "Is this correct, Ardiana? I keep you very busy, do I not? Freddie, she does not speak much English, I'm sorry to say."

Ardiana flicked her long black hair and extended her pale hand to Milonakis. He kissed it.

"*Faleminderit shumë*," she said.

"Police officer?" Milonakis asked her.

Ardiana turned her head toward Dragusha. "*Ç'është ky?*" she said.

"*Mos u bëj merak*, Ardiana," Dragusha said. "No, Fred, she is not. Or perhaps she is very, very deeply undercover! Ha ha, Fred? Haha!"

The former Miss Serbania looked bewildered.

"Cover, Valon? Or covers?" Milonakis asked with a wink.

"Ha, Fred. Ha!" Dragusha shouted.

"Drinks this evening, Valon? Let's meet in the cocktail lounge, I will buy you an ouzo or two," Milonakis said. "There is much to discuss."

"Police business only, of course."

"Of course."

"And my little friend Broussard, he will join us, no?" Dragusha said.

"We'll have to see," Milonakis said. "He's a very busy man."

Inside the hotel, Interpol Events Manager Antonio de Caldevilla was carrying a clipboard and looking for someone to humiliate. But the German police had done such an excellent job of preparing, and of anticipating all possible requirements and eventualities, that Caldevilla was hard-pressed to find a victim. And the BKA officers assigned to oversee preparations were not people who cried easily, if at all.

Caldevilla spied Adolph Fenstermacher in the lobby and went over to him with a question.

"Our welcome sign, Officer Fenstermacher?" Caldevilla said.

Interpol always arranged for a giant banner to be hung from the front of the General Assembly host hotel, emblazoned in the organisation's four official languages with words to the effect of: *Welcome to the World's Police.* Every year this was the subject of much debate, inside Interpol and among those in host countries who were uneasy about advertising to terrorists and other ne'er-do-wells that police chiefs from some 190 countries were all sitting down together in one place.

Fenstermacher was one of those who thought such advertising of police business to be unwise.

"It will be installed at the last moment, as agreed," he said curtly.

"I was not consulted," Caldevilla said.

"Clearly not," Fenstermacher said.

Caldevilla pored over his clipboard. "Water glasses for all delegates?" he said.

"Do you think the *Bundeskriminalamt* would forget about the importance of delegates' hydration requirements, Mr Caldevilla?" Fenstermacher said, his right hand going unconsciously to his hip where he would be carrying a sidearm if in uniform.

"Just checking," Caldevilla said haughtily.

At that moment, the Zambezin police delegation arrived in the lobby. Among them was Miss Namwene Mwanze, niece of Zambezi's Interior Minister. Ms Mwanze was not crying on this occasion. However, when she spotted Caldevilla she froze. She whispered something to an elegant uniformed police officer walking beside her. The officer turned to look over at Caldevilla and Fenstermacher, and glared menacingly.

"Trouble," the Interpol Events Manager said. "Africans."

"I beg your pardon?" Fenstermacher said.

Caldevilla chose that moment to hurry off to the Interpol souvenir stand, always set up in hotel lobbies for General Assemblies. His youngest secretary was expected to be on duty at the stand virtually non-stop for the next few days, selling a range of Interpol-branded sweatshirts, pens, beer steins, bottle openers, coffee mugs and ash trays. Visiting police snapped up these items, as well as hundreds of bottles of Cuvée d'Interpol wine, with their brightly coloured labels showing an aerial view of the Lyon headquarters building. That the red and white Côtes du Rhône wine on offer in any given year was of extremely dubious quality seemed of little importance to delegates, such was the Interpol mystique.

Caldevilla's youngest secretary could always be driven to tears; he knew this from long experience. He fired a couple of warning shots her way to make sure she understood what was ahead.

"Solange, Solange, do you have no idea how close we are to the opening?" Caldevilla shouted. "Surely you don't think this display is in any way ready for the first day?"

Solange, gratifyingly, stood trembling as she waited for more verbal blows to rain down.

Inside the cavernous main conference hall, hotel staff and German police still scurried around, though to the unpractised eye it appeared that all was ready, that the ghost of Albert Speer had worked his event-staging magic. Frank Franklin, reasonably sober, was performing yet another walk-through, inspecting preparations and imagining disaster scenarios. He was accompanied by young Phoebe Jackson, on her first foreign mission for Interpol.

"The TV crews will be on those risers at the back, Phoebe, but just for the opening ceremony," Franklin said. "Then things go into closed session and you'll have to escort all of them out as fast as you can."

"That's going to be a bit hard," Phoebe said.

"Just tell them it's time to go. We'll have briefed them before. They'll know they can't shoot during the closed sessions."

"What if they don't want to go?"

"Phoebe, for Christ's sake, you'll just have to make sure they do go."

"Where will you be?"

"I don't know. Running around somewhere else in the hall, probably."

"I'll call you on your mobile if it starts to get crazy."

Two uniformed German policemen brushed by them with a straining sniffer dog on a stout leather leash. The dog stopped briefly to sniff their feet and legs and Phoebe's small backpack.

"No bombs in there!" Franklin said.

The cops were not at all amused. They carried on without a word.

"What happens if they actually do find something?" Phoebe said.

"Call your mum in Vancouver really fast and then run for the exit. Or maybe run first and call her after. Maybe that's the way."

They headed up onto the main stage. Franklin checked that a little platform had been constructed for the Secretary General to stand on. The German carpenter had done a splendid job, giving the carefully sanded wood a coat of lacquer and stapling a little square of red carpet on top. Franklin tested it out. It made him six inches taller and far more imposing at the podium.

"See, Phoebe?" he said, grinning. "This is going to make my career."

Adolph Fenstermacher came up to join them. "All is in proper order, Mr Franklin," he said. He paid no attention at all to Phoebe.

"Yes, thanks, looks good to me," Franklin said.

"Will everyone stand on that thing?" Phoebe said. "What if they're already tall?"

"We've got that figured out already, thanks to Officer Fenstermacher here."

"Chief Inspector Fenstermacher," Fenstermacher said.

"Right, of course, sorry," Franklin said. "Look, Chief Inspector, sorry but just a last question about the honour guard and the security detail—"

"Yes, yes, yes, yes, as we have told you before, all will be of average height. It is arranged," Fenstermacher said.

Phoebe smiled. Fenstermacher glared at her and then at Franklin. Franklin glared at Phoebe only.

"And average height in German is what, approximately?" Franklin asked. "Just approximately."

"Please," Fenstermacher said.

"OK, alright, sorry. I'm just a bit of a details guy," Franklin said.

"As am I," Fenstermacher hissed. "And all of my BKA colleagues. Always."

Franklin left Phoebe in the main hall. He went out into the lobby where another of his press officers, a bespectacled young Brit, was manning the press accreditation desk.

"Any media so far, Stanley?" Franklin asked. "Tell me there's none as early as this."

"A couple, Frank," Stanley said. "But that CNN guy Henderson is one of them."

"Christ," Frank said. "Where is he now?"

"In the press room. With his cameraman. The camera guy is a bit of a strange one."

"Christ."

On his way to the press room, Franklin ran into Milonakis near the hotel reception desk.

"CNN is here," Franklin said.

"Henderson?"

"Yup."

"I'll speak to him," Milonakis said. "I've been wanting to speak to him."

"Fred, no, I don't think so. Let's just let him do his work like any other reporter who's coming. That's the best way, I think."

"I want to have a word with him, Frank."

"Easy does it, Fred."

Henderson and Jacoby were lounging in the press room with a couple of German local reporters, and the Agence France-Presse correspondent in Munich. Henderson was sipping on a can of Coke.

Jacoby was smoking a little cigar. There was no sign of the depressive CNN sound man. Henderson jumped up when he saw Franklin and Milonakis come in.

"Hey Frankie, how's tricks, buddy?" Henderson said, offering his hand. "I figured you'd be in Munich."

Franklin shook his hand. "This is Freiderikos Milonakis, Rob. The Chief of Staff."

Henderson offered his hand to Milonakis. Milonakis did not offer his.

"Yeah, sure, Fred Milonakis," Henderson said. "Too bad we didn't get a chance to talk while I was in Lyon, Fred."

"There are other people you should have talked to as well," Milonakis said. "The Secretary General, for example."

"Yeah, that was a shame, we just sort of ran out of time. I guess you guys weren't too happy with my piece, right? I kinda figured you'd call us up after it went to air."

"I did try," Franklin said. "Your producer wouldn't give me your mobile number."

"Here we go," Jacoby said, exhaling a stream of acrid cigar smoke. "Battle stations! A-oogha! A-oogha!"

The AFP man looked up from his laptop.

"Surely you don't think your report was fair and accurate, Henderson. Surely not," Milonakis said quietly. When he was angry, his voice got very low. Franklin had seen this before.

"It told a story," Henderson said.

"You did Interpol a disservice, my friend," Milonakis said.

"So does the SG want to do an interview, maybe? Try to set the record straight?"

"You can't be serious," Milonakis said.

"Sure I'm serious. Right of reply. Hear his side of the story."

"A bit late for that, Rob, wouldn't you say?" Franklin said.

"Naw, never too late," Henderson said. "Unless you're now refusing to put the SG forward."

"Henderson…" Milonakis said.

"We're not refusing. He's just not going to be available," Franklin said.

"Secretary General Didier Herriot-Dupont refused on Tuesday to comment on allegations of…"

"Henderson…" Milonakis said, his voice even lower.

"A-oogha!" Jacoby said. "A-oogha! Take cover, Robbie boy."

At that moment the *Tempo of London*'s Christopher Winslow-Hague walked into the press room, wearing an emerald green blazer.

"Aha, Franklin, just the man," Winslow-Hague said. "What's the latest on the Zimwabse matter? Will Matonga attend?"

"What's up with Zimwabse, Frankie?" Henderson asked.

Jacoby reached for his bulky camera and hoisted it to his shoulder. The AFP man walked over to join the group, carrying his notebook. Milonakis tried to put his hand over Jacoby's lens.

"Easy does it, Freiderikos," Franklin said.

"Rolling," Jacoby said.

The InterContinental's cocktail lounge on the night before the General Assembly was fashionably dim, all surfaces shimmering discreetly in shades of polished black, red and silver. A plump woman with unruly blonde hair and wearing a black ankle-length dress generated vaguely recognisable melodies on a grand piano and occasionally burst into unintelligible, heavily accented song. The room was filling up fast with police from dozens of nations and their associates. Weighty law enforcement matters were being debated in many languages. Some alcoholic beverages were being consumed.

In a cramped circular booth done up in tufted red vinyl sat Milonakis, Dragusha, the former Miss Serbania and Gilles Broussard. Frank Franklin was not among them. He was sitting at the bar along with press officer Phoebe Jackson, surveying the lounge with the air of someone very much off duty. Franklin was relaxed but alert.

"The vote must be unanimous, Valon, for DHD's re-election to have the sort of moral authority he needs to carry on his work effectively," Milonakis was saying to the group in the booth. "You see that, don't you?"

"Moral authority?" Dragusha said. "I'm not familiar with that expression. Can you explain please perhaps?"

"*Ç'është ky?*" the former Miss Serbania said. She was drinking a Kir Royale and looking splendid in a slinky gold lamé dress.

"*Mos u bëj merak, mos u bëj merak,*" Dragusha said, patting her hand.

"I mean to say that the Secretary General needs the absolutely unequivocal support of all member countries if he is to continue the work of transforming Interpol," Milonakis said.

"That is what Monsieur Herriot-Dupont has said often to me also," Broussard offered. He was drinking a mucous-green glass of Pernod and water.

Milonakis looked sharply at the computer man. "And why would he discuss such matters with you, Gilles? With all due respect."

"Oh, we talk of many things, Monsieur Herriot-Dupont and myself," Broussard said proudly. The Pernod was working its magic on his inhibitions.

"As we do also, no?" Dragusha said, slapping Broussard heartily on the back. "I enjoy our conversations very much, Broussard. You are a good man. Very good. I will steal you away from Interpol one day and you can come to work with me in Virana, a very excellent place. This is a very excellent man you have here, Freiderikos. A true professional. Very excellent."

Dragusha raised his fishbowl-sized glass of red wine. He clinked Broussard's glass and shouted, "I propose a toast! I propose a toast to moral authority and to the future of international police cooperation!"

Some other delegates at another table heard the toast and roared their approval. They were Fijian police, trying hard to spend all of their expense money as quickly as possible. Dragusha stood up with some difficulty between the booth's table and bench and shouted even more loudly, to the entire room, "To moral authority and the future of international police cooperation!"

A cheer resonated through the lounge. Glasses were hoisted; police backs were slapped. Milonakis looked uneasily around, then raised his glass without much enthusiasm. He did not like Dragusha taking centre stage like this. He did not like Broussard's latest remarks. He did not have a good feeling at all.

"Valon, Valon, thank you very much. Please let me buy you a drink," Milonakis said. "And of course your lovely assistant, and Gilles."

"I am drinking Bordeaux," Dragusha said. "The best the waiter could offer. Waiter! Waiter!"

"No, Valon, no, allow me, please. I'll go to the bar and see whether there's any proper ouzo for us to drink together. We will drink a toast with the finest ouzo to the future of Greek and Serbanian police cooperation. I'll go, please."

Milonakis squeezed himself out of the booth and strode up to the bar. He stood beside Franklin and tried to get the barman's attention.

"That Dragusha's pretty darn cheery tonight," Franklin said, only slightly slurring his words.

"Too cheery," Milonakis said sullenly. He placed an order for four double ouzo shots. "Put them in tall glasses," he told the barman. "Give me a small tray. I'll carry them over myself."

"You know, Fred, I've been thinking," Franklin said.

Milonakis said nothing, appearing preoccupied as he waited for the drinks to be poured.

"I've been thinking, Fred, and I've been telling Phoebe here – haven't I been telling you, Phoebe? – that I think we've got to tell the Secretary General there's something nasty going on, and urgently."

Milonakis turned to Franklin. "What?"

"Something nasty's going on. Something's not right. I feel it right here." Franklin thumped his chest hard with his fist. "In my heart, like."

"Franklin, you've had too much to drink."

No, not really, not too. I just really, really, really think, Fred, there's a conspiracy. Look at all the things that have gone wrong lately."

"A conspiracy?" Milonakis said impatiently.

"That's my theory," Franklin said, motioning to the waiter to bring him another whisky.

Phoebe giggled.

"Frank, how many's that now?" she said.

"No, Phoebe, really. Really, Fred. You've got to listen to me – we've got to warn the Secretary General. People don't like him. You see? Some people. Not everyone. Some. They're out to get him. You see? Things are going wrong. There's a conspiracy against him. You see what I'm saying?"

"Frank, you better go up to bed," Milonakis said. "We have a big day tomorrow."

"No, seriously, Fred. Someone's got to warn the guy. You've got to warn him. Or I can do it for you. How's that, eh? I can tell him. I'm not afraid."

Franklin tried to stand up. "Is he here yet? What room's he in?"

"Frank, settle down," Phoebe said.

"Thank you, Phoebe," Milonakis said. "Frank, just go to bed. We don't want you hung over tomorrow."

Milonakis picked up the small, circular tray with four glasses on it and walked off. Franklin and Phoebe watched him go. He appeared to be having trouble carrying the tray without spilling any ouzo. He was Chief of Staff of the world's largest international police organisation, after all, not a waiter. He stopped momentarily and placed the tray down on a long wooden sideboard at the side of the room, with his back to Franklin and Phoebe.

"What's he doing?" Franklin said.

"He's going to spill those drinks," Phoebe said.

Milonakis fumbled around in his little leather shoulder bag. What was he looking for? He fumbled around some more, stood for a while longer, hunched over his bag and the tray, and then, finally, lit a cigarette. He put various things away in his bag and picked up the tray again. He looked back at Franklin and Phoebe, then walked toward his booth, squinting though the smoke curling up from the cigarette in his mouth.

"He's nervous," Franklin said knowingly. "I've seen that a lot of times. He smokes like that when he's nervous."

"What's he so nervous about?" Phoebe asked.

Secretary General Didier Herriot-Dupont arrived in grand style at the InterContinental the next morning, riding in a small convoy of gleaming black vans amidst a shrieking gaggle of gleaming white motorcycles. The Germans had been reluctant to provide a motorcycle escort, arguing that the Munich traffic flowed perfectly well without special intervention, and that in any case, motorcycle escorts were usually reserved for visiting heads of state. Chief of Staff Milonakis had prevailed, however, thereby providing Adolph Fenstermacher with one more reason to despise Interpol staff.

A small group of officials and staff waited at the hotel entrance for DHD to descend from the police van. Milonakis was there, of course, and Jean-Marc Moulin, as protocol required; Events Manager Caldevilla, Frank Franklin (not looking well), Dragusha (not, at this hour, accompanied by his assistant, and also looking most unwell), Belixico's Alonso Gomez, Japan's Executive Committee member Yoko Watanabe alongside a uniformed Japanese policewoman, the Deputy Director of the German Federal Criminal Police, plus Adolph Fenstermacher and some other BKA officials, the hotel manager and the hotel's catering manager and head of security.

Also crowding the forecourt were journalists of various persuasions and a few newspaper photographers and TV cameramen. Among them was Rob Henderson of CNN.

The strapping motorcyclists dismounted and grouped themselves to the side, next to one of their powerful BMW bikes. They did not remove their helmets. Herriot-Dupont emerged from his van, accompanied by Julia Smith. BKA Deputy Director Ulrich Holstein grasped the Secretary General's hand in a warm greeting. Brilliant white camera flashes began to punctuate their encounter. A German photographer called out, "Please, gentlemen, a group shot. With the outriders. Please."

Herriot-Dupont looked around in alarm as the little group was herded by a BKA press officer closer to the motorcycle and the group of riders. Cameras flashed, videos were recorded. Nice picture, with a nice piece of police equipment for added interest. But wait. The Interpol Secretary General appeared to be in distress. He looked, in fact, like he was trying unsuccessfully to move out of the shot. Behind him, towering above him, towering even higher in their helmets than they normally would have done, was the impressive group of what were surely Germany's tallest motorcycle policemen.

Indeed, Deputy Director Holstein himself was a man of far more than average height. Holstein looked bewildered when the Interpol Secretary General stalked angrily away and pulled two Interpol officials aside.

"Freiderikos," DHD hissed, "those shots cannot be used. Do you understand me? Franklin, you buffoon, speak at once to all of those photographers and tell them those shots are not to be used."

"What's wrong, Secretary General? It's a great shot, with that motorcycle in the background," Franklin said. "It tells people right away this is a police event. Police business. Uniforms, helmets, a big police bike. That'll get good play. Sure, maybe they're a little taller than we would have liked, but—"

DHD was livid. He turned to his Chief of Staff. "I thought all the advance work had been properly done, Fred," he said. "You must know our requirements well enough by now."

"We made our requirements very clear to Fenstermacher," Milonakis said. "Am I right, Franklin?"

"Yes, oh yes. But we didn't specifically mention the motorcycle guys," Franklin said.

"This is a bad start," Herriot-Dupont said. "Franklin, make sure those pictures are not used."

"I'll try to speak to the BKA press team," Franklin said.

*

In the lobby, DHD calmed himself sufficiently to exchange a few pleasantries with delegates. His exchange with Valon Dragusha, however, was extremely brief.

"Secretary General, I wish very much to remain here with you and speak with you, yes, of course, but I really must run," Dragusha said, his face red and exuding great volumes of perspiration. "I am truly not well. I am very uncomfortable. Something I ate has disagreed with me, I think."

"What a shame, Valon," DHD said.

Dragusha's face was contorted with effort. He shook the Secretary General's hand and then rushed off, calling out to the desk clerk, "Where is the nearest toilet? Please, it is urgent I find a toilet."

"Too much Bordeaux," Milonakis said.

"No, he's in bad shape," Franklin said. "He's got a terrible case of the runs. He told me at breakfast. He's been racing off like that all morning."

"I see," Herriot-Dupont said.

"What a shame," Milonakis said.

Yoko Watanabe of Japan was very formal and all business. She bowed slightly from the waist when greeting DHD, then said, "The proposed budget, Secretary General. Please allow me to say that this still requires much discussion."

"We will talk of this as soon as possible," Herriot-Dupont said. "Fred, set up some time for me to meet the Japanese delegation. Alright, Yoko? We can talk soon."

Watanabe nodded curtly.

A couple of African police walked DHD's way, before he had got to the front desk.

Colonel Lumumba Kayembe of the Congolese police said, "Regarding Zimwabse, sir. We must speak urgently before the General Assembly begins. Mr Matonga has apparently been pre-vented from attending. Some of the African delegations are most unhappy."

"Mr Matonga informed me personally on the telephone that he

would not attend in order to avoid an unpleasant diplomatic incident that would distract all of us from our important police work here in Munich," DHD said smoothly. "It was a selfless gesture, which I will try to make up to him in some way as soon as possible."

"Some of us would like to have a word nonetheless," Colonel Kayembe said.

"Fred, please set up some time with our African friends," DHD said, moving off.

He gave a friendly wave to some Belixicans, and another to Stefan Timmermans of the Dutch police, which was not returned. He then briefly stopped at the front desk to sign a small form before heading to the elevators.

"Fred, Franklin, I will see you in my office, if you have remembered to arrange one for me. In ten minutes," the Secretary General growled. He stopped before getting into an open elevator. "And Julia?"

"Over there, sir," Franklin said.

On the other side of the lobby on a giant sofa sat Julia Smith, deep in conversation with Gilles Broussard. As if suddenly aware of a gaze upon him, Broussard looked the Secretary General's way. He raised his hand in a cautious gesture of greeting, a crooked smile appearing on his lips. Julia Smith waved also.

"Broussard, too," DHD hissed to the Chief of Staff. "My office. Ten minutes."

On the evening before any Interpol General Assembly begins, there is always a gala dinner in the hotel. It is the highlight of the world law enforcement social calendar. Dozens of police and police officials gather for a sumptuous meal, and some, particularly those from Africa, attend in their national dress. Others wear splendid dress uniforms with all regalia. Others merely wear their finest business suits and agency ties.

Very few women attend, but those who do are either senior police officers in their own right or the partners (de jure or de facto) of senior police. Whatever their calling in the world, the women at an Interpol gala are much sought after for dinner conversation, for networking, or, when festivities have progressed sufficiently, and if appropriate in the host country, for dancing.

Interpol Secretary General Didier Herriot-Dupont, head, leader, helmsman of the world's largest international police organisation, invariably used conference dinners to network, to shore up his position on matters of global law enforcement significance, to pitch or defend costly new projects, and essentially, to persuade attendees that he was the greatest leader the world's largest international organisation had ever had, or could ever possibly hope to have. At the InterContinental, therefore, after dinner had been served and much wine had been consumed by virtually everyone, DHD could be seen moving resolutely from table to table, beaming at one and all, shaking hands and patting shoulders in the warmest possible way.

Others, of course, saw such gala dinners in the same way. Who was sitting or standing with whom could often be of major significance. That the police representatives of certain nations were seen in the company of police from certain other nations was something to be noted and evaluated. Chief of Staff Freiderikos Milonakis, a true professional where noting and evaluating was concerned, stood discreetly to one side of the vast room, noting and evaluating.

There, for example, was Valon Dragusha, deep in conversation with a cluster of European police. Milonakis noted the presence of a grim Albanian man, and some others from Europe's eastern frontier. There was Miss Serbania, drinking a Kir Royale, looking like a million lek, seated beside a very attentive Polish cop and doing her bit for international police cooperation. Suddenly, however, Dragusha jumped up and rushed from the room. Milonakis noted this. He allowed himself a discreet smile.

There were the Japanese, still deadly serious and nodding incessantly to each other. Discussing weighty budgetary matters, no doubt, or the latest statistics on cross-border shipments of drugs and stolen cars. Yes, quite possibly. And there were the Americans, sober but cheery, speaking to no one from any other tables. Who knew what the Americans could ever be discussing in private at an international conference?

There, somewhat more disturbingly, was Jean-Marc Moulin, seated at a giant round table with many African policemen and their wives. He was leaning forward and making some important point, a hand in the air for emphasis. This was very odd. Moulin was not the most sociable of men, normally. Milonakis noted, and evaluated. DHD's afternoon meeting with the Africans had not gone at all well, but neither had Moulin been assigned to smooth things over. Noted. Evaluated.

But wait! Could that be Julia Smith, Madame DHD, dancing with a somewhat sheepish Gilles Broussard? Yes, indeed it was. Milonakis looked over to where the Secretary General was standing with some Latin American police. He had not yet observed what was occurring on the dance floor. Milonakis moved closer to the dancers, unsure whether, or how, to intervene.

Then Julia stopped dancing, and waved to someone at the entrance to the room. Milonakis looked over at the doorway. Could it be? No. Impossible! But yes, there in the doorway, in her usual figure-hugging black cocktail dress, was none other than former Interpol intern Evangeline. Milonakis glanced over his shoulder toward DHD, then rushed to the door, arriving there at the same moment as the Secretary General's wife.

"Evangeline, what are you doing here in Munich?" he asked.

"Evangeline is here at my invitation, Fred," Julia said. "She's a former intern as you know, and she's been working with me on a research project in my capacity as a criminologist. I thought she would find a General Assembly quite educational."

"Julia, I really don't think…" Milonakis was for once at a loss for words. Nervously, he looked again over toward the Secretary General. "Evangeline is not a police officer, Julia. She's not accredited to attend."

"She's a member of the Interpol family," Julia said.

"I'm very interested in what goes on here, *monsieur*," Evangeline said.

Milonakis rubbed his hand through his hair. Then suddenly, also appearing in the doorway, was CNN's Rob Henderson and his cameraman. Impossible! Milonakis moved immediately to block their entry.

"Henderson, this is a private function. No journalists are allowed," he said sharply. "You can't film in here."

Jacoby already had his camera on his shoulder. He switched on a very bright spotlight attached to the top. It startled groups of diners and dancers abruptly captured in an illuminated circle. There were murmurs of protest from some.

"Phoebe Jackson said it was OK," Henderson said. "Just for a couple of shots."

Phoebe, at that moment, was running down the hallway toward them. "I told them they couldn't come in!" she shouted. "I never said it was OK!"

Behind her, also running, but more slowly, was a puffing Frank Franklin, his tie and tinted aviator glasses askew.

Jacoby turned to film the two new arrivals. "Whatcha gonna do now, call the cops?" he called out to them.

Far across the room, Milonakis saw that Herriot-Dupont had interrupted his conversation with Peru's chief of police and was walking quickly toward the TV light and the commotion. Milonakis suddenly had a very bad feeling about how things were going. Maybe Franklin was right. Something nasty was going on. Something was not right. He felt it right there, in his chest.

FOURTEEN

It was, everyone agreed afterward, not a good thing for the giant Interpol welcome banner to suddenly fall off the side of Munich's InterContinental hotel just before dawn on the first full day of General Assembly proceedings. The vast expanse of canvas and ropes had inexplicably cascaded down from where it was affixed to the side of the building and entangled itself on the edge of the glass awning over the forecourt. It flapped wildly from there, lashing at the doorman and some other startled staff and a couple of waiting taxis below.

Few who inspected the aftermath or were told of the incident later that morning ventured the opinion that perhaps it was an omen of some sort. Interpol Chief of Staff Freiderikos Milonakis, however, watching workmen hurriedly remove the fallen banner before proceedings began, experienced the deep foreboding that comes to anyone who believes they may have been party to an omen, and a terribly bad one.

Milonakis had slept very little before being awakened by a call from Adolph Fenstermacher informing him about the fallen banner. He had got to bed extremely late, after a difficult emergency meeting with the Secretary General and Frank Franklin in the InterContinental's rooftop bar. DHD had been angry about various alarming developments, and Franklin had rambled on about conspiracies against Interpol, against the Secretary General, and against himself.

It was difficult to say what had enraged the Secretary General most. Milonakis thought it must have been the appearance in Munich of the youngest of his mistresses, in the company of his wife. Or perhaps his wife's continued assignations and consultations with Gilles Broussard. Or the repeated intrusions by CNN and the inability of his communications staff to control the activities of the media generally speaking. At that point, during the meeting in the early hours of the morning on the hotel roof, the Interpol banner had not yet fallen off the building. It would be Milonakis' task later to inform Herriot-Dupont of the next bit of worrisome news.

"I can't understand why this Evangeline would come to a General Assembly anyway, when she's just a former intern," Franklin had said repeatedly on the roof, apparently unaware of, or feigning ignorance of, the Secretary General's extramarital appetites. "But why get so fussed about it? Who cares?"

Herriot-Dupont and Milonakis both glared at Franklin with deadly intensity.

"You should instead be asking yourself why we are so worried about a hostile television crew getting into the ballroom last night and filming me and the delegates going about our private business," DHD shouted. He too had had a fair bit to drink before coming to the roof. Milonakis hoped this would not affect the Secretary General's performance in the all-important speech he was to deliver in just a few hours' time.

"That was Phoebe's fault," Franklin said.

"She's on your staff!" DHD shouted.

"She's scared of journalists," Franklin said. "And those CNN guys are out to get us."

"I know they are, fool!" DHD shouted. "Your job is to stop them!"

"They didn't get much footage," Franklin said.

"Only of security trying to force them out," Milonakis said. "And of the Secretary General shouting at them. And delegates drinking and dancing. Police delegates."

"I did not shout!" DHD shouted.

"Secretary General, you really must compose yourself," Milonakis said. "You should just go down to your room now and get some sleep. You have to be at your best for your re-election speech. Being tired isn't going to help."

Herriot-Dupont ran his palms over his hair and leaned back in his chair to stretch wearily.

"The speech is one of the very first items on the agenda," Milonakis said soothingly. "Then the voting, and then you can relax. The rest of the day and the day after that is routine General Assembly business. I can look after things once the vote is over, and you can relax."

"Relax?" DHD said bitterly. He looked at Franklin and said suddenly, "That's all."

Franklin stood up and prepared to leave. "Good luck tomorrow, sir," he said.

"Pah!" Herriot-Dupont said.

When Franklin had gone, Milonakis said, "It will be alright."

"How do we know that, Fred?"

"Trust me," Milonakis said. "I've been in difficult situations before."

The Secretary General grew pensive. "Where is Julia now?" he asked suddenly.

"I believe she registered for a room of her own."

"That's a small blessing, I suppose."

"Yes."

"And Evangeline?"

"I'm not sure. I assume she's in her room. It's very late."

"My wife's room?"

"No, no, her own."

"Another small blessing."

"Secretary General, I would advise very strongly against…"

"Of course, of course, I'm not stupid. Tonight of all nights. With my wife in this very hotel."

Herriot-Dupont, however, looked wistful, disappointed. Was any chambermaid in the hotel safe?

"And Dragusha? What mischief was he up to tonight?"

"He's still not well," Milonakis said. "His socialising with the delegates was, let's say, often interrupted. He's not well."

"Excellent."

"I've been sending some very special ouzo to his room since he fell ill. To help settle his stomach. An old Greek remedy."

Herriot-Dupont looked for a long time at his Chief of Staff. "It has to be unanimous, Fred," he said at last. "The vote."

"I know that, sir. That's my objective also."

"I have tried to make Broussard understand what a crucial role he'll play. I've tried to make him understand that dark forces are at work that could—"

"I'll watch over things, Secretary General. That's my job."

"Broussard is our man, Fred. Am I correct in this?"

"I believe so, Secretary General. Yes."

Very late, after Herriot-Dupont had finally gone to his room, Milonakis decided to take a last stroll alone through the main meeting hall. Two uniformed German policemen at the entry peered at the photo on his security pass; then let him in. In a few hours, hundreds of police from around the globe would crowd the long tables and the place would be abuzz with debate, ideally on weighty law enforcement matters. For now, the cavernous room was extremely still, in perfect order.

Then Milonakis spied a lone figure seated almost dead centre in the middle of the room, at a special table laden with Interpol audiovisual and computer equipment. It was the table where technicians would operate the microphones for keynote speakers and ordinary delegates, screen videos and photos and charts as required, and where Gilles Broussard would compile and make public the results of various votes. Could it be Gilles Broussard himself sitting there alone at this extremely late hour?

It was. Milonakis approached him quietly from behind, the better to observe things closely before announcing himself. Broussard, cardigan-clad, was peering at a laptop computer, tapping a single key occasionally. He appeared to be looking at Interpol's Red Notice pages again. Poring over mug shots of the world's fugitives, in the middle of the night, just hours before the General Assembly was to begin.

"What are you doing here so late at night, Gilles?" Milonakis said suddenly.

Broussard leapt to his feet and wheeled around, badly startled. "*Mon dieu seigneur, monsieur*, you have frightened me almost to death," Broussard said breathlessly.

"What are you doing here?" Milonakis asked again. "Why are you always looking at wanted persons notices in the middle of the night?"

Broussard seemed extremely nervous; flustered. A glass of red wine sat beside his computer and two empty glasses were on a small tray.

"I'm checking all equipment one last time to make sure everything works as it should," he said. "Connections with headquarters, connection to the Internet, checking picture files – everything people might need, *monsieur*."

Milonakis looked dubious, but said, "Commendable."

Broussard looked exhausted, stricken. His new hairstyle was no longer perfect. His newfound self-confidence appeared to have waned substantially.

"I'm finding the pressure on me is very heavy now, *monsieur*," he said.

"Everything will go well, I'm sure."

"Everyone is counting on me. They all say this to me all the time."

"We're all counting on you, that's true."

"Everyone has suggestions. The pressure is very…"

Broussard sat down abruptly. Milonakis thought for a moment that he would burst into tears.

"You shouldn't be here so late, Gilles. You need to rest. Tomorrow is a big day."

"Everybody says the same thing," Broussard said. "Just what you have said. I know tomorrow is a big day. I know that." He reached for his glass of wine.

"That's not a good idea," Milonakis said. "Drinking wine won't help. You need to be rested and have a clear head for tomorrow."

"That's what everybody says, *monsieur*," Broussard said morosely. He put his glass back down on the table.

"Be strong, Gilles," Milonakis said.

"I will do my best. It's hard."

"We're counting on you, Gilles."

"Please don't keep saying that, *monsieur*. It is very hard. The pressure…"

The opening ceremony went quite well, and not just because it was organised by Germans. Police like a bit of military-style pomp and pageantry from time to time, though some more than others, and the opening ceremony of an Interpol General Assembly is nothing if not military.

The long rows of tables in the InterContinental's conference hall were jammed with police from 190 nations, resplendent in their best uniforms and regalia. The wives of the chiefs of police, seated in a section of reserved chairs to one side and at the back, were no less splendid in their finest attire or, in the case of those from many African nations, their wildly colourful national dress and headscarves.

Germany's police band did a magnificent job on Interpol's anthem, and of course the German national anthem. Delegates and senior officials, their partners, and all those seated high on the stage at the front of the hall, stood up. Many snapped to attention. Some saluted smartly. Flashes from news photographers' equipment cast sudden bursts of light over the scene and TV cameramen scurried here and there, heavy cameras on shoulders, to get the best vantage. The Interpol flag, and that of Germany, were placed at the front of the room by two solemn police cadets. The flags were to remain in place until proceedings ended officially in two days' time.

At the front of the room, in two long rows of chairs placed immediately before the first line of delegates' tables, was the VIP seating. This was reserved for senior German and Interpol officials and their guests. Julia Smith sat there, literally front and centre, almost immediately in front of the speakers' podium. Young Evangeline sat to her right. Interpol's Chief of Staff, grim-faced today, was to Julia's left. To Milonakis' left were other key Interpol staff: Jean-Marc Moulin, Chief Legal Counsel Cynthia Payne, Antonio de Caldevilla and others. At either end of this line of Interpol people sat members of the Executive Committee, including one very bilious Valon Dragusha.

Frank Franklin, looking, for anyone with experienced eyes to see, exceptionally hung over, stood unsteadily to one side watching the unpredictable movements of photographers and cameramen and preparing to herd them to the cordoned-off press area at the back of the room. There they would be allowed to stand with an unruly gaggle of reporters to record the opening remarks before being escorted out to allow speeches and voting and General Assembly deliberations to truly begin behind closed doors. Phoebe Jackson stood at the ready in the back, waiting to help corral and eventually muster out the media pack.

Behind the stage, high and imposing, were the two massive digital TV screens on which were now being projected images of the opening ceremony as it took place, and on which, later, would be shown close-ups of speakers and delegates as they went about their important police business. Charts and videos and photos and other information would also be projected there. On the left-hand screen, at the moment, was a tight shot of an expressionless Secretary General Didier Herriot-Dupont seated onstage in a bespoke navy blue suit with a hint of pinstripe. He wore, of course, the Interpol tie, in red and discreetly embroidered with the organisation's official crest.

From the front row of seats below, Chief of Staff Milonakis tried to catch the Secretary General's eye, to give him an encouraging signal. The Secretary General did not look down. Could this be because his wife and youngest mistress were seated there just to the Chief of Staff's right? Quite possibly, Milonakis thought ruefully. Please, he said to himself, please, God in heaven, let this day unfold as it should. Milonakis was by no means a religious man, but some days, on this day, he very much yearned for the protection of a beneficent higher power.

Frank Franklin had not gone to bed immediately after the tense encounter with the Secretary General and the Chief of Staff on the roof of the hotel the night before. He had gone back to his room and tried his best to empty the mini-bar and to fend off the demons that now followed him everywhere, cackling in delight at his ruined career and his imminent return in disgrace to the barren wastes of Ontario.

He had slept for perhaps two hours, and opted for three stiff vodka and orange juice bracers for his breakfast. Days of accumulated alcohol, coursing through his blood at various metabolic and digestive stages, now put him in the sort of gently disordered state that only the very, very skilled drinker can enjoy. These people do not stumble; they do not fall. They go about their business as they must, and as best as they possibly can. Not always successfully, perhaps, but always very well insulated against unwanted stress.

Franklin succeeded, with some difficulty, in guiding the photographers back to the cordoned-off riser at the rear of the hall. Phoebe was there to assist, as arranged. Franklin did not return Rob Henderson's cheery greeting, nor did he make eye contact with the menacing cameraman Jacoby. He merely herded and mustered as required, then stood rocking gently on his heels as the German Interior Minister and the BKA Director welcomed delegates and made the requisite declarations about the challenges of international police cooperation and the grave threat of cross-border crime. Law enforcement platitudes wafted pleasantly over Franklin like a warm breeze.

By the time he and Phoebe had managed to get the last of the journalists out of the hall after opening remarks and the doors closed for the start of official business, Franklin was approaching euphoria, a state of grace. He began to feel wonderfully safe and cosy in his booze cocoon. The stress level had fallen with the media now expelled and his work, for the moment, was done. He could simply take a chair at the back of the room and listen peacefully to the Secretary General's speech. He smiled contentedly at Phoebe. She smiled happily back.

The keynote speech by the Interpol Secretary General, insiders agreed afterward, did not begin particularly well. Didier Herriot-Dupont smiled warmly after being introduced by the German chief of police. He raised his right arm in an elegant, self-effacing gesture to acknowledge the applause from delegates. He rose, carrying his notes. Then he looked in vain for the little platform that had been arranged for him so that he could see, and be seen, to best advantage over the imposing podium. The little platform was not there.

Herriot-Dupont paused. He looked uncertain. He looked down at his Chief of Staff in the VIP section of the room. He looked over at Adolph Fenstermacher at the far edge of the stage. Fenstermacher looked to where the platform should have been, where it had been just a few short hours ago. He looked down at Milonakis and turned up both of his hands. Milonakis looked back at Fenstermacher, not knowing from where he sat what problem was being signalled. He looked at the Secretary General, who grimaced briefly before making his way, somewhat reluctantly, to the podium.

The Chief of Staff then immediately saw the problem. On both giant TV screens were identical close-ups of the Secretary General, now dwarfed behind the podium. He looked very much like a short schoolboy trying to make a speech at a grown-up event. The German police cameraman, shooting from the back of the hall with a long lens, did his best to frame the difficult shot but from a low angle the Secretary General's on-screen head barely appeared over the microphones. Milonakis looked frantically around for Franklin, but Franklin was nowhere to be seen.

Herriot-Dupont looked extremely unhappy, and unsure of what to do. He looked over his shoulder at his image on the two screens. He looked down as best he could over the podium at his Chief of Staff. Milonakis tuned up both of his hands and shrugged, shaking his head. Herriot-Dupont looked down at his wife and his youngest mistress. Julia was whispering something into Evangeline's ear. Evangeline listened intently, nodding and smiling. Then, farther along the line of VIP chairs, Executive Committee member Dragusha suddenly leapt to his feet and ran to one of the hall's side exits. This, too, was disconcerting to someone about to deliver a crucially important speech.

From far at the back of the hall, even with his eyes closed in a dream-like state, Frank Franklin could sense that something was amiss. The Secretary General was taking too long to begin. Franklin looked up at the stage and saw, all but hidden behind the podium, part of DHD's head looking out at the assembled police. He could see that all was not well. And it appeared that the audience was beginning to grow restless.

Franklin's mobile phone beeped once. A text message appeared. It was from Chief of Staff Milonakis at the front of the hall. The message said simply: *Fix this!* Franklin's addled brain could see no immediate solution to the problem of the Secretary General's less-than-average height. He looked over at his young colleague Phoebe. She had a quizzical look on her face. She shrugged her shoulders and raised her eyebrows in a silent interrogative gesture. Franklin shrugged also, then closed his eyes again, waiting for the speech to begin.

Even when Secretary General Herriot-Dupont had composed himself and started to speak, things did not go well. There was an immediate, excruciating howl of feedback from the ballroom sound system that startled Franklin from his reverie. Gilles Broussard and various Interpol and German technicians scurried around the audiovisual table, trying to find the source of the problem. Far off in the distance, Franklin saw Chief of Staff Milonakis stand up in the front row of seats, turn, and glare in Broussard's direction.

The feedback eventually subsided. Then DHD's properly amplified words wafted episodically into Franklin's waking moments, as from far, far away.

"Real police work is a very simple matter," the Secretary General began. "It is to find and apprehend wrongdoers. That is all."

Even in his dreamlike state, Franklin knew that those words would bring joy to the hearts of Jean-Marc Moulin and other like-minded cops listening intently to the speech in that vast room. Had DHD undergone a sudden conversion on the road to Munich?

"Everybody in the worldwide brotherhood of police is striving for the same goal," DHD continued. "Yes, at times we will disagree. Yes, at times some of you may have questioned the direction Interpol was taking. Change is not without risk, not without controversy, not without expense…"

"The old Interpol… The new Interpol… The post-9/11 world… Dangerous place… Safer place… Exciting new projects… New tools, new techniques… Policemen everywhere must blah, blah, blah… They must be equipped with state-of-the-art blah, blah, blah… It is Interpol's task to… I have been doing my utmost to…"

The inspirational words were having a hypnotic effect on Frank Franklin, and perhaps on others in the room. Unidentifiable emotions welled up in his chest. Then, paradoxically, a sudden silence roused him.

The Secretary General was looking over his shoulder, glaring at two very blank TV screens. The collage of law enforcement images collected by Franklin at great cost from world news agencies was not being projected as planned. Neither were any charts or graphs. There was more frantic scurrying at the audiovisual table. Another ferocious glare in Broussard's direction from a now-standing Chief of Staff.

DHD waited no longer. He proceeded without visual aids of any sort.

"Yes, there have been some robust budget discussions... Healthy sign of... Nevertheless, the genuine support of my esteemed Executive Committee colleagues... Without whom neither I nor Interpol could ever... Salute their selfless devotion, dedicated efforts, countless hours of etc. etc. etc...."

More, on a touching personal note.

"Since I was a young boy in Normandy... Wanted a career in... Joined at first opportunity... Firsthand knowledge of the trials and tribulations of the... Devoted my career to... Like to think I am still at heart a police officer who can... Hope colleagues will agree... Life on the frontlines of Interpol is every policeman's... Under my stewardship... And stride confidently together in the direction of blah, blah, blah..."

Franklin opened one eye, but could not gauge the reaction of the room without shifting himself. He closed the eye; listened again.

"Outraged by recent irresponsible media coverage... Hope you will all agree that... Unfettered freedom of the press is of course... Scurrilous accusations and unfounded allegations... Damaging not just to...

"Outraged also by the treatment of our esteemed colleague from Zimwabse... Commissioner Matonga has very kindly... Hope African delegates will agree that I... Naturally, I will now take up this matter at the highest diplomatic...

"As for Europe, I would like to... My dear friends in Eastern Europe... A special vote of thanks to EC member Valon Dragusha, who is sitting right there with us today in... And my Western European colleagues, who of course also...

"Dedicated Interpol headquarters staff, also of course must blah blah blah... Vote of thanks... Unstinting efforts... All pulling together despite the occasional... As in any group of dedicated professionals, there will be from time to time...

"And to my dearest wife Julia, herself a respected... Value always her professional etc.... Without her support I could never hope to… From my heart I say to Julia today…"

Franklin sensed a finale coming, a crescendo.

"And so, dear friends and colleagues, I… Therefore, I hope I can count on your… The opportunity to continue to serve… In closing, I… Allow me to… Naturally, would see it as a vote of confidence in… A strong signal that I may… I thank you all very much for your attention."

Secretary General Herriot-Dupont walked stiffly back to his place on the stage and sat down. There was a moment of silence. Then there was applause. Franklin was in no condition to be able to judge whether the applause was heartfelt or enthusiastic, or merely warm. Surely it was more than simply polite applause. From Franklin's perspective. Perhaps it was not sustained applause. No, perhaps not. But who was he to judge?

He looked to the front of the room. Freiderikos Milonakis was on his feet, the first inspired to a standing ovation. One by one, other members of Interpol staff got to their feet to join in. Franklin couldn't see if Julia Smith and her young friend were standing. Some of the other police delegates in the room rose also. Not all, but a number. Franklin was not the best one to judge whether one could correctly say that the room *erupted* into applause, and that the Secretary General received a *thunderous* standing ovation. Perhaps words like 'erupt' and 'thunderous' were not quite correct. But Franklin was really in no condition to judge.

Freiderikos Milonakis turned around where he was standing and surveyed the audience; tried to gauge their reaction. For Milonakis, too, the speech had wafted over him as if in a dream; in his case a troubled dream. It was hard to know what to think of the delegates' reaction. Some, certainly, had followed his lead into a standing ovation. Some. Was it mere politesse? Who could say? Milonakis was tired, very tired. In his fatigue, in the overheated ballroom, the sea of delegates now swam before him like some sort of waking nightmare.

What could they be saying to each other? Could they all be

conspiring? There, over there, was a cluster of African policemen; clapping, yes, but talking earnestly, even gravely, amongst themselves. None standing. And there were the Japanese, only one of them standing, all clapping politely, but none of them with the slightest expression on their faces.

There was Alonso Gomez of Belixico, already circulating among his Latin American colleagues, distributing what appeared to be souvenir medallions of some kind. There was Valon Dragusha, back in the room but still looking rather pained. There was Timmermans from the Netherlands, looking ill at ease. There was Jean-Marc Moulin, looking smug. There was Julia Smith, not standing, locked in conversation with young Evangeline. There was Gilles Broussard, seated at his table, not clapping, holding his head disconsolately in his hands.

Police from 190 countries couldn't agree afterward about exactly what happened next, how the incident actually unfolded. It was a hot topic in police circles and in the media for a very long time afterward. In some circles, it still is.

The German police director, chairing the meeting as protocol required, invited delegates to vote on the first order of business: that Secretary General Didier Herriot-Dupont, his speech now having been delivered, be confirmed for a second five-year term as head of Interpol. All delegations had already been given their little electronic voting devices and had been instructed on how to use them. Delegates, seated at the long tables ranged throughout the hall, whispered to each other each other as the voting began. Dignitaries at the head table onstage chatted amongst themselves or busied themselves with paperwork or their mobile phones.

DHD looked pensive, as one might imagine. He sat in his place, gazing out at the sea of small national flags positioned on the tables of each delegation. He glanced down to where his senior Interpol colleagues were seated or standing, waiting for the result. He exchanged a glance with his Chief of Staff. His Chief of Staff gave him a thumbs-up signal and a wan smile.

DHD turned his attention to the technician's table, far off in the exact centre of the vast room. He saw Gilles Broussard poring over his computer, no doubt watching the electronic results coming wirelessly into the system for tabulation and transformation into graphical form. Other technicians moved around in the area, going about their work.

On the TV screens mounted high up behind the stage, only twin images of the Interpol logo appeared. Soon, however, projected there for all to see, would be the results of the vote. Soon the suspense would be over.

A vote of this nature at an Interpol General Assembly can sometimes take a little while. Delegates do not always hit the Yes or No button on their devices immediately. A number of them will deliberate on the matter at hand for some time. Others fumble with the equipment. Some may need to be shown again how to register their vote, though the equipment is extremely simple to use. Voting can sometimes take a little while.

In this case, in the case of the vote to confirm Didier Herriot-Dupont as Secretary General of Interpol for another five-year term, the voting seemed to be taking an inordinately long time, an excessively long time. On this at least, many delegates were agreed afterward.

When most delegates had apparently completed their voting, when many had begun chatting or exited the room for refreshment or a smoke, it began to appear that the process really was taking too long. A restless buzz began to build slowly in the hall.

Chief of Staff Freiderikos Milonakis looked from his position at the front of the hall back down to where Broussard was working. Broussard appeared to be in distress. Milonakis could see that even from afar. Broussard was seated bolt upright, one could almost say that he was frozen, in front of his terminal. He did not appear to be doing anything at all except staring at the screen.

Milonakis then began walking down to where Broussard was

seated. At that moment, Julia Smith, who had apparently also decided there was an inordinate delay and noticed Broussard's distress, also began walking from the front. Valon Dragusha, too, seeing where Milonakis and Julia were headed, moved in the same direction. From the stage, Herriot-Dupont observed these movements, this inexplicable convergence of key individuals, and stood up. He came to the edge of the stage and peered in the direction of the technicians' table. The BKA Director and Adolph Fenstermacher also stood up.

What happened next is still somewhat unclear. Even senior police from 190 countries still cannot agree on exactly what happened next. Media reports are contradictory.

Milonakis was the first to reach Broussard. He came around from behind. Broussard now sat with his head buried in his hands, in deep distress, still frozen in his place. Milonakis looked over Broussard's shoulder at what was on the screen, what could at any moment be projected onto the two TVs at the front of the hall.

It was an Interpol Red Notice. It showed two very uncomplimentary head shots, in black and white, what could only be described as mug shots, of Secretary General Herriot-Dupont. Milonakis gave a shout of alarm. The Red Notice was laid out precisely as genuine notices are laid out. It said, to the right of the famous red logo, *Wanted by Interpol!* It contained all the police-like information that a genuine Red Notice would contain. *Name: Didier Herriot-Dupont. Date of Birth... Place of Birth... Height... Weight... Wanted for: Adultery. Criminal mendacity. Deception. Breach of trust. Fraud. Incompetence. Interfering with police. Attention! This man has access to deadly weapons. He must be considered dangerous. Approach with extreme caution. This man is not to be trusted.*

Milonakis gave another cry of alarm. "Gilles, no! What on earth?" he shouted.

He tried to push past Broussard to get to the keyboard. The Secretary General had at this point already descended from the stage, and was now running toward the commotion as fast as his short legs could carry him. Julia Smith arrived at the table before him.

"Do it, Gilles!" she shouted. "Do it! DO IT! Remember what I said would happen to you if you don't!"

Dragusha arrived at the table as well. He pushed his way in front of Milonakis and Julia. He, too, saw what was on the screen.

"Gilles, Gilles," he shouted, lunging at Broussard. "That's not what you said you would…"

Broussard covered his head as if he expected to be attacked. He began sobbing uncontrollably. His cardigan was being trampled underfoot.

Armed security officers rushed to the table. The Secretary General rushed to the table.

Suddenly, at the back of the room, there was another commotion. A TV crew, CNN, had pushed open the main back doors and a cameraman was filming. A spotlight from the camera shone a circle of light onto delegates, tables, chairs. Other security guards rushed to the back, shouting and waving their arms. Frank Franklin was seen shoving a tall, blazer-clad reporter. The reporter was shoving back. Phoebe Jackson was wringing her hands, pacing back and forth.

A police officer smashed the spotlight off the CNN camera with a nightstick. The hot, breaking light globe exploded with a very loud bang and a blinding flash.

"Gun!" someone shouted. "Gun!"

"Terrorists!" someone shouted.

Delegates raced in panic for the exits. Some dived to the floor. A German policeman fired two warning shots into the ceiling. Glass and plaster dust rained down. At the technicians' table, Secretary General Herriot-Dupont lunged for the computer, scrabbling for the keyboard. Gilles Broussard collapsed off his chair. Herriot-Dupont fell to his knees.

"Someone has been shot!" a bystander shouted.

"Officer down!" shouted someone else.

More police and security ran to the technical table. Herriot-Dupont was knocked completely over in the melee. Milonakis was knocked over. Then Dragusha suddenly ran at top speed away from the scene. He was pursued energetically by German police.

"I need a toilet urgently! Please!" he shouted as he was wrestled to the ground. "Let me go, please!"

No one listened to his protests. Dragusha writhed and kicked, to no avail. It took a number of police from a variety of countries to subdue him. At the back of the room, the CNN crew had by now been hustled out, handcuffed and detained. In the distance, there was the sound of sirens in the Munich streets.

Police medics rushed to assist the victims. The Secretary General and his Chief of Staff were still conscious. Gilles Broussard lay very still where he had fallen in the line of duty. The computer screen on the table above him now displayed only the Interpol logo. Eventually, a semblance of order was restored.

EPILOGUE

Armed Attack Disrupts Gathering of World's Senior Police

MUNICH (Reuters) – German police on Thursday foiled an apparent attack by terrorists or a criminal gang on the Interpol General Assembly, where senior police representatives from 190 countries had gathered for their annual conference.

Interpol Secretary General Didier Herriot-Dupont, a career French police officer, personally intervened during the attack, in which at least three shots were fired and several people were slightly injured. Eyewitnesses said Herriot-Dupont threw himself in front of a member of his own staff to protect him from harm.

The exact circumstances of the attack, which sent General Assembly delegates and support staff diving for cover, are still not clear. Three people, including a senior police official from Ser-bania, were arrested at Munich's luxury InterContinental hotel, where the incident occurred. Eyewitnesses said a number of perpetrators had apparently escaped.

A German police spokesman said an urgent investigation was underway, and other arrests may follow.

Two members of a CNN television crew arrested at the scene were questioned and later released. They have been charged with trespass and resisting police, and are to appear in a Munich court next week.

An Interpol computer technician injured during the attack is still in hospital. No official details of his injuries or his current condition were immediately available. A medical source said the man, a French national, was suffering from shock but had not been wounded by the gunfire.

"This was a cowardly attack at the very heart of international law enforcement, an attempt to disrupt the police cooperation that is essential in a dangerous post-9/11 world," the Interpol Secretary General said in a brief statement after the incident. "Interpol will not be deterred, however, from carrying on with its crucial work under my leadership.

"I applaud the swift and effective response by the German police, without which this appalling incident could have had far more serious consequences," Herriot-Dupont said.

The Interpol General Assembly resumed after order had been restored, with a delay of some five hours. Proceedings continued into the night as delegates attempted to make up for lost time. The conference, held by the organisation in a different city each year, is to conclude today.

"If we were to postpone or cancel this General Assembly, the criminals will have won," Herriot -Dupont said.

In the first order of business, which had been interrupted by the attack, delegates voted unanimously to endorse Herriot-Dupont for another five-year term as the head of the world's largest international police organisation.

Several media organisations quoted anonymous police sources as saying that despite Herriot -Dupont's heroic actions during the attack, there had been a large number of abstentions in the vote to endorse him for a second term. One well-placed source told Reuters that abstentions had totalled almost a hundred, and that the vote was "not exactly a ringing endorsement".

In a statement issued after the vote by the Interpol press office, spokesman Frank Franklin said the organisation never released detailed breakdowns of General Assembly votes, calling the information "confidential police business". However, Franklin pointed out that according to widely accepted rules of order, abstentions are not taken into account when determining whether an Interpol vote on any issue can be considered unanimous.

No one in the Interpol press office was immediately available for further comment.

ALSO BY MICHAEL E. ROSE

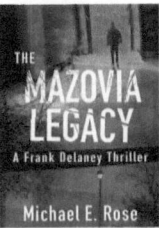

THE MAZOVIA LEGACY

In the icy depths of Quebec, investigative journalist Frank Delaney is drawn into to help find the truth behind a mysterious death that the authorities seem to want covered up.

"Murder, betrayal, international intrigue… Rose's tale has it all."

THE BURMA EFFECT

The search for a missing Canadian secret service agent brings Frank Delaney first to London, then to Thailand and Burma, where evidence points to an elaborate plot to destabilize the Burmese military regime.

"Strong writing, compelling plot… A thriller that truly lives up to the name."

THE TSUNAMI FILE

In Phuket, Thailand, after a tsunami kills thousands, Frank Delaney makes a bizarre discovery that leads him through Thailand's seedy child sex trade to an elaborate cover-up in Europe.

"A layered, evocative action thriller… An accomplished work."

For more about Michael E. Rose and his books visit
www.michaelrosemedia.com

www.ingramcontent.com/pod-product-compliance
Lightning Source LLC
Chambersburg PA
CBHW031215260626
47169CB00007B/2072